GOBLIN QUEST

AZUL GREGORSON

EDITED BY
WREN L. HELGREN

CONTENTS

Preface	v
Chapter 1 *The Cliffs of Kol'Grathu*	1
Chapter 2 *Honoring Tradition*	9
Chapter 3 *The Hunt*	18
Chapter 4 *The Bargain*	25
Chapter 5 *The Discovery*	35
Chapter 6 *The Betrayal*	50
Chapter 7 *Warface*	64
Chapter 8 *The Quaking Hills*	71
Chapter 9 *The Dread Marsh*	86
Chapter 10 *Enemy of my Enemy*	103
Chapter 11 *Crown of the Glyphwood*	113
Chapter 12 *The Briar King*	124
Chapter 13 *Old Battles*	141
Chapter 14 *The Challenge*	147
Chapter 15 *The Warrior's Fate*	158
Chapter 16 *The Veteran*	166

Chapter 17 *Prejudice and Pride*	181
Chapter 18 *The Hermit*	192
Chapter 19 *Chronostones and Wondrous Things*	203
Chapter 20 *The Thunderbird*	211
Chapter 21 *The Raid*	224
Chapter 22 *Rewards*	239
Chapter 23 *The Moot*	246
Acknowledgments	269
About the Author	271

PREFACE

Life is made of stories. They give us joy, meaning, and purpose. Whether the characters in those stories are real or live only in the theatre of the mind, we are moved by them and can learn a great deal from their trials, triumphs, and failings. I am blessed to live a life suffused with stories, and some of the best I have lived or imagined in concert with my friends.

I am a second generation tabletop role-play game nerd. In such games, and in many classical fantasy stories, goblins are often the antagonists. There are goblins in the folklore of many cultures around the world, sometimes they are portrayed as helpful, as in the case of the goblins of Europe who warned miners deep underground if there was danger of a cave-in, or the tengu of Japan who guarded mountains and forests. People were telling stories about goblins long before John Ronald Reuel Tolkien wrote his iconic series where thousands of unfortunate goblins were pressed into the service of the Dark Lord. There is even a word for goblin in chunik-wawa, the indigenous trade language of the Pacific Northwest, (but we are not supposed to say it, or it might summon them to cause mischief).

The world of this story is a different world from our own, and different from all other worlds you might have read about in fantasy stories, though some things will seem familiar. This world has a name, though I will not reveal it just yet. It contains many mysteries, and how its goblins, humans, and other humanoid people came to be there are among them.

Many years ago, I sat down with friends at my kitchen table and orchestrated a role playing game on this fantastic world I imagined. On a whim, I encouraged everyone to play as goblins, because we were fomenting ideas about creating a biannual volunteer-organized festival called the Goblin Market; where people could learn, barter, and play together as if the seelie and unseelie fae courts came together twice a year, when spring turns to summer and when summer turns to autumn.

The story that emerged took three years and some months to tell, altogether about four hundred hours of collaborative storytelling, and it was a privilege that gave me great joy. It was also a pleasure to weave that experience into a narrative that I am proud to share with you in the coming pages.

CHAPTER
ONE
THE CLIFFS OF KOL'GRATHU

Limestone cliffs towered above the crashing waves of Shipwreck Bay, illuminated by the soft, bright light of the waxing moon. Whitewater rapids plummeted from the mouth of a cave into the churning surf below, the waterfall fed by the torrential rain of late spring.

Silvorn moths fluttered out of the shadowed cavern, where rough-hewn wooden bridges criss-crossed over the subterranean river. Moth-hugged paper lanterns bobbed in the breeze, dimly illuminating the boardwalks leading into natural tunnels carved, long ago, by rushing water, the floors well-worn by countless generations of goblins.

Vilayne fussed with her copper wire-wrapped earrings in the main common chamber of the goblin warren. Kol'grathu had been her home since birth, and for all thirty years of her life, she had never left their tribe's territory. The world was a dangerous place, especially to goblins, whom "civilized" people demonized and regarded as stupid, evil creatures, little more than beasts.

The bat-like features and short stature of goblin folk were often exaggerated into ridiculous stereotypes by the folklore of humans. Human myths maligned their intelligence and portrayed them as tricksters and thieves, but it was true that goblin bands raided villages and settlements, ambushed travelers on the roads, killed and did other nasty things, from the merely mischievous to the profane.

And why not, Vilayne thought, when human adventurers had wiped out entire goblin warrens? They killed the young and the old without prejudice. Only a few well-defended or well-hidden enclaves remained, scattered across the known world.

Goblin raiders would come and trade with their warren; Spiderclaw and Thunderbite goblins, and some of their own, would sometimes leave the tribe to join these roving bands of robbers and killers. Vilayne didn't have a problem with this, as those who joined such pirates annoyed her, and she was glad she wouldn't have to suffer their presence in the warren anymore. It was especially peaceful at home during the moons when the war-chief was gone with volunteers for the summer raids.

She ignored Fumble, who was eyeing the wares spread out on the leather before her; goblins did not steal from other goblins—though there was unexpected borrowing, sometimes. He was interested in trading something for his hair-care products, specifically a collaboration on making decorated earthenware to put his formulas in. Fumble himself was bald, perhaps due to one of his early hair-care experiments. His scalp was speckled with shades of green —like the rest of him—and his leather vest was stained from various spills and scorched in places, too. He was a thinker, which was why they called him "Fumble the Wise," genuinely and sarcastically, depending upon the situation.

Across the enormous chamber, she could hear Trokar slurping up a large bowl of mein noodles, which were made from the hanging spore-tendrils of a glowing cave fungus. He was seated at the polished driftwood slab bar, almost certainly waiting for an opportunity to flirt with Cavesong, who usually tended the bar. She was considered one of the most attractive goblins in the warren, for her musical skill was unmatched.

Trokar, "Eater of Mein" as he was jokingly called, was not like most goblins. He was obsessed with appearances, particularly his own, and ate more noodles than anyone to keep up with his exercise regimen, keeping him exceptionally strong. By goblin standards, he was handsome, and he possessed a good singing voice. He took immaculate care of grey skin and his straw-colored hair, which he treated with Fumble's special moth oil. He and Fumble spent years developing the hair treatment using the ample supply of moth wings from their tribe's subterranean moth ranch.

Vilayne found Trokar's optimistic view on life and cheery attitude mildly annoying. She suspected it masked his loneliness. He never hunted or raided, and avoided confrontations, which made him unpopular with the more rough-and-tumble crowd. He had a reputation as a coward, and yet, he visited the sparring chamber daily to lift weights, enduring the jeering of Warface and his lackeys.

She felt a tug on her skirt and looked down to see a fluffy black spider about the size of her head, one leg gently pulling on the edge of her quilted robe. It was one of The Wise Woman's pet spiders. She was being summoned.

Vilayne rolled up her wares in the leather they were displayed on. "I have to go," she announced plainly, interrupting Fumble.

"Ah"—Fumble scratched his hairless head—"you can think it over, yes? Let me know if you want to join our enterprises?"

"I'll let you know," she said as she tucked her things under her arm and left. She definitely wanted nothing to do with either of them.

She walked through the network of caves, across a bridge and into the secluded chamber that was The Wise Woman's lair. There was no door, only a threadbare curtain hung from an arch of driftwood. None dared to enter without The Wise Woman's permission.

Old cobweb-covered tapestries lined the walls about the cluttered, oblong space; they hung across the chamber, making two separate spaces. Quilts sewn from human and elven fabrics, stitched with Kol'grathu embroidery, told stories of their history in the fashion of goblin pictographs.

The Wise Woman's other young pupil, Ezme, was sitting on a pillow, surrounded by The Wise Woman's pet spiders, who patiently waited in hope of a gifted treat. Ezme's dark hair was tied back in a tail above her gaudy headband, which was studded with black quartz. Her outfit was stitched with pictographs of her own design, and her toe and finger claws were painted black, as was her style. She gave a slight nod of greeting to Vilayne.

Ezme had been receiving lessons alongside Vilayne for three years, half as long as Vilayne herself had been The Wise Woman's pupil. It was considered rude to ask someone directly about their age, but Vilayne guessed Ezme was about a decade younger than she.

Ezme had been something of a loner when Vilayne noticed her inventing magic symbols to hex the young goblins that teased her, and they found comfort in each other's company, if only because they shared a general disdain for the warren's dominant social circles.

"I have something important to tell you," The Wise

Woman said to Vilayne without looking up from an array of divination bones on the rug.

The Wise Woman was broad of stature, but that might have been from layers of furs and other garments beneath her cozy robe. Her ears were very large, one of the largest sets of the whole warren, which spoke to her great age. They were tattered, with many piercings of red gold and pearls. Her white hair was also adorned with pearls, woven through her netted headdress.

"Is it also what you said you would tell me?" Ezme asked, trying to sound patient.

"Yes, now shut your yap and listen. I have had a vision." She looked up and met Vilayne's gaze. "The voices of the long dead call to me. They speak of the Goblin King."

"*The* Goblin King?" Vilayne asked.

"I thought the Goblin King was just a myth," Ezme remarked, scrunching her nostrils.

"A myth that holds the truth!" The Wise Woman exclaimed. "Ten thousand years ago, the Goblin King walked this world."

"Were you alive to see it?" Ezme teased.

"I'm not *that* old, sprat!" She jabbed at Ezme with her cane which swiftly emerged from the curtains of her robe. "But I am old enough to discern the meaning of the oldest stories."

"What version of the story do you know?" Vilayne asked, smiling to herself as Ezme's ears drooped. They were obligated to listen to the most respected elder of the warren.

"Long ago," The Wise Woman began, "the Goblin King ruled all goblin-kin. He spoke to the gods and the earth and learned their secrets. But then, he turned his back on the wheel of life and death. He forsook his ancestors and tried to reach for immortality. Many fell under his spell, and there was war. At the end of it, those loyal to their ancestors broke his crown, and he was banished from the world of the living."

"That's it?" Vilayne asked after a pause. "I was expecting a longer story."

"Me too," Ezme said with relief.

"There are many stories about him, but it doesn't matter. What *is* important is that the ancestors speak of him, and of Zalenthas."

"Who's that?" Ezme asked.

"Not 'who,'" The Wise Woman replied, "but '*where.*' It is one of the very first warrens of our ancient ancestors, and it was believed to be somewhere in this region."

"Could it be an older name for Kol'grathu?" Vilayne asked, pondering the possibility.

"No, it is distinct from our warren. Its entrance is not by the cliffs, but deep in the forest. I have seen it in a dream. It has been sealed since the Goblin King's banishment, but something has made the spirits there restless. Something has happened, or is happening, or is soon to happen . . . and there are *humans* involved."

"How do you know?" True worry began to tinge Vilayne's mood.

The Wise Woman jabbed her cane at the bones on the rug, as if it were the obvious answer.

"The bones speak of outsiders," the old woman went on. "Who else would go digging up our sacred places?"

"Humans are bigly greedy," Ezme agreed.

"This is why you shall both go there and ensure its secrets do not fall into the wrong hands."

"What?!" Emze cried in alarm. "Why me? I barely know how to sing a spell that can move a feather!"

"Why not send warriors?" Vilayne took an assertive step forward. "Surely they would be able to deal with any humans."

"I do not command the warriors," The Wise Woman said, "Warface does. He is the warren war-chief, and if I ask him to go on this quest, I foresee disaster. The omen specifically warns against the use of a warrior, and that goes double for one as warg-headed as Warface."

"So you're sending *us*?" Vilayne asked in disbelief.

"Despite my *best* efforts, you two are the only ones in the warren who have any appetite for spellcraft. It is in you, I must place my trust, for it is magic and cunning you will need in spirit-guarded places."

"What about Fumble?" Ezme offered. "I've seen him do magic."

"Illusions!" The Wise Woman scoffed. "Puff and potions and glamour! His vain ambitions would best stay in the company of that muscle-head, Trokar."

"Can't we bring anyone else?" Vilayne asked. "There's safety in numbers."

"Of course, I am not sending just the two of you. My apprentice will guide you."

"*Bonewise* will lead us?" Ezme asked.

"Yes."

A serious matter then, Vilayne thought. The Wise Woman would not send her apprentice and both of her student-servants unless the stakes were truly high.

"Isn't there anything you can give us that might help tilt the odds in our favor if we find trouble?" Ezme asked hopefully.

The Wise Woman glanced at a heap of ritual oddities on a table and stroked the fuzz around her lips.

"There is *something* I can give you," the elder said,

retrieving a crooked, charred stick from a pink crystal holder. She held it out for Ezme, but the young goblin didn't take it right away. She examined it closely in the old woman's wrinkled hand.

"A wand?" Ezme asked. "What does it do?"

"I'm not sure," The Wise Woman replied. "It is from a zohar tree that was struck by lightning in a strange land. Its energy is . . . confusing, but the power is there."

Ezme took the wand, and The Wise Woman stepped back with a wary glance, as if she were afraid it might discharge its power at once, but nothing happened.

"Do not use it unless you need to," The Wise Woman warned.

"Don't I get something?" Vilayne asked.

"No," The Wise Woman said abruptly. "Ezme needs it more than you, Vilayne. Just remember what I've taught you."

Vilayne sighed. "The war-chief will need to approve of this mission," she commented. "The Moot is soon, isn't it?"

"You are correct," The Wise Woman answered. "It has been three years since the last Moot, and he should begin his preparations soon. He will agree to this mission, if asked in the right way. Bonewise knows. A gathering will be called tonight. Prepare for your journey."

CHAPTER
TWO
HONORING TRADITION

Bonewise marched up the tunnel toward the great chamber of the warren, his large headdress of bones and the clack of his wooden sling-staff on the stone signaling others on the path to step out of his way. Some were grabbing food from the eatery on his left, others were dumping garbage down the bottomless pit on his right.

"Gathering is now," Bonewise said gruffly to them. "You heard the call."

They nodded and said they were coming.

"Do not tarry," he added. Everyone who heard the call was supposed to join the gathering, but Bonewise knew some tried to skip out on meetings.

The Wise Woman had told him what was to come. He was to undertake a journey to find a long-lost warren. Something of great importance was nigh: An event, a turning point, a nexus of destiny, however the omens were unclear. The visions were mysterious, but that was the way with mysticism. The ancestors never gave straight answers. At least, not to him. He suspected The Wise Woman knew more than she was telling him, but such was to be expected, for she was practically an ancestor herself. She had been old even when he was a little sprat.

He remembered his younger nights fondly, when he would go hunting rabbits through the briars with his friend, Thorn-Snub. Creamfoot went with him sometimes instead, but when she did, it wasn't to actually hunt for rabbits. Those were happy nights under the moon, before Creamfoot disappeared on a fishing trip, and a few years after Thorn-Snub was killed by a lone warg during a dangerous hunting expedition with Warface.

Bonewise had stood on the cliffs for days and nights, hoping to see his lover's little boat return from the cove, but it never did. He agonized over the thousand unthinkable ways she could have died. He had been mired in his grief, but The Wise Woman taught him how to accept her death, and later, even how to commune with the dead. To speak with Creamfoot again.

Creamfoot had not told him how she had died. He was to accept the mystery of death, to find a purpose in life that included his pain, and went beyond it. If he could help others, even if only to carry their own pain, then he would honor the ancestors as well as those who were yet to be born.

He took a private vow of celibacy and dedicated himself to learning the wisdom of his ancestors. How strange, he thought, that even after all these years, he had difficulty feeling compassion again, most of all for himself. Tears had not come to him in many years. Putting the dead to rest was so much easier than finding peace for the living. Now the time had come to put his training to use. He would find the dwelling place of his ancient ancestors, and find out why their spirits had become restless.

He entered the central chamber. It was crowded with the goblins of Kol'grathu, as disordered and beautiful as the graffiti on the walls. The assembly was a shifting mosaic of speckled green, blue, and grey bodies in colorful garb, each leaf-nosed face unique and known to him. They packed the floor and balconies, raucous with gossip and laughter.

The cave ceiling wafted with the smoke of varied musical smoking implements, for blue cave lichen was plentiful and helped loosen creativity. It was common for gatherings to generate several jam sessions where the players tried to smoke each other out.

Bonewise smoked a flute, but this was not an occasion for celebration. He saw a dozen hunters clustered in the center, outfitted with their weapons and armor, and amongst them was Warface, who stood on the speaking stone, already trying to command attention. The war-chief's visage was tattooed, as was the fashion for many hunters, but they accentuated an earlier mark: two claw gashes from the warg that had taken Thorn-Snub's life.

The warg had gotten away, and Warface had never succeeded in tracking it down. It was a sore subject for the war-chief, and there were unpleasant consequences for bringing it up in public, as his critics had learned.

Warface's purple-jeweled chin piercing flashed as he jabbered a strident call for attention, which cut through the riotous chamber and echoed along many connecting tunnels.

"We are here to plan for the summer raids!" Warface growled as everyone reluctantly turned their ears to hear him. "Kol'grathu, let me hear you!"

The great chamber thrummed with a chorus of voices singing their own names, as was customary to begin an official gathering.

Warface gazed proudly across the assembly as the echo of their voices traveled into the far reaches of the warren.

"The Moot is next moon!" Warface announced as the singing ceased, breaking the sudden silence. "The more warriors we can commit to join the other warrens in raiding the enemy, the more hands we have to bring back loot!"

"Loot! Loot! Loot!" Many goblins chanted.

"The Moot is for loot!" Warface recited. "Who is brave enough to join the war band?"

"War-band War-face!" His hunting friends chanted.

"Who will show the worth of Kol'grathu by the prizes they take from the sprat-murdering humans?!"

Many called out that they would join, and hunters went through the crowd with planks and chalk for volunteers to scribble their personal insignia, as was customary to keep account.

Bonewise made his way to the speaking stone, even as Warface continued to bark atop it.

"Finally going to add some humie bones to your collection, spirit-speaker?" Warface asked him smugly.

"There is another matter of the Moot that has not been addressed," Bonewise announced loudly.

Warface scowled. He did not like anything that sounded even remotely like a challenge. Bonewise walked half-way up the dome of the speaking stone and stopped, his sling-staff clacking loudly in the quiet. It was customary for the speaking stone to be shared with whomever was addressing the assembly, but Warface did not budge.

"What might that be?" Warface asked, agitated.

"Each warren represented at the Moot brings a fantastic gift. As you all know, the war-chief who presents the best gift is awarded the position of Big War-chief and leads all the clans on the raids."

"What's your point, Bonewise? Spit it out!"

"Not only that," Bonewise continued loudly, "but the leading warren is awarded *all* of the gifts the others gambled in the bid to win the position! Why should it not be us?"

Hearty cheers answered him from the crowd, but also incredulous laughter.

"In all your years, you have never *been* to a Moot, Bonewise," Warface accused. "If you had, you would know that the bigger warrens gamble with powerful relics stolen from the humans and the elves. We do not have such things! Perhaps your headdress possesses great magic? Give it to me, and I shall offer it!" He gave a sour grin.

"It is true our warren is small," Bonewise said, turning to address the crowd. "But we do not need great numbers to prove we are a great clan, nor do we need to present the work of non-goblins as a measure of our own worth! Our ancestors created *wonders*, and it is known to me that an ancient warren of our people is hidden in the forest to the south. I shall go there and recover these wonders for Kol'-grathu and the Moot."

"You?" Warface asked, amused. "All by yourself?"

"Others skilled in the art of magic shall accompany me."

"I will go with him," Vilayne announced as she approached the speaking stone.

"And me," Ezme said from nearby, briefly raising her hand.

"So"—Warface grinned—"it was The Wise Woman who put you up to this, was it? Very well, Bonewise, you and your volunteers can go, but you need to take a warrior, as well."

"The omen warned against taking a warrior," Bonewise cautioned.

"Is that so? Why?"

"I do not question the advice offered by the spirits." Bonewise thunked the foot of his sling-staff on the stone for emphasis.

"Perhaps the warrior would be ill-fated?" Warface slanted one ear thoughtfully. "I cannot spare any of my hunters, but you really ought to bring some *muscle* with you. I insist." Warface turned toward the bar, an expectant look on his face. "Trokar!"

Nearby goblins stepped aside, opening up a space around Trokar, who had been leaning on the sleek bar in the midst of whispering something to Cavesong, who was pouring him a drink. At the sound of his name, his ears went flat and he jolted upright, whirling around.

"That's me!" Trokar answered reflexively, pushing his ears back up with effort. "I'm here! Just getting a drink . . ." He reached over and awkwardly lifted his mug from the slab. "Yep. Grog is good tonight! How are you?"

"You are *strong*, Trokar, are you not?"

"I-I am! It's so nice of you to notice!" He flexed one bicep. "You usually call me a weakling, so I—"

"You will go on this 'mission of wonders' and protect The Wise Woman's pupils."

"Uh . . . The what? Oh, I don't think I should," Trokar said uneasily.

"They need a strong warrior to protect them. You have trained hard. Now make yourself useful!"

"But . . . I'm not a warrior! I just do exercises to stay healthy. I don't believe in violence. I—"

A sudden crack and puff of smoke interrupted him, and the shiny, bald head of Fumble appeared beside him.

"I've seen Trokar crush rocks to powder with his bare hands!" Fumble declared, sparkling motes of light falling from his palms. "Yet his skin remains soft and his hands uncracked, thanks to our specially-formulated work'n-goblin's skin-care oil!"

"We don't have time for your perfumes and potions, Fumble!" Warface snarled.

"Ah, but I know magic!" Fumble exclaimed from his perch atop the bar. "Since those skilled in the art of magic are going on this mission to uncover ancient secrets and whatnot, I feel strongly that I should accompany Trokar, for he is in peak performance with my help, you see!"

"Fine! Just shut up! You can go as well, but no others!"

"Then it is decided," Bonewise stated.

"Yes," Warface affirmed, turning back to Bonewise. "You shall leave at sunset. Now, who will show their worth in the raids?" His hunters resumed pressing planks upon anyone who was fit to travel.

THE SUN WAS SOON to rise, and most goblins would be going to their nests to sleep for the better part of the day. Trokar and Fumble, however, scrambled to stock their packs with useful and extra-useful items. Trokar stuffed one of his pack's side-pockets with dried noodles, and on the other side, pouches of paprika, salt, and other spices.

Fumble pointed out that Trokar needed a weapon, so they spent the better part of an hour looking through the stock of Jaxxfang, the trader. Fumble traded for a simple shortbow and quiver of hunting arrows, even though he had no skill in archery to speak of. Trokar bought a cuirass of old, cracked leather armor that he thought accentuated his biceps, then finally selected a chipped, double-edged iron sword the length of his forearm, but he didn't have anything left Jaxxfang wanted in exchange. Fumble made the trade with a "special" potion, and in return, asked Trokar if he would carry some of his heavier camp gear, which Trokar graciously accepted.

At last, Fumble took a sleeping potion and got some rest in his den a few hours before sunset, making sure to set his home-made, water-clock alarm. Trokar, however, was too excited to sleep. He sat on the narrow beach at the bottom of the cliffs around Shipwreck Bay, making sure to slather himself with Fumble's anti-sun ointment. The sword in its scabbard on his belt felt uncomfortable, so he removed it and stuck it point-down in the sand.

Trokar had never killed anything bigger than a moth before. What would he do if he had to use his sword, he wondered? He had tried to learn how to fight in the sparring chamber when he came of age, but after two years of bruises and ridicule, he focused exclusively on strength training. The ridicule did not stop, but at least he had not been in physical pain. For five years, he channeled all his anger into his workouts, and it had made him one of the most muscular goblins in the warren.

He watched coconut-sized hermit crabs and the sun-bleached skulls they used for shells comb the beach for washed-up morsels. He reflected on his life, and realized that he had never ventured far from home, though he dreamed of selling beauty products in distant and wonderful places. He believed that if he could trade such things to the humans and elves, then he could claim true success. Goblins were considered ugly by the other races, but if he could help the other races become more beautiful, perhaps they would see the beauty in goblins as well.

He trembled with anxiety about what dangers might take his life on the quest that had been thrust upon him, but also with excitement of what it could do to propel his dreams into reality. He leaned back on the sand in the shadow of the cliffs and thought about it until he closed his eyes and drifted off under the bright blue sky.

CHAPTER
THREE
THE HUNT

Fumble stepped through the round wooden door to exit his laboratory, which was the size of a coat closet. It closed with a harrowing squeak, as it had upon opening. He glanced up at an air shaft that went from the cave to the cliffs, and saw the slant of afternoon light. He quaffed a bit of go-juice, then strapped on his pack and traipsed to the central chamber.

Bonewise, Vilayne, and Ezme were already there. They were outfitted in sturdy traveling gear in addition to their ceremonial garb, such as Bonewise's elaborate headdress and Vilayne's colorful, chain-clasped cloak with a fur mantle.

Acrid, the scullery worker, was busy cleaning up in preparation for a new night, and a few sprats were up early to hunt for bugs skittering over leftovers of food.

"Where's Trokar?" Ezme asked.

"You haven't seen him?" Fumble asked.

They shook their heads.

"Hang on, I think I know where he is."

"We will meet you at the leaning stones," Bonewise said.

Fumble went to Trokar's sleeping alcove, but his hammock was empty. Next, he scampered to the training room, but as soon as he arrived, the door to the war-chief's chamber opened. Fumble ducked back around the corner, nearly tripping over a dumbbell. Warface yakked to rouse Rusthead the runner from the cot beside the weapon rack. Not waiting to see if he had been noticed, Fumble retreated back up the tunnel.

Finally, he spied Trokar's pack behind the fermentation barrels, and went down the drainage tunnel to the beach, finding Trokar asleep in the sand.

"We gotta go, Troak!" Fumble called.

"Wh-wha?" Trokar mumbled.

"Let's hit the trail before Warface changes his mind!"

"Oh, crud!" Trokar exclaimed, remembering the mission as he woke. "But I haven't washed yet, and there's sand in my hair!"

"No time for that, moth-mouth! The others are waiting for us!"

Trokar nearly forgot his sword, but turned back and grabbed it as he followed Fumble to retrieve his heavy pack. They went up the spiral tunnel to join the others at the entrance to the warren. Killgap the old, one-eyed guard gave them a nod as they passed him and the giant trapdoor spider trained to guard the camouflaged cave entrance under the leaning stones atop the coastal plateau.

"Twilight is soon upon us," Bonewise announced as they arrived. "Let us make our way."

They headed east but soon turned south on the sinuous trails through the brambles that arched over the path protectively. They all knew the labyrinth of the briar well, but then they entered the deep, dark wood that was Duskfen Forest.

Moonlight filtered through the canopy, cast in hues of deep purple from the flowering jacaranda trees. It would have been too dim for a human, but goblins had keen vision in the dark. The air was filled with the music of cicadas and floral fragrance—honey-sweet, mixed with the earthy musk of decaying fleshy pedals on the forest floor. Briar patches and arid scrub obstructed the trail here and there, but most of the time movement was easy between swordferns, and they trekked many leagues.

Fumble elucidated how he distilled the fragrance of the flowers, though Trokar was the only one of the group who expressed any interest as he obsessively scratched the sand out of his hair. Fumble jumped from one related subject to the next without missing a beat, broadcasting copious information like he always did when he was excited or nervous.

While Fumble and Trokar were distracted, Vilayne walked up close behind Bonewise.

"The Wise Woman said not to bring a warrior," Vilayne whispered to him.

"By his own admission," Bonewise replied with a sidelong glance, "Trokar is not a warrior. So we need not worry."

Fumble was describing his process for creating fully reacted pure salts, when the cicadas stopped singing, and his voice was heard in stark contrast to the silence.

"Hey, Fumble," Ezme addressed as she swiveled around in agitation, cutting off his next words as well as his next steps. "Clamp your tongue before every creature in the forest—"

"Be silent and still!" Bonewise called from the front. He

grabbed a stone from his rock pocket and quickly placed it in the sling of his staff. Everyone turned to face where he was looking.

A hulking, spiny animal stepped out from the cover of tall pech grass in a clearing just ahead of them. It was twice the height of Bonewise, and that was including his headdress. Its shoulders were massively muscled; its back arched up in a hump between them. The bristles on its long, thick tail prickled, and it bared its sharp yellow teeth. There were old scars on its face, and Bonewise knew: This was the warg that had killed Thorn-Snub all those years ago.

"Spread out! Be threatening!" Bonewise shouted, puffing his chest.

They moved out of single-file to present their numbers, and Trokar unsheathed his sword shakily. They shouted and yakked, but the warg snarled louder and louder, drool dripping from its massive mouth.

It took a step closer.

Fumble violently shook a vial then popped the cork with his thumb, and a bright flash of light shot out from it at the warg. It flinched, crouched, barked angrily, then charged at the meatiest member of their assembly —Trokar.

At that moment, Trokar wanted to run, but he was too terrified to turn away. He yelped in panic and threw his sword with all his might. The warg ran straight toward the twirling blade, which pierced its eye and lodged deep in its brain. It made a guttural groan and collapsed as it skidded to a halt a few paces from its perceived prey. The warg's tongue flopped out of its mouth, then it was still. It drew no breath, and after a moment of stunned silence, they realized it was dead.

"*Woo!*" Trokar shouted with upraised arms. "Did you see that?!"

Bonewise could scarcely believe his eyes. He poked at the warg's body with his sling-staff.

"My flare blinded it!" Fumble declared. "That's probably why it ran into your sword, Trokar."

"I saw it staring into my soul!" Trokar retorted, posing with his bicep flexed. "I slew the terrible beast with the skill of my strong arm!"

"That was *luck*," Vilayne said.

Trokar paid her no heed and basked in the afterglow of victory.

"Be at peace, old friend," Bonewise prayed solemnly, laying a hand on the warm head of the warg. He was speaking to the spirit of Thorn-Snub, who had a connection to the creature that took his friend's flesh.

"That thing was your friend?" Ezme asked incredulously.

"No," Bonewise answered dourly. "It killed someone close to me, long ago."

"Oh. I'm sorry. Who was it?"

Bonewise didn't answer. He turned his gaze to Vilayne. Did she know, he wondered? Goblins did not always know their parentage, for the young were raised collectively by the warren, usually in the care of a few dedicated mothers and sprat-herders. Vilayne had been very young when her father had died.

Vilayne met his gaze and Bonewise looked away, back to the corpse.

"We should not linger," he said. "Death draws attention."

"Wait," Trokar protested, "we have to take proof!"

"Even if we took the time to flesh its hide, its stink

would alert other beasts. And, it's a big hide, it would burden our journey."

"I can carry it," Trokar declared confidently, and he dropped his heavy pack with a clatter.

"Take a trophy, if you must," Bonewise grumbled. "But I will not skin this for you. I advise you to leave it for the scavengers."

"I want its teeth," Fumble said.

"I'll have its head, then," Trokar decided. "You can have the teeth after we get back, Fumble. I can't present a toothless monster!" He pulled his sword free of the head with a firm tug. "Gross," he muttered.

He chopped at the neck, but the chipped blade practically bounced off the thick spines and scruff. He tried chopping at it more forcefully, his frustration overriding his disgust of the gore his efforts created.

"Gross, gross, gross!" Trokar cried as he hacked and slashed, working himself into a frenzy. Finally, the head separated from the spinal column.

"Congratulations," Vilayne sighed. "You have your trophy. Can we go now?"

"Just a sec . . ." Trokar poured salt from a bag over the cleaved meat, then stuffed it in the canvas sack that had been holding his sleeping roll. He tied the sleeping roll to the top of his pack, then strapped the trophy bag, already stained with blood, to the back of it. He grunted with effort as he lifted the pack to his shoulders. The head almost doubled the weight of it, but he was committed.

They traveled on, and at midnight, they came within earshot of the Duskfen River, its mighty current snaking around natural canals and river islands of limestone.

Bonewise knew they had veered east, away from the coast, so they put the sound of the rapids behind them as they turned south once more. They hiked for hours, and the moon marched across the night sky. It was almost full, and cast long, deep shadows through the forest as it squatted upon the horizon, soon to disappear. Trokar was exhausted, and lagged behind.

"Gobs?" he called ahead breathlessly. "If we could stop for a snack... I just need a breather."

"Shouldn't we set up camp, or something?" Ezme complained, her weariness evident as she stumbled on snagging, thorny vines. "Do we even know where we are?"

"Not to be overly skeptical," Fumble piped in, "but how do we know where we're supposed to be going?"

"I'm just following Bonewise," Vilayne clarified.

At the front, Bonewise blinked out of a trance. He realized he had been pressing on without really knowing what to look for. He needed a sign. He stopped at the foot of a huge jacaranda tree and looked up. A breeze rippled through the mauve canopy high overhead. The quivering trees stretched tall, reaching toward the light. This part of the forest was old, he realized, and the stink of the tree's flowers was overpowering.

"I think I smell... smoke," Vilayne announced.

Bonewise sniffed—once, twice, and a third time, deep. He had thought the smokey-scent was from the rotting petals, but she was right, there was smoke in the air.

"Be wary," Bonewise cautioned. "There may be humans near. We follow the smoke to its source." He turned northeast, almost entirely back the way they had come. He passed Ezme, tangled in vines.

Vilayne unsheathed a knife and cut her free.

Trokar had just set down his heavy pack, and groaned as Bonewise gave him a look. He shouldered it again and followed.

CHAPTER

FOUR

THE BARGAIN

They criss-crossed the breeze, following the scent of smoke, until, near dawn, they encountered a campsite in a grassy clearing beside a low hill. There was a small, pyramidal canvas tent hung from a tree branch by a rope, with a stack of dry, broken branches nearby, and a fire-pit faintly ablaze beside a cloaked figure hunched next to it.

The goblins huddled behind some squat, flowering quince trees at the edge of the glade, which were no taller than themselves.

"That looks like a human," Fumble whispered, "and look, it's sleeping!"

The woman's face was a deep mahogany color, her black hair naturally twisted into curls, the tips dyed purple. Her eyes were lidded, her head propped up on her hand, with her elbow on her knee. Her feet, clad in scuffed, knee-high boots, were perched upon the stones of the fire-pit, as close as possible to the warm coals. Beneath her cloak were purple robes with blue trim. A shoulder-slung scroll case was propped against the log she was sitting on, with a dark bottle beside it.

"This is the perfect opportunity to set up an ambush!" Fumble declared.

"Now, hold on," Trokar whispered back. "Why do we need to ambush her? She's just one human, and there's"—he paused to count—"five of us! Maybe we can talk to her?"

"Talk?!" Fumble whispered incredulously. "That's a dirty, filthy human, Trokar! You can't trust them! I bet there's more humans crammed in that tent, and as soon as we show ourselves, a dozen of them will pop out of it like a bunch of murder clowns!"

"One or two, perhaps," Bonewise reasoned.

"Attacking them is just what they would expect us to do," Trokar argued. "I say we throw them off by being friendly."

"Ah, and *then* attack them." Fumble nodded. "Very devious."

"No attacking! What if we can make a trade with them?"

"We need more information," Vilayne said.

"Vilayne is right," Bonewise announced. "We do have the element of surprise, but we may be able to learn more with words than with violence."

"Don't say I didn't warn you," Fumble said.

"You gobs hang back," Trokar said. "I'll put myself out there and you can rescue me if you need to."

"Smart not to reveal our true numbers right away," Ezme said agreeably.

Bonewise gave Trokar a nod, then they all watched as Trokar crept out into the open.

As he drew near, he noticed the creeping twilight illuminating a shadowy arch in the background, set in the low hill. At first, he thought it was an old tree bent over to the ground, but he saw it was of a grey stone, and a flat rock wall was sheltered beneath it.

He turned his attention back to the human woman. She didn't look like a warrior, Trokar thought, eying her. He told himself there was no need to feel afraid, and yet his heart pounded in his chest. She dozed, unaware of his approach. He stopped, thinking he should not get too close before announcing himself.

He cleared his throat, but she only stirred a little, and didn't wake up.

"H-Hello? Hello," he said, unsure if she could understand his native language. He only knew a few words in the common speech humans used, and they were all from dirty jokes.

The woman slowly opened one eye, then the other, her gaze soft and unfocused.

"Hello," he said again, and waved at her.

The woman inhaled sharply and leapt to her feet, grabbing up the bottle beside her as she flung her cloak open. She popped the hinged stopper off with her thumb.

Trokar put his hands up, presenting his open palms to show he wielded no weapons, and he took a step back.

"Peace!" he said, and much to his relief, the woman took no further action. She blinked, peering at him with a face twist with alarm and confusion. He told himself that she must be fearful of what he might do because he had startled her awake, and not because he was a goblin.

"Baga-ki," the woman said in cautious salutation, but she kept her guarded stance. "Hûvu?"

"Hû...vu?" Trokar echoed back, unsure of its meaning.

"Peace," the woman translated, speaking his own language.

Trokar's ears went up.

"Yes, peace!" Trokar repeated. "You speak goblin, that's great! My name is Trokar." He pressed a hand to his chest.

"Name..." the woman said in recognition, "Trokar. My name... Sueda."

"Sue-da," Trokar repeated back. "Nice to meet you, Sueda. Are you here alone?"

He flattened his ears. In retrospect, he thought the question might be interpreted badly.

"No," she answered.

"I have friends nearby," Trokar said slowly, so she could understand him. "We come in peace. We were just... wondering... what you're doing here?"

Sueda hesitated. She seemed about to speak, but then a man appeared between her and the tent. He was tall and thin, with gaunt shaved cheeks. His hair was black and straight, the hue of his skin much paler than the woman's, and his robes were silver with red embroidery of geometric shapes. A shiny blue gem was set in a leather headband over his forehead like a third eye.

"What business is it of yours, goblin?" the man asked. He spoke Trokar's language easily, much better than Sueda, though it still sounded strange from a human mouth.

Trokar quashed his fear, noting that while rude, the man did not seem threatening.

"Uh, well..." Trokar began, "these are *our* ancestral lands."

"This land is a territory of the Faladian Republic. We have every right to be here."

"Who *are* you, exactly?"

"I am Audrel, magnate of archeology for the Republic and leader of this expedition."

"Expedition? Expedition for what?"

Adurel stared at Trokar with a mixture of intensity and serenity. He seemed to be calculating something in his private thoughts.

"I will be happy to tell you," Audrel said at last without emotion, "if your friends would come out and join us."

"It's alright, gobs!" Trokar called to the bushes, and he gestured them over.

Bonewise, Vilayne, Ezme, and Fumble emerged from the edge of the forest and came to stand near Trokar. He introduced them each in turn.

"Charmed, I'm sure," Audrel said flatly.

Trokar wasn't familiar with the phrase, but he sensed Audrel's sarcasm.

"As I said," the man continued, "I am Audrel, of House Meklar, and this is my assistant Sueda from the Atrium Academy. She is not of noble birth, but she is sponsored by my House as one of our water priestesses." He gave Sueda a glance, but she kept her eyes on the goblins, eyes roaming from one to another.

"Ah," Trokar said, "that sounds very . . . big." He had meant to say something like "prestigious," but couldn't think of the word in that moment.

"You were going to tell us what you came searching for?" Vilayne asked. She was tired and had even less patience for pleasantries than usual.

"We are studying ancient cultures," Audrel explained. "We have visited many ruins suspected to be of goblinoid origin. The feats of architecture we found, it was difficult to believe that goblins could have built them. Indeed, some of my colleagues believe that goblins only occupied or vandalized the works of others. Elves, or perhaps the dwarves, but—"

"How do they know what goblins are capable of?" Ezme asked, irritated.

"It is well known that goblins dwell in natural caverns. If your kind ever built cities, you have not done so for all of recorded history."

"Maybe if humans stopped killing us," Ezme accused, "we would live above ground!"

"No fight!" Sueda pleaded.

"Let us not argue," Audrel said, waving his hand dismissively. "There is a wall, over there"—he pointed to the stone arch behind him—"which bears pictographs particular to goblinoids. It is far less impressive than what we found in the Crown Spires, but it is very old, and we are having difficulty interpreting it. Perhaps you could make sense of its meaning?"

"Why do you want to know?" Bonewise asked pointedly.

"For posterity, of course," Audrel said, his lips curling up slightly in an almost imperceptible smile.

"What does that mean?" Ezme whispered.

"It means he wants to share what he learns," Vilayne answered.

Bonewise huffed. "My posterior! You can't go sharing our people's culture for your own benefit!"

"If there were greater understanding between us and your kind," Audrel said, "would you not benefit as well?"

"Not necessarily," Vilayne said.

Fumble, who had been silent the whole conversation up until then, stepped forward. "If you humies want our interpretation, it will cost you."

"But of course," Audrel responded. "I have silver."

"Silver is good. How much you got?"

"Greedy goblins!" Audrel seethed, his calm facade

cracking. "I have a modest sum allocated for trading. I shall give you fifty silver for your service."

"Make it eighty and I'll give you an alchemist-grade translation."

"Ten silver for each of you is a generous offer! Unless you want to haggle with each other, as well?"

"Fine—fifty," Fumble said. "A good sum for up-front payment."

"Up front? Oh, very well! Since you have such a *deep connection* to this place, I expect a stellar translation!" He slipped his hand into his robe and plucked out a small, clinking cloth bag, which he tossed to Fumble.

"We can count it later," Fumble said, tucking the pouch away for safekeeping. "Let's have a look at these glyphs."

Audrel and Sueda led the goblins the short walk to the tree-like stone arch holding up the foot of the hill, and beneath it was a wall with deep, precise inscriptions. The inscriptions were a procession of symbols and images, with triangular-headed figures in the depictions.

The first symbol was a circle with two dots beneath it intersecting a smaller circle, a number. The next glyph showed a gathering of figures within the swirly, reed-bordered symbol for a small body of water. The third symbol showed the figures being submerged, and then the same symbol inverted. The fifth symbol was much like the first, except the smaller intersecting circle had four triangular heads connected to it. The final symbol was reminiscent of a shrug.

Fumble started his interpretation, but Bonewise disagreed with his impression of the second symbol, interrupting him to say so. Vilayne offered some ideas, and everyone got involved by the time they discussed the fifth glyph. The birds were singing to the rising sun.

"Clearly," Bonewise said, "it is a question of how do you get twenty-four people coming out of the pond when only twenty went in?"

"Maybe they had babies underwater?" Trokar wondered.

"I thought this, also," Sueda chimed in. "It is sacred technique of water priestesses."

"We don't do that," Fumble said dismissively.

"You . . . do not have babies?" Sueda asked quizzically.

"Of course we have babies, but goblins lay eggs, you see." He gave a wink to Trokar.

Trokar did his best to keep a straight face.

Sueda looked skeptical, dark eyes narrow.

"Maybe it means literally four heads," Vilayne pondered. "Like they were decapitated when they went underwater and then floated to the surface."

"How macabre," Audrel commented.

"Do you mind?" Fumble asked, annoyed. "Twenty-four . . ." He mused, rubbing his bald top. "Twenty-four . . . and the four is represented as heads . . ." He rubbed his hand down where his eyebrows would have been, if he had any hair. Suddenly, he looked at his hand, then touched his brow with a wide grin.

"That's it!" Fumble declared. "It's not a number puzzle, it's a word puzzle! They only came up out the water partway, showing their four heads! Twenty *foreheads*!"

The stone wall rumbled, then slowly slid down into the ground, revealing a dark, square passage through solid rock into the hill behind it.

Audrel slapped his forehead. "You mean the answer was a pun?! I should have known goblins would come up with something so ridiculous!"

"And *we* should have known you were hiding the fact that this was a doorway!" Ezme accused.

"I suspected as much!" Fumble added.

"I could not be sure it was anything," Audrel said defensively. "But now that we know there is more here, we are obliged to investigate."

"You got your interpretation," Vilayne said, "but fifty silver doesn't buy you our heritage!"

"Yeah," Ezme said, "we won't let you steal from our ancestors!"

"A goblin," Audrel scoffed, "telling *me* not to steal? Outrageous!"

"Hûvu, Audrel," Sueda said to him.

"How about another job, goblins?" Audrel offered, straightening his posture. "I'll give you *ten* times my former offer . . . to hire you to investigate the interior in our stead. There is only one thing I desire from within."

"What might that be?" Bonewise asked.

"A stone. A very special grey or silver stone. It might not look like more than a pebble to your eyes, but we believe it is connected to an ancient relic of our ancestors"—he paused for dramatic effect—"the Bloodstone."

"What's that?" Ezme asked.

"It's a magic gem, also known as a philosopher's stone, which is said to have mythical, life-giving powers. It was spoken of by Dustameus himself."

The goblins looked at each other and shrugged, none of them knew what he was talking about.

Audrel rolled his eyes. "Dustameus," Audrel clarified, "the prophet that led my people to the light of Utu."

"Who to?" Fumble asked.

"Utu! The Sky God!"

"Riiight," Fumble said patronizingly, "the invisible sky-god that talked to that one guy. Of course."

"Do you want the pay, or not?"

Trokar cocked his head. "Give us a moment to talk it over?"

Audrel made a permissive gesture, and the goblins huddled around the smoldering ashes of the fire pit to whisper amongst themselves.

Fumble was convinced it was a trap, but Bonewise could not abide allowing the humans to explore the tunnel. Fumble agreed they needed to keep the humans out, and Trokar wondered if some should go inside while others stayed outside to keep an eye on the humans.

Vilayne and Bonewise were against splitting the group, then they all agreed to deal with the humans after they explored the passageway. They broke the circle and turned to face Audrel and Sueda.

"We agree to your terms," Bonewise announced.

"Yeah," Fumble added, "but we want to see the silver!"

Audrel went to the tent and emerged carrying a small wooden box. He flipped the lid open. It was almost filled to the brim with neat rows of silver coins. Half of one full row was missing.

"It will be waiting for you when you return," Audrel said, then closed the lid.

"So be it," Bonewise said.

Trokar untied the bloody bag containing the warg's head from his backpack, setting it down by the archway.

"Don't touch!" Trokar demanded, pointing to the bag, and then he and his companions walked into the dusty, lightless tunnel.

CHAPTER
FIVE
THE DISCOVERY

As they walked deeper into the hill, a nauseating breeze of stale air blew by, escaping toward the entrance. Something was unsettling about the squareness of the tunnel, the flatness of the walls, ceiling, and floor, which would have been indistinguishable from one another were it not for their feet planted firmly on the ground.

"I feel strange," Ezme said, rubbing the inside of her ears.

"Did your ears pop?" Fumble asked.

"Yeah, they did," she replied.

"Mine, too."

Trokar flexed his jaw, yawned, and he, too, felt his ears pop.

"There is power here," Bonewise stated.

"There aren't any seams in the rock," Vilayne said, running her fingers along the wall.

"How long could this tunnel be?" Trokar asked, looking back at the diminishing square of light in the distance.

"Are we going down?" Fumble asked. "How big is this hill?"

"Fumble," Bonewise addressed, "give us some light."

Fumble took a vial of liquid in hand and lightly shook it. It glowed with a yellow light, illuminating a fork of the square passage in front of them. One tunnel went to the left and the other to the right. Bonewise thunked his staff on the floor a couple times, listening to its echo.

"The path there comes to an end," he announced, pointing to their right, "while the other way opens into a large chamber. Let us avoid the dead end."

After a short walk through the curved tunnel, they came into a circular chamber with a ceiling so high they couldn't see it. Fumble shook his glowing vial again, with more vigor, and it shone brightly. The pale yellow of old bones peeked out from goblin-sized burial alcoves all around the chamber and up the walls, stacked tier upon tier, hundreds of them, up into the darkness. They still could not see the ceiling.

"The hill didn't look this tall from the outside," Ezme said.

"It wasn't," Fumble affirmed. "Maybe it's an illusion?"

"It's real," Bonewise said. "We are deeper underground than that tunnel would have us believe. Do not disturb the dead where they rest."

There was an ornate, bronze door on the other side of the chamber. Trokar urged them to caution, and carefully inspected the dusty floor for tripwires, pressure plates, or markings, but found nothing. He scrutinized the bronze door, too, finding nothing. No divots, no cracks; not even a lock. He gripped the handle and took a deep breath.

He pushed, but the door didn't budge. Even with all of his weight, the door still held. He pushed a third time, putting every ounce of strength into it, and the door groaned a little but did not open. He stepped back and took a tired breath.

Vilayne stepped forward and pulled on the handle; the door swung open with a creak.

"Uh, after you," Trokar said, gesturing for her to go before him.

Vilayne rolled her eyes and went into the room, the others following. Fumble shook his vial again, but it was growing dim. The room appeared to be for preparing the dead, with stone slab tables, surgical tools, and bolts of threadbare cloth tattered from age. There was another door on the left side of the room, and a torch holder on the wall beside it.

Vilayne perused the surgical tools, which, besides a veneer of dust, looked remarkably untarnished.

"Ooh," Fumble exclaimed, "are those forceps? Very nice." He plucked them from their resting place.

Trokar took the torch from the wall mount and blew the dust from it, shaking it softly. As if responding to his action, it flared to life with a green flame and he yelped, dropping it. It clattered to the floor but stayed lit.

Vilayne picked it up and gazed into the green fire, noting smoldering glyphs in the strange lacquered wood.

"Ah, good," Fumble said, tucking away his glowing vial. "I can save my light potions. Did you check this door, Trokar?"

"Oh, right!" Trokar skittered forth, checking the door for traps. Like before, he couldn't find any. "The doors aren't even locked, so I doubt they're trapped."

"Why don't you open it then?" Vilayne asked.

Trokar gripped the handle and pulled, but just like the other door, it didn't move.

"They open *away* from the room," Vilayne informed him.

"I was going to try that, next," Trokar replied, somewhat embarrassed, and he pushed it open.

Another curved passage took them to another intersection within the square tunnel system. Bonewise thunked his staff to echolocate again, then said: "There was a cave-in to the left. To the right, the tunnel extends far."

They turned to the right and walked for many minutes, their scuffing footfalls echoing along the flat stone. At last, they came upon an octagonal intersection of eight tunnels.

"Oh, great!" Ezme cried. "We're going to get lost down here!"

"Mark the passage we came from," Bonewise suggested.

Vilayne used her knife to scratch an X on the wall. "If we take the rightmost passage, it should take us back in the direction of the burial chamber."

"If that burial chamber was any indication," Fumble argued, "it's that these tunnels don't follow the usual tunnel rules."

"Be that as it may," Bonewise said, "let us start with the rightmost passage."

The rightmost passage was short, compared to the one they had just traveled, and multicolored light emanated from the great chamber it took them to. The light came from a garden of wondrous growing things, and none of them were plants. There were mushrooms, some as tall as jacaranda trees, their delicate gills slowly pulsing with red light. Glowing molds, stretching dainty filaments in every direction, possessed a light of the faintest blue. Some fungus seemed to cast fiery yellow nets from under their caps, while others were like transparent bubbles on the ground and milk balloons hovering on strings of mycelium.

Silvery, luminescent moths fluttered gracefully to and from spore-producing flower cups.

An arched bridge of clear glass stood broken above the mushroom canopy, two arms of razor shards reaching toward each other from walkable shelves of stone jutting from the walls. High above, the cave ceiling glistened with resting moths on silk-clothed stalactites.

"This place is amazing." Trokar gaped. "I've never seen anything so filled with beauty."

"This place is special." Bonewise nodded, a tear coming to his eye as he imagined what Creamfoot would say were she alive. "The life here is very old and very delicate. Do not disturb—" He turned around at a crunching sound of someone chomping.

Ezme had a glowing moth wing dangling from her lip.

"I was hungry," she said. "It's *really* good."

"This is a self-contained environment!" Bonewise scolded. "Any action we take disrupts the natural balance that has sustained this place for thousands of years!"

"Too late," Fumble said. "It's already disturbed, so we might as well have a snack!" He began jumping after a moth.

"I'll only eat a couple," Trokar reasoned, and he, too, began chasing a glowing moth.

Everyone but Bonewise was snatching a morsel, and he sighed, relenting. "Just a snack wouldn't be too harmful, I suppose." He plucked a moth from a flowering cup beside him, popping it into his mouth to crush it between his molars. An explosion of buttery flavor filled his mouth and he closed his eyes, savoring it.

"They're so *good*!" Ezme declared with glowing remnants of moth between her teeth. She scrambled up the branches of hanging mycelium like a rope ladder, reaching for more.

"That's enough!" Bonewise commanded with a clack of his staff.

Ezme sighed, slipping down from the smooth fungal flesh. She landed upon a springy mushroom cap beneath and slid from it, feet first to the ground below.

"Alright, fine," she said, brushing off the dusty red spores that had powdered her.

Bonewise pointed up. "Let's see if we can get up to that broken bridge."

After a bit of searching, Vilayne found stairs that had been overgrown with mushrooms twice her height. They squeezed between the rubbery stalks and ascended to the stone ledge by the foot of the glass bridge.

It looked as though it had been cast as a single piece, broken by some violent force. From their vantage point, they could see across the chamber to the ledge walkway on the other side, where there was a caved-in tunnel; something squat and wide in front of it, overgrown with fungus. Beside their end of the bridge was an ornately-carved tunnel into darkness.

Bonewise clacked his staff, turning his ears to the tune. "Two rooms opposite each other at the end of this tunnel."

The green light from Vilayne's torch showed them two antechambers as they came to the end of the tunnel. A bronze door glowed in the light on the far wall of the chamber to their left, and a pile of rocks and smashed statues heaped against the far wall on their right. Whatever furnishings had been contained in the antechambers had long ago been removed or destroyed.

Trokar went into the left antechamber, checked the door, determined it was safe, then opened it with a push.

The circular room inside was barren except for a dusty, complicated red symbol painted on the floor, half the span of the room itself. There was a twisted rib cage laying on a pile of ashes in the center of the symbol.

"*Nope*," Trokar said. "That's a big nope. I'm not going in there."

Vilayne poked her head in the room, assessed it, and said: "Looks like whoever was standing in the middle of that magic circle had something go wrong."

"Yep. No need to fix it. Let's check the other room."

In the other antechamber, Fumble climbed up the pile of broken stones, dislodging a jutting statue, which toppled to the floor and broke into smaller pieces.

"What are you doing?" Ezme asked as he slipped and stumbled his way up the slope.

"Since when do statues fall into a pile of rocks? This wasn't a cave-in, but made to look like one. Sloppy! The other room had a door, and I bet this one does, too, hidden behind this rubble. See?!" He revealed the top of an arch by pushing away the broken bottom half of a statue from the top of the heap. Trokar dropped his backpack, climbed up, and helped Fumble move the debris while the rest stood clear of the tumbling stones. At last, the upper half of a large, intact bronze door was uncovered. Jagged, rough carvings marred the arch over it. They were crude pictographs, but Fumble scrutinized them.

"These look hastily made . . ." Fumble muttered. "Opposite of refusing . . . some kind of meat?"

"Forsake not the flesh," Bonewise interpreted.

"Huh," Fumble exclaimed quizzically. "Is it telling us to engage in some sort of carnal pleasure?"

"It is a warning. You recall the story of the war of the Goblin King?"

"He wanted immortality," Vilayne answered. "To escape the wheel of life and death. Is that what this is referring to?"

"Perhaps," Bonewise said thoughtfully. "Something is hidden behind this door. The question is, should we open it?"

"Unless we can do a better job of hiding it," Fumble said, "sooner or later, someone is going to find it. I think we have to look inside."

It took them hours, but they moved every stone blocking the door. Most of the heavy lifting was done by Trokar.

"I need a serious nap soon," Trokar declared, exhausted from the exertion.

Bonewise grasped the handle and pulled on the door. The metal hinges whined and groaned, and he stopped when the opening was just wide enough for him to pass through. Inside was a spherical polyhedron chamber that seemed not quite as large as the mushroom garden, but far more strange by its baffling construction. The domed chamber was defined by an array of cubic stone blocks, which were held tightly together by some unseen binding. In the center of the chamber was a red crystal pedestal holding a silver pebble no bigger than a thumbnail. Bonewise cautiously approached as everyone else entered the chamber.

"That must be the stone Audrel was talking about," Fumble said.

"How do we know it's not a fake?" Ezme asked.

Bonewise hovered his hand over the pebble. It was perfectly smooth and oval. His hand felt heavy. There was power there, Bonewise knew. What that power was, he did not know, but he felt a gravitas to the moment, that once he took it, there was no turning back.

"Wait!" Trokar called.

Bonewise turned to look at him.

"It might be trapped!" Trokar warned. "Let me try the ol' switcheroo?" He picked up some pebbles of rubble left from the barricade.

Bonewise shrugged and stepped aside, gesturing for Trokar to proceed. Trokar brought his pebbles and held up each one in turn near the one on the pedestal, judging if they might weigh the same. He selected one and discarded the rest, then, after taking a breath to steady himself, deftly plucked the pebble from the crystal with one hand and replaced it with the other.

He held his breath for a moment, but nothing happened. He stood up straight with a grin, pinching the smooth stone between his fingers.

Suddenly, a shiver ran through the whole room. The cubic blocks began to fall from the center of the ceiling, as if whatever had been holding them together had suddenly dissolved.

"*Run!*" Fumble exclaimed, and he scrambled through the exit along with Ezme and Vilayne.

Trokar cried out in panic as he looked up at impending, crushing death. He wanted to run, but his aching muscles seized up. Bonewise yanked him by the collar, sprinting toward the door.

Square blocks bounced and cracked open at Trokar's heels as he was swiftly dragged across the floor, then flung through the doorway. Bonewise's headdress deflected bouncing rubble as he leapt through the crack, then the door swept forward as it was broken off its hinges by the avalanche.

Trokar hyperventilated, half buried in cracked blocks, still pinching the pebble aloft.

Bonewise grumbled as he pulled himself out of the debris, then plucked the stone from Trokar's grasp.

"Are you alright, Bonewise?" Vilayne asked.

"Nothing broken," he replied. "Trokar?"

"I . . . I can't feel my legs," Trokar wheezed.

Fumble and Ezme grabbed Trokar's meaty arms, pulling him from the rubble; though, Trokar yelped in sudden pain.

Bonewise stashed the pebble in a nook of his headdress, then laid his hands on Trokar's bloodied legs and chanted. Trokar's bones cracked as the fractures mended themselves, and again he cried out in pain.

"You'll be able to walk," Bonewise assured him, then he reached up to retrieve the stone.

He paused when he touched it, feeling *something*—a power seeping through his headdress and settling into his own bones. He felt more sturdy on his feet, more grounded, and healthier, like how he felt when he roamed the briars in his youth. As he took the stone from its place in his headdress, the feeling diminished. Bonewise then tucked it into his rock pocket, certain he could distinguish it from his sling stones by both look and feel.

Once they had collected themselves, they returned to the mushroom garden.

"What now?" Vilayne asked.

"We could go back and explore those six other tunnels," Ezme suggested.

"I think we should check the other side of this bridge," Fumble said.

"How will we get over there?" Vilayne asked.

"We could climb?" Ezme suggested.

"My legs feel great!" Trokar exclaimed. "I could jump!"

"You'll fall," Bonewise grumbled. "I'll not mend your legs twice in one day."

"I won't fall. Watch this!" Trokar ran to the end of the ledge and leapt onto the top of a tall mushroom. He bounced off the rubbery flesh and onto the top of the next cap, and from there to the rock ledge of the other side.

"I guess that works," Bonewise shrugged.

Vilayne did the same, as did Ezme and Bonewise, but Fumble slipped on the first mushroom top and bounced down, falling from one cap to another until he crashed into a soft patch of mold. He ran back up the stairs and tried again, but slipped and fell the same way as before, right into his fresh mold print. On his third try, he made it across, by which time the others were already examining the fungus-covered thing by the ancient cave-in.

It was a bronze ballista, pointed away from the glass bridge at the caved-in passage. There was also the broken end of a metal cart that was half-buried in the rubble, one of its wide, metal wheels askew on its snapped axle.

"Maybe there's still stuff in that cart!" Ezme pointed.

Trokar was quick to pull out his crowbar. He pried a bronze panel away to discover what was evidently a weapons locker with a spear and an untarnished sword of a metal similar to that of the ballista, though the leather-wrapped handle had long since rotted away.

Trokar unsheathed his chipped iron sword and cast it aside, replacing it with the bronze-colored one and wrapping its handle in scrap leather from his pack. Upon closer inspection of the spear, he saw that its bronze-like shaft was inscribed with glyphs. He held it, believing it was meant to be used as a javelin. The most prominent glyph resembled a lightning bolt.

"Ah-ha yeah!" he cried in triumph. "A Javelin of Lightning! We can offer this for the Moot! Bonewise, look!"

Bonewise ran his hand over the glyphs. He felt an energy, dim and shapeless, but there was some kind of spell upon it, he was sure.

"Hmm," Bonewise murmured. "There *is* some magic within it."

"I knew it!" Trokar exclaimed happily.

"Toss me that crowbar, Troak?" Fumble asked as he inspected the crushed cart.

As Trokar tossed it, Fumble grasped only air as the crowbar clattered against a rock. Fumble picked it up and began to prod along the corners on the inside of the weapons locker.

"Just as I thought!" Fumble exclaimed, and he pried open a metal panel, revealing to him a long, narrow cavity containing three arrows. Instead of being tipped with bladed arrowheads, they had glass bubbles that shimmered faintly with multicolored light. When he grasped them, ripples of electricity reverberated along the smooth, ebony metal shafts.

"This is wild," Fumble said with a tone of awe. "I found arrows, and I have a bow! It's like some destiny shit."

"What about the pebble?" Vilayne asked. "Are we really going to hand it over to the humans?"

"*Sprat-splats* to that!" Fumble cursed distastefully as he slid the arrows into his quiver. "We can give them a different pebble. How would they know the difference?"

"This Audrel," Bonewise said, "he has the scent of a wizard about him. He would be able to tell the difference between a rock and a stone of power."

"What's so special about this stone, anyway?" Ezme asked.

"I do not know," Bonewise admitted, "but the ancestors called us here to protect it, I think."

"So, what are we going to tell the humans?" Vilayne asked.

"That we must refuse their offer."

"Why can't we just tell them we didn't find it?" Trokar asked.

"We could try," Bonewise answered. "Something tells me Audrel will not take us at our word, however. We should be ready for a fight."

"I'm not ready," Trokar complained, his ears drooping. "I've barely slept for two days and I need a rest!"

"Me too," Ezme said.

"How long do you think the humans will wait for us?" Vilayne wondered out loud.

"That's a good point," Fumble said. "What if they come looking for us?"

"Then we deal with them," Bonewise answered. "That is, if they don't get lost down here. We will rest for the remainder of the day, though it is hard to say from here when the sun will set."

They laid out their bed rolls and dozed. Bonewise volunteered to keep watch. He was tired as well, but he could rest in a trance and still become alert if there was danger. He palmed the mysterious pebble, and relaxed into its deep, grounding power, thinking of the music of home. After he felt a few hours had passed, he roused the others.

Ezme wandered into the cover of the mushrooms to relieve herself, and when she emerged, she waved everyone over.

"Hey," Ezme called, "I think I found something!"

Bonewise approached and brushed aside the rubbery growth by the wall where Ezme indicated.

"Watch your step," she warned.

There was an inscription in the cave wall—two triangles, one inverted beneath the other, each possessing six "faces," or sections. There was an indent in the middle where they joined, about the size and shape of the pebble. Bonewise fished out the pebble from his pocket and placed it in the depression. It fit perfectly.

At once, the stone wall vanished, and the pebble fell to the ground. Bonewise scooped it up and gazed down a dark square tunnel.

"What is it?" Trokar asked, trying to see around the fungal overgrowth and Bonewise's headdress.

"Another passageway like the one that brought us here. Let us see where it leads."

The goblins entered the tunnel, and this time, thumbing the pebble in his hand, Bonewise felt the distortion of distance. Though the way seemed flat, their depth changed dramatically. Each step brought them many leagues through solid rock. Everyone but Bonewise felt nauseated by the journey.

At last, they approached the end of the tunnel. It was a dead end, but an inscription greeted them on the wall by the green light of Vilayne's torch.

"It cannot be seen," Bonewise interpreted, "cannot be felt . . . cannot be heard, cannot be smelt; it lies behind stars and under hills, and empty caves it often fills."

Fumble looked like he had an idea and raised his hand, but then frowned and lowered his hand, muttering to himself: "No, you can smell that."

"Were you just thinking what I think you were?" Trokar asked Fumble.

"Yeah," Fumble answered, "but you can smell that kind of gas."

"How can gas be behind stars?" Ezme asked.

"Depends on what kind of star we're talking about," Fumble said with a waggle of his hairless eyebrows.

"You dirty gob."

"Vilayne," Bonewise addressed, "put out your torch."

Vilayne squinted at her bright torch, then swiftly shook it downward. The green flame snuffed out. They were instantly enveloped in complete darkness. Bonewise stretched his hand out to touch the wall at the end of the tunnel, but it wasn't there.

"Everyone," Bonewise called, "clasp hands and walk forward."

They all reached for each other and grasped hands, then shuffled together into the darkness. The sound of their feet was too muffled for echolocation, and after a few paces, Bonewise bumped into a wall.

"Light," he said.

"Ask me nicely," Vilayne demanded casually.

"Please?" Bonewise grumbled.

Vilayne shook her torch and the green flame sprouted anew. They were in an intersection of two square tunnels, one behind them, and one on their left.

"That was some good thinking, Bone-dome!" Trokar praised.

"Thank you," Bonewise muttered.

CHAPTER

SIX
THE BETRAYAL

After a short walk down the adjoining tunnel, they came to a familiar intersection with the tunnel that had taken them to the burial chamber. Further on, they could see a glimmering light coming from the entrance, and after a short while, they emerged back at the glade under the night sky. Sueda was sitting on the log by the crackling fire, sipping from a bottle. Nearby, Audrel stopped pacing—noticing the goblins—and gestured for Sueda to rise.

"So," Audrel said, "you are not dead, after all. I was beginning to wonder."

"It wasn't easy," Bonewise commented.

"All well?" Sueda asked.

"I broke my legs," Trokar answered, "but I'm better now!"

"The stone," Audrel commanded. "Give it to me."

Bonewise said nothing, simply staring up at the pale human.

Trokar nervously cleared his throat and stepped forward. "Uh, regrettably, we didn't find it. There's nothing but bones and mold down there, and traps that break your legs!"

"You *lie*," Audrel stated gravely. "I can *feel* its presence. Hand it over, and I shall reward you your silver, as promised."

"There will be no trade," Bonewise said in a tone of finality.

"We had a deal!" Audrel seethed.

"The value it has to our ancestors is great," Vilayne retorted. "Its value cannot be matched by any weight of silver!"

"You little imps do not understand, nor deserve, such power!"

"You don't *know* us, man!" Fumble exclaimed.

"We are leaving," Bonewise stated. "Let us pass."

"You shall not be going anywhere," Audrel said, and he produced a brass wand from the confines of his robes. "*Sruv-sekka!*" He recited his spell loudly, and gestured widely with his free hand.

Trokar reached to unsheathe his new blade, but his arm felt like damp clay. He moved only half as fast as he should have.

Bonewise had already concealed a sling stone in his palm, but his movement to place it in the leather cradle of his sling was as slow as Trokar drawing his sword. Ezme blinked in slow-motion and began to recite a spell of protection. Fumble began to slowly shake up a potion while Vilayne shrugged off her backpack and began weaving her hands about in a dance, untangling herself from the snare of magic.

"He's ensorcelled us!" Vilayne warned.

"Sueda!" Audrel shouted without looking at her. "*Urid xänpak!*"

Sueda popped open the hinged stopper of her wine bottle with her thumb and swept her other arm in a circle. Red wine floated out of the bottle in front of her as she sang a word and it swirled into a disc as wide as her arm was long.

Bonewise grasped his staff with both hands and flung it forward. Though the movement was only half as fast, the loose end of the leather cord slipped off the top of the staff as it should have and released the rock from its cradle. Audrel stepped aside and the rock sailed past him.

"*Mosu-kekkera!*" Audrel recited, pointing his brass wand at Trokar. Purple light, painfully bright, shot from the wand in two bursts and zapped Trokar in the chest.

His leather tunic was instantly charred where the light struck. Biting pain sank into his skin, and the smell of burning hair from the smoldering leather filled his nostrils.

Sword in hand, heart racing, Trokar willed his legs to move with all his might, but he felt like he was trying to sprint through waist-deep syrup, and the heavy pack he carried seemed to pull him backwards. It was just like in his nightmares where he could only run slowly from the monsters chasing him, except this time he was running toward the monster.

Fumble popped the cork of his agitated potion and blinding light shot out at Audrel, who shielded his eyes.

"Sueda!" Audrel called in aggravation, but Sueda remained where she was by the fire, holding her disc of wine in the air.

Her expression was focused yet sad, and it gave Trokar hope that perhaps she would only defend herself and not her boss. He pushed on, still several stretched strides away from the wizard. He let the heavy pack slip from his shoulders.

Fumble dropped the spent vial, raised his bow, and reached for his quiver. Unable to see the arrows, he picked one of the conventional hunting arrows, rather than one of the three with glass tips. He notched it with more grace than he was accustomed to, perhaps because the imposed slowness allowed him more control. Even so, he overcompensated the arc, and when he released the bowstring, the arrow sailed up into the trees.

Ezme completed her protection spell, untangled herself from Audrel's hindering web of magic, and wielded the charred zoharwood wand The Wise Woman had given her. She pointed it right at Audrel's head, and tried to imagine his skull exploding.

Audrel braced himself against whatever the wand might unleash, but nothing happened to him. No one noticed, but behind him in the night sky, a distant star exploded into a supernova.

Ezme shook the wand in frustration, thinking she had failed to activate it.

Audrel smirked and shook his head. "*Goblins,*" he sneered condescendingly, pointing his wand at Ezme. "*Mosu-kekkera!*" He recited again, and purple bolts of light leapt from the brass.

Vilayne darted in front of Ezme and intercepted them. She seemed to guide them around her body as she pivoted, singing a bent note with her voice. In a flash, she sent them back toward Audrel, but in the same instant, he flicked a ring on his free hand and a semi-transparent circle of runes manifested like a shield, deflecting the bolts of energy.

At last, Trokar was upon Audrel, and though Trokar felt trepidation to cause harm, he thrust his sword up at the wizard's neck, hoping he would be fast enough.

He was not.

Audrel dodged aside and hissed a volatile spell that pulled the flame from the fire pit to the tip of his wand, directing it at Trokar. It whooshed at him with the intensity of a blacksmith's forge, and Trokar was not quick enough to back away from the thrashing flames. It burned his arm as he raised it to shield his face and his precious hair.

Trokar didn't know if the burning smell was from his leathers or his hair, and his fear was blurred into frantic, survivalist rage. He lashed out with his sword, hacking and slashing with wild abandon as fast as he could, but Audrel's magic shield deflected each strike with crackling multicolored sparks.

With Trokar too close to Audrel for a clear shot, Fumble fired another hunting arrow at Sueda, but her spinning disc of wine knocked it away. He threw down his bow in frustration and rummaged through his pouches for another potion.

Bonewise had thought to grab another sling stone from his rock pocket, but without meaning to, he grabbed the pebble they'd found in the tunnel, his fingers drawn to it like a magnet. He felt its power course through him, connecting him to the world as if he were a conduit of its deep energy, and a resonance rang in his consciousness from both the blue gem on his enemy's headband and the stars above, stone magic reflecting sky magic. He knew the ancestors were with him, and on an impulse, he began to sing a song of their home:

"The cliffs of Kol'grathu, thorny and cleat,
    Fierce are the waters that beat at their feet,
    And sweet are the echoes—the warm caves above,
    Sweet are the echoes of goblins thereof!"

. . .

Vilayne joined in the singing, adding her lyrical voice to the gravely base of Bonewise, then Ezme and Fumble joined in as well. Trokar felt bolstered by their voices, and he sang with them, flowing with their rhythm. He felt quickness come back to his limbs, the restricting magic unraveling. He sliced below Audrel's magic shield, and the blade struck the wizard's knee, drawing blood.

Audrel, enraged by the injury, directed the fire-flow of his wand to roar upon Trokar once more. Trokar cried out in panic as the blaze closed around him like jaws, but Sueda sliced the stream of flame from the fire pit with her wine disc, severing Audrel's magic. The others stopped chanting, perplexed.

"Hûvu!" Sueda pleaded, a determined look upon her face.

"Tratarè!" Audrel accused spitefully.

In that moment, while Audrel was distracted, Trokar thrust his blade forward and pierced the wizard's chest. Audrel gasped in agony, but Trokar looked as surprised as he. Trokar had acted on impulse, and now the reality of his planted sword, and the flowing blood, was plain to see. It horrified him.

Audrel staggered back, and Trokar forgot his strength, letting the sword handle slip from his grasp, leaving the blade wedged between the wizard's ribs.

Vile hate boiled up in the wizard's visage, and he began whispering words laced with it. His voice rose even as his body convulsed in tremors, and a deep blue, gloaming light sparked within the jewel upon his headband. The fire beside Sueda snuffed out, and even the stars overhead dimmed. The shadows of the surrounding forest gathered around the glade, deepening.

"Audrel, no!" Sueda cried in her language, her eyes brimming with tears even as they widened with terror. "It is forbidden!"

"Trokar," Bonewise called. "Stop him!"

Trokar heard the desperation in the elder's voice, and it frightened him beyond all trepidation. He leapt forward and hooked one leg behind Audrel's ankle, then shoved him hard, sending him toppling over onto his back. The wizard's mouth began to leak blood and his voice became hoarse, but still, he continued chanting. Trokar pulled his sword from the human's chest as worms writhed up out of the earth around them, twisting and thrashing. He raised the bloodied blade, unsure if the nauseating feeling in the pit of his stomach was from the dreadful magic at work or from the revulsion of violence. He was primed to strike the killing blow, yet he felt paralyzed.

Sueda sprinted toward them from the fire pit, crouching beside the man as she brought her hand down upon his face, speaking a word through gritted teeth that sounded like it was pronounced backwards.

Blood erupted from Audrel's nose, mouth, and eyes, even as he gurgled the last drawn-out syllable of his spell. The dull light faded from the jewel at his forehead, and after a tense, terrible moment of silence, it was clear that he was dead.

Trokar slowly lowered his sword and Sueda looked up at him; he could see the tears dripping down her cheeks. There was a look of horror upon her face, then she seemed to look past him, at the tunnel into the hill.

The goblins turned their large keen ears to the tunnel.

They heard it echoing from the darkness: scraping, grinding, shambling, clacking of bones.

"Death magic!" Sueda cried, using goblin words.

This was what Bonewise had feared: Necromancy. Hundreds of the long dead had risen from their graves, animated by a power too terrible to name. He knew they brought death. He might be able to ward off some of them, but not that many. Despite having no muscles, they moved with great speed, and they would show no mercy.

"We need to run!" Bonewise shouted.

Fumble stepped close to the stone arch, standing directly in the path of the dead.

"Fumble!" Bonewise called, wondering what madness had possessed him.

Fumble could barely see what was coming in the shadowy tunnel, but there they were, goblin skeletons rushing like lemmings, ancient daggers pointed for the attack. The drumming of their bony feet was thunderous. He was ready to bet everything that his plan would work.

"Twenty foreheads!" Fumble called, arms outstretched.

The thick stone wall that answered his voice slid smoothly back up from the ground and assumed its old station, sealing the passage with a dull thunk.

Everyone held their breath.

The wall remained closed, and all was silent. Crickets began to chirp in the emptiness of night.

Bonewise soothed Trokar's burns with a cooling salve and wrapped them with cloth; he and Fumble were uncharacteristically silent as they processed what they had just seen.

Sueda used a small, collapsible spade from the tent to dig a shallow grave for Audrel in the thin, stoney soil of the glade. Trokar offered to help, but Sueda insisted that she do it alone.

When the hole was dug, he offered to help drag the body, which she allowed. He took the opportunity to slip the magic ring of shielding from Audrel's finger. Ezme had already plucked the brass wand from the wizard's dead hand, and Sueda removed the headband which held the blue gemstone. She placed a covering of rocks over the veneer of soil that covered the body, said a prayer, then tied the headband around her forehead.

She remained kneeling, holding a long moment of silence before standing.

"How did you kill him?" Vilayne asked Sueda.

Sueda gazed down at the grave for another long moment before answering.

"I am a healer," Sueda finally said, speaking in the goblin's language much more eloquently than before. "We are not to use our power to cause harm . . . unless absolutely necessary. I inverted a healing spell, so that it took life instead of giving it. I . . . had never done it before—and I hope I never have to again."

"Hey," Ezme remarked, "how come you speak goblin so well, all of a sudden?"

"It comes easier to me now, with the magic of the Skystone." She tapped the headband at her temple.

"The Skystone?"

"We found it in the Crown Spires, in a place built by goblins, long ago. It was well-guarded by traps. We lost the other members of our expedition to that place. It was there we also found information pointing to the location of two other Source Stones. It is why we came here."

"Can you tell us more about these stones?" Bonewise asked.

"Hold on!" Fumble interjected. "I want to know why you betrayed your boss. Just who's side are you on?"

"I'm with the rebellion," Sueda answered.

"We don't keep up on human politics," Vilayne said. "Who are you rebelling against?"

"The Faladian Republic is an unjust, corrupt empire," Sueda said tersely. "It upholds institutions of slavery. It uses the military to enforce and expand their control under the pretense of deterring an invasion from Vorn. Goblins, ogres—anyone who isn't human—is treated as an enemy. As for the desert elves, the Republic treats them as second-class citizens, if not outlaws, and doesn't care to send any help to them in their war against the forces of the Witch Queen."

"Which queen?" Fumble asked.

"The Queen of Vorn. She is a witch, and also undying, filled with the same power Audrel used to call up the dead."

"I have heard of this queen," Bonewise said. "They say she lives in a fortress city to the north, across the Sea of Dreams."

Sueda nodded. "Long has the Republic used her to scare the people into accepting the injustices of their own government. The lesser of two evils. I can no longer turn a blind eye to the evil that rules over us. That's why I joined the rebellion."

"Was he a part of the rebellion?" Vilayne asked, pointing to Audrel's grave.

"No, he claimed to be loyal to the Republic, but I knew him to be loyal to no one but himself. That is why we did not return to the capital once we found the Skystone. He wanted to use it and the other Source Stones for his own."

"These stones are a part of our heritage," Vilayne said. "Will you share with us what you know about them?"

Sueda nodded once more, wrapping her cloak about herself more tightly.

"I'll start the fire back up," Trokar said, and they all gathered around the fire pit as he stacked twigs and dry branches, sparking them with flint and blowing on the smoldering coals to get it going again.

"The Source Stones are said to be the keys to the forces of creation," Sueda explained. "The one you found here is the Geostone, blessed by Ged, Lord of the Earth. The Skystone was blessed by Utu. The Bloodstone was misused by the ancients of Karn to bring demons to life—so they say—and Utu smote them with fire from the sky. There are only vague references to the others . . . the Daystone, the Nightstone, and the Songstone. Six, in all."

"Audrel was obsessed," Sueda continued, "and his persistence paid off. The Republic gave him funding for his research and an expedition, but the rebellion couldn't let such power fall into the hands of the government, so I was assigned to get close to Audrel, learn what he knew, and stop him."

"You said you found out where two other stones were hidden," Vilayne recalled. "This Geostone was one. What was the other?"

"The glyphs were not specific as to which one," Sueda answered. "Or at least, we could not interpret it precisely, but we were sure the pictographs told us where we could find it. 'The Crown of the Glyphwood.'"

"The Glyphwood," Vilayne echoed. "You mean the Glyphwood Forest?"

"That's not far from home!" Trokar said excitedly.

"That's elvish territory," Bonewise remarked.

"If it's a literal crown," Sueda said, "then the elves probably have it. I need to find out."

"No way I'm going anywhere near those creepy elves!" Fumble declared.

"Please, I can talk to them. I can speak elvish. At least guide me through your territory?"

"These stones," Trokar said, "they are clearly *super* important to our ancestors, right, Bonewise?"

Bonewise reached into his pocket and palmed the Geostone. He hummed deep in his throat and turned his gaze to the campfire, opening himself to some sign, some inner tug from the ancestor spirits.

"I know it is asking a lot," Sueda admitted, "but I believe these stones connect both of our people. We lost our entire expeditionary force obtaining the Skystone. I don't know what you did to get the Geostone, but none of you died!"

"Well," Fumble chimed, "we *are* extraordinary individuals, but we also know how to choose our battles!"

"We'd have to cross the Quaking Hills," Ezme said.

"And the Dread Marsh after that," Vilayne added.

"But these stones are our heritage!" Trokar exclaimed. "We already have two, and three is the magic number!"

"It's been hidden for ten thousand years," Fumble said. "You somehow expect to find it in a vast, ancient forest? And what about the Moot? What about Warface?"

"Warface is so much smaller than this! This is about all goblin-kin! *A goblin quest*! We can reclaim our history and maybe finally get some respect from the other races! Don't you see? This is why the ancestors called us here! Isn't it, Bonewise?"

Bonewise stared into the flames of the campfire, smoothing the Geostone with his thumb. He could still feel a resonance between it and the Skystone. He felt more comfortable in his body than he had in years, and he had always been taught to listen to his bones.

"Perhaps," Bonewise said at last. "Now that the secret is known, it is only a matter of time before others seek it out. I feel... anticipation from the spirits. Time is of the essence."

"Last I heard," Sueda said, "the war between the elves of the Glyphwood and the forces of the Witch Queen had escalated. The Glyphwood is now considered contested territory."

"Oh, great!" Fumble lamented. "It's a war-zone as well?! Trokar, think about this!"

"I have," Trokar said, "and I realize now how small my dreams were before tonight. This is our chance to really make a difference! Think of the possibilities!"

"What about you?" Vilayne asked Sueda. "What's your stake in all this?"

"I will help you reclaim the Source Stones for your people," Sueda said. "In return, I ask that you help the rebellion. Help us overthrow the Republic, and your people will stop being hunted. The rebellion works with people of all races. There can be a place for you, and all goblins, at our table in the new order we wish to build."

"You hear that?" Fumble asked. "'A New Order.' That's always how it starts! Next thing you know, dissidents are disappeared by secret enforcers!"

"Oh, come on, Fumble," Ezme said. "It couldn't be any worse than the way it is!"

"Things can *always* get worse," Fumble retorted.

"Let's put it to a vote!" Trokar said. "I say we give Sueda and her rebellion a chance! With the relics of our ancestors, we can sway the other clans to coordinate with us at the Moot. Then goblins wouldn't just raid for loot, but bring down a whole evil empire! Free the slaves! We could usher in a new beginning for everyone! All in favor?" He raised his hand.

"What the hell?" Ezme said, raising her hand. "I'm for it!"

Vilayne's expression remained stoic, but she raised her hand as well.

Bonewise grunted and thunked his staff, then raised the Geostone in his other hand; something had been set in motion, he realized, and there was no turning back.

For the first time, they saw Sueda smile, and she raised her hand.

"Well, fine!" Fumble declared. "But don't say I didn't warn you!"

CHAPTER
SEVEN
WARFACE

They agreed to undertake the journey back to Kol'grathu after more rest and Bonewise asked to be roused from sleep before the sun reached its zenith. None of the goblins were used to being awake so early during the day, but Sueda was eager to leave the glade —and Audrel's grave—behind. She had packed everything she wanted to carry neatly into her pack, but left the shovel and heavy canvas tent.

The silver was counted and distributed out in equal portions amongst the goblins, then they began the hike north. Sueda could tell that everyone but Bonewise seemed unaccustomed to traveling. Trokar looked strong, but his pack was overloaded. She did not even want to know what was in the blood-soaked sack.

Sueda had walked for months during the expedition, and she had lightened her pack continuously as she shaved off things she hadn't really needed. She had lost much of her figure as well, yet she felt denser, walking farther and farther without tiring like she used to.

The only other goblins she had ever met before were goblins who worked the dock in the Faladian capital. She was forbidden to converse with them by her sponsor House, as it was considered unseemly, but she had gone to the lower docks in disguise several times and paid a blind goblin called Chumbucket—a fishing net weaver—to help her practice goblin speech. She had plenty of academic sources to study, but there was nothing better than learning from a native speaker.

Considering she only had two years to learn a non-human language before departing with Audrel on his expedition, she felt she had done reasonably well. Her knowledge of the language was crucial to convincing him to take her along. Simultaneously, she had to seem ignorant so that she would not arouse suspicion. Other water priestesses of House Meklar gossiped that Sueda was ditzy, selected to serve only because of her looks. She told herself that they derided her intelligence only because she was playing her role so well. Now, with the Skystone upon her brow, her mind as it had been without its magic seemed to her as clumsy as the gossipers had claimed. She also realized how understanding complex languages had seemed so effortless to Audrel.

Her thoughts were so clear, the words and meanings swam instinctually from the depths of her memory like fish racing upstream, remembering exactly the mountain pools where they were spawned.

Her greatest difficulty was in pronouncing goblin speech. There were rolled R's and other, more subtle variations that her voice could not easily reach. She was certain there were nuances of the language lost to her, too, due to goblins having a much broader and more sensitive range of hearing.

Though the goblins seemed to understand her very well, understanding the goblins was more elusive.

She found the basic elements of goblin speech easy to grasp intuitively, but difficult to define. The meaning of a phrase was sometimes determined by the sentence structure, other times by which words were used first or last, and, other times, it was determined by a certain word's relationship to the action expressed by the verb. Certain words had a permanent trait of agency, like "runner" or "biter," but such words were not necessarily the agent of a sentence, and placement was important for it to convey the intended meaning.

She was happy to listen to the goblins banter and bicker with each other, already finding them to be better company than Audrel had ever been. Even after so long together in isolation, he had remained cold and guarded.

Certain members of the goblin band didn't trust her, that much was obvious, and neither did she trust them; a part of her mind squirmed nervously as they led her deeper into Kol'grathu territory. But she trusted the goddess and the path she guided her to follow. So many people were suffering in the world, and she was convinced that drastic action was needed to break the stranglehold of slavery. And if she was to die, she reminded herself that her soul would be borne by the River Mawwu to the goddess, and she would be cleansed of all memory of her pain, and made new again.

During the latter half of the afternoon, Trokar asked if Sueda would teach him her own language. She was happy to oblige, and started explaining the singular and plural forms of basic words.

"Ay kpi̖mṷkhi," she said, pointing to herself and then her temple. "I learned. Ṷ ja mṷkhi. You will learn."

By the time it was getting dark, Trokar had made a little progress, and she had him repeating a tongue twister her mother had taught her: "Da nyu̱ nyu̱ṉu̱ gichi nyu̱ huju̱zu da nu̱nyu nyu̱ chi̱pu bimu ha mu̱na. And he stood holding his cloak and turned his wet face to the wind."

Trokar huffed and puffed between words as they hiked along, and eventually said he would go over it in his head so he could breathe easier. It wasn't long after that Bonewise turned to face everyone from the front, bringing their movement to a halt. They could hear the ocean, but could not yet see it.

"Alright," Bonewise grumbled. "How do we want to proceed? It might be unwise to have a human seen in our company."

"It'll be fine!" Trokar said cheerfully. "We'll just say we captured her!"

"Wait, what?" Sueda said, blinking.

Bonewise frowned. "What do you think Warface might do to a human captive?"

"Well, uh . . ." Trokar began. "Couldn't we just say that she isn't to be harmed?"

"Handling captives falls to the war-chief. We can forbid nothing, nor can we claim ownership over her."

"I should say not!" Sueda scoffed.

"I didn't mean actually hold you captive," Trokar assured her. "Just pretend."

"It would be real to Warface," Vilayne explained. "And he would be cruel."

"Okay, fine," Trokar relented. "Bad plan."

"Why doesn't she just wait outside until we come back?" Ezme suggested. "Aren't we trying to go north as soon as possible?"

"That's right," Fumble said mockingly. "We need to find

the nondescript magic rock and get back in time for the Moot!"

"No problem!" Trokar said. "There's no way Warface can say no once we show everyone the loot we scored, not to mention the warg!"

"I'm fine with waiting," Sueda said.

"You'll need to stay hidden from patrols," Bonewise told her, "away from commonly-used trails. This way."

Bonewise led everyone to a sinkhole in the limestone where the forest met the briars, which gave a glimpse of the rushing subterranean river below, like a pulsing artery of the world's landscape. There was a rock shelf just within the sinkhole with a deep recess in the wall, a perfect hiding spot which he and Creamfoot had used long ago.

"The river will mask your sound and your scent," Bonewise said, "but don't slip, and don't start a fire. We will return as soon as we can."

WARFACE LOOKED like he had been caught with his pants down; eyes wide, ears flat. He had not been expecting Bonewise to return so soon, much less with actual treasure. He had hoped at least that Trokar would have perished, but instead, the misfit rolled the head of a great warg out of a bag at his feet. It reeked of decay, but the scar was unmistakable. It was the same warg that had killed his friend and eluded him all those years.

He looked up at Trokar's smug grin, and in the sudden, stunned silence of the gathering chamber, Warface could hear his own breath whizzing through his nostrils as his face became hot with indignation.

The warg was old, and probably sick, he thought. Weak.

Starving. How else could it have been killed by the likes of Trokar? Rage festered in his heart that this liar, this *fraud*, would humiliate him in this way.

Trokar kept up his grand smile and regaled the crowd with how he had delivered the fatal blow. Vilayne rolled her eyes at Trokar's obvious exaggerations and embellishments while Bonewise watched Warface carefully.

Warface tried to think of an excuse to cut Trokar down right then and there, one that the rest of the warren would accept. He came up with nothing, because no rules had been broken. He forced his ears up.

"What is this treasure you claim to have found?" Warface asked, interrupting Trokar's long-winded story.

"Ah!" Trokar exclaimed excitedly as he untied the cloth-wrapped weapon from his pack, "I found it deep in the ruins of an ancient warren, crafted with mastery by our ancestors! Behold, a javelin that strikes with the power of a lightning bolt!" He hoisted it high and the crowd murmured superstitiously.

"Lightning, eh? Let's have a demonstration, then."

"Oh. Well, the thing is . . . it might be the kind of thing that you can only use once, you know?"

"So you have not used it? How do you know, then, what it can do?"

"It has a lightning bolt on it, see?" Trokar pointed to the engraving.

Warface looked incredulous. He flicked his gaze to the javelin, to Trokar, then to the crowd, wondering how anyone could be so naive.

"Give it to me," Warface growled.

Trokar presented the javelin, and Warface took it. He scrutinized the short spear-like weapon, his brow furrowed in consideration. It was of a strange metal, a burnished bronze color, but it wasn't heavy enough to be bronze. He wasn't sure how, but as he grasped it, he felt certain it did indeed possess the power Trokar claimed.

"I shall take it to the Moot," Warface declared at last. "We shall see how it compares to what other treasures the clans will bid."

"But wait, there's more!" Trokar announced. "We found clues pointing to more treasure in the Glyphwood forest."

"What treasure?"

"Uh, it wasn't specific," Trokar replied, "but it's something really good! Something powerful! We'll leave right away. With your permission, war-chief."

"The Moot is in a fortnight! You plan to travel that far north, find this treasure in the vast Glyphwood, and make it back in time?"

"That's right. And if we don't, at least you have the javelin!"

Warface burst out laughing. It was a cruel laughter, a hateful delight. Trokar kept up a nervous smile.

"Sure, sure!" Warface announced. "You have my permission. Don't come back empty-handed!"

Another opportunity to be rid of an embarrassment to the clan, Warface thought. And if The Wise Woman's apprentice didn't return, or any of them, that would be okay with him.

CHAPTER
EIGHT
THE QUAKING HILLS

"It hurts to walk!" Ezme complained, reluctant to unwrap herself from her blanket. "Can we sleep just a little longer?"

They had made camp shortly after midnight, sheltered from the morning sun by the crumbling slope of a rocky ravine. Bonewise had insisted they get moving.

"We shall have no shelter from the sun once it crests that hill," Bonewise said. "We are running out of water. We must press on to the marsh."

They had restocked their supplies and rejoined Sueda three days prior. Ever since, they had spent most of their waking hours traveling north. The Duskfen Forest had diminished into oak savanna, then they crossed a few leagues of scrubland before reaching the stoney reaches of the Quaking Hills.

The place lived up to its name. Every few hours the land trembled, making sleep tenuous.

Sueda, however, seemed to be a heavy sleeper. She was not used to sleeping the way goblins did, bedding down just before dawn and sleeping until the afternoon, but the rigors of their journey, and the need to split their sleeping hours into shifts, had warped their sleep schedules. Only Bonewise ever seemed to be well-rested.

Vilayne spent her watch shift familiarizing herself with her magic torch, finding she could control the green flame if she sang to it.

"Wake up, human!" Fumble shouted, brows scrunched in discontent.

"Ugh," Sueda moaned, opening her bleary eyes. "At least with Audrel I could get a full night of sleep."

"Well, *you* murdered him."

"I did not!"

Fumble sucked his teeth. "Oh, I saw it. His eyes exploded."

"You're exaggerating! I'm not proud of what I did, but I did what I had to."

"Right, and now you have to get up and get moving! I don't plan to die of thirst on your account."

"Oh, you need water?" She stood, dusting herself off.

"I'm pretty sure all life needs water."

"I can bring up some water for you."

Sueda walked into the middle of the dry ravine, where a stream might have run with enough rain, and crouched down, placing her hand atop the pebbles that lay there.

"*Garû*," Sueda sang, "*vûhi m'bi bi-chipu—bi-chipu.*"

Before their eyes, a waterskin's worth of clear water bulged up from the ground, drawn to her hand, swirling an inch above her palm.

"Why didn't you do that yesterday when I said I was thirsty?" Fumble asked accusingly.

"There wasn't need. Trokar gave you some of his water. You didn't ask me."

"Can you teach me how to control water like that?" Ezme asked.

"It takes years of meditation," Sueda replied, "and it's not even really my own magic. I'm a priestess. Mawwu grants me some of her power."

"Your shield that deflected my arrow didn't look like water," Fumble commented.

"That was my sacramental wine. I blessed it to protect me."

"Is that the same wine I see you sipping from every day?" Vilayne asked as she shouldered her pack.

"Yes," Sueda said with a good-humored smile. "It renews my connection with it, helps keep my energy flowing."

"What if you run out?"

"Oh, that never happens." She giggled. "I'm very frugal. Just a sip keeps the blessing!"

Sueda filled everyone's water containers, then took a sip of wine from her bottle, uttering a prayer. With that, they resumed their journey, hiking for many leagues until they reached a chasm so deep they couldn't see the bottom.

"Don't get too close to the edge," Bonewise warned. "Never know when a quake will strike. We need to go 'round."

To clear it, they traveled east for hours, finally rounding the end of the great rift, then headed north again. The sun was low in the west, obscured by the trees; it was hard to tell exactly how close to sunset it was with coastal clouds moving in too.

"Look"—Ezme pointed—"a cave!" A slab of rock jutted askew from the tumbled landscape, a dark recess beneath it.

"Can we stop to rest?" Vilayne asked no one in particular.

"A snack and a nap do sound nice," Trokar sighed.

"Those clouds bring rain," Sueda remarked.

"You hear that, Bonewise?" Fumble asked. "The water witch says rain is coming. We better find shelter."

"I would be wary of being under a slab of rock in the Quaking Hills," Bonewise grumbled.

"Let's just check it out," Trokar proposed, and without waiting for agreement, he approached the shadow of the cave.

"Trokar, wait!" Vilayne hissed, and she shook her torch to produce its green flame.

He ventured inside, and when his eyes adjusted, he noticed three spiny lumps, breathing.

The spines, stiff like quills, slowly heaved as whatever the creatures were slumbered. He froze in his steps.

"What do you see?" Ezme asked from the entrance.

Trokar whirled around and shushed her, but it was too late. One of the spiny forms reared its head, eyes wide and black, screeching a horrible sound that hurt the goblin's ears. The other two creatures jolted awake too. They were ape-like, with short legs and strong arms.

"Ravenous gibberers!" Bonewise warned, readying his staff.

Trokar came running out of the cave with the creatures on his heels, gnashing their pointed teeth. Bonewise smacked one in the head as it came close, sending it reeling back.

Ezme tried to dodge the second creature's swiping claws but stumbled, and Fumble wasn't fast enough to notch an arrow, so he tried to beat back the third gibberling with his bow; he creature charged through the whipping wood and knocked him off his feet.

Vilayne shrieked at the gibberling bearing down over Ezme, and the green flame of her torch shot toward the snarling creature. It cringed in fear as the searing flame melted some of its spines.

"They fear light!" Vilayne called out.

Fumble summoned an illusion of swirling lights to swarm the gibberling clawing at him, and it swatted angrily, shrieking. It gave Fumble enough of an opportunity to scramble away.

Trokar found his courage and unsheathed his sword, charging the one standing over Ezme, running it through with his blade.

Bonewise beat down the beast he had previously dazed, cracking its skull, and Sueda blinded the eyes of another with a whip of stinging wine to its face. After a few more violent seconds, the three beasts were killed by sword and staff.

"That was hairy," Fumble commented as he checked his scratches. "Those things were disgusting! It feels like these wounds could get infected."

"Is everyone alright?" Sueda asked as she guided her wine back into its container.

"I'm not!" Fumble complained.

The ground then trembled beneath their feet.

"Quake!" Ezme announced.

"That's no quake," Bonewise said with severity, and he glanced at the last dim rays of sunset reaching over the clouds. "They're coming out! *Run!*"

Bonewise took off to the north while everyone else looked south to the rift, where they saw a great shaggy host of the creatures charging up over the ledge.

Adrenaline made them forget their weariness, but their packs swayed and their shoulders ached under the straps as they fled. The snarling creatures were fast, and every time Fumble glanced back, there were more of them, moving like a carpet of spines across the land. There must have been hundreds, perhaps thousands. He knew they would not outrun them.

"We need cover!" Fumble shouted.

"You want to hide under a rock?!" Ezme shouted back.

"I can try something!" Sueda announced.

Sueda had caught up with Bonewise thanks to her longer stride. She came to a stop, took a deep breath, and chanted something similar to what she had sung in the ravine. Drops of water rose from tufts of grass and cracks in the rock, and she drew it around her.

The goblins passed by and Sueda started running again, drawing more and more mist, creating a ground-skimming cloud that followed them.

Vilayne didn't look back, but she—as well as the rest of the goblins—could hear the horde of ravenous gibberers still running toward them, gaining.

"They're still coming!" Vilayne cried.

"Maybe I can throw them off our scent!" Trokar exclaimed. He tried and failed to reach for a side pocket of his pack as he ran. "Fumble, get into this pocket and pull out the paprika!"

"Unless those things are *very* allergic," Fumble replied, "I don't think that's going to help! We need light! Lots of it!"

"Your potions, Fumble! Use your potions!"

As if a light went off in his head at Trokar's words, Fumble pulled out all five of the light potions that he'd collected before they left the warren. With his other hand, he grabbed twine from one of his vest pockets and clamped the end of it in his teeth while he wrapped it around the bundle of vials several times. Fumble then held the rest of the twine ball in his mouth along with the other end, palming a firebomb potion, almost dropping it, as he tried to tie them together.

"Clove hitch," Fumble muttered as he fussed with his assembly, "then wrap six times, make two fraps in the middle..."

The sound of the stampede had grown louder behind them, the shapes of the howling creatures faintly visible through the mist.

"Just tie a granny knot!" Trokar cried.

"What's a granny knot?!"

"Fast and *simple*, Fumble! Just throw it!"

"For this to work," Fumble huffed, "it has to blow up *before* it hits the ground!"

"I can do it!" Vilayne called. "Throw it!"

Fumble spun around and hurled it high, tripping backwards as soon as it left his hand.

Vilayne planted her feet, barked a note of magic, and a green bolt of fire leapt from her torch. It shot straight at her target and shattered the glass.

Rays of blinding light illuminated the landscape as if the mid-day sun had suddenly appeared. The gibberling horde stopped in their tracks and shielded their eyes, screeching in fear as the light flowed down to the ground, along with tumbling flames, and splashed against the rocks.

Sueda bid the mist to stay in place, and it formed a thick veil that concealed their retreat.

The beasts did not follow. Still, the party kept up their pace to put as much distance between them and the creatures as fast as possible, and after a few minutes of jogging over rough terrain, they laid low in a channel thick with sedges. Even Bonewise was exhausted, and they hunkered down to catch their breath; the air putrid and salty.

"Looks like we found the marsh," Fumble said, squishing the mud beneath the sedges.

They turned to follow the widening channel in the rock until all stones disappeared beneath reeds, mud, and saltwater. Dead trees peppered the landscape as rain pattered the spans of standing water, rippling its surface.

"I think we are deep enough in the marsh now, so we can rest," Bonewise said after a tired yawn.

"So much for shelter," Ezme said morosely as she threw off her pack and collapsed into the mud. Others made their beds more carefully as they discussed the order in which they would take watch. Vilayne looked for material to start a small fire. She broke twigs and small branches from a split tree, its dead fibers grey with age.

She noticed more than a few scaly, pale mushrooms growing out of the trunk and larger branches. She sniffed one, scrunching her nose at its briny odor. She had once asked The Wise Woman about the salty mushrooms kept dry in a jar, to which the elder explained that they were valued for inducing visions. Seeking clarity, Vilayne pointed it out to Bonewise.

"It is not often we come across these," Bonewise said. "They will keep for a few days before drying."

As she harvested some chunks from the fruiting bodies, she noticed the flesh of the fungus flush red after it was broken, the color spreading faintly to other mushrooms that had not been disturbed. They were all connected, she realized.

They cut sedges and laid them down on the soft mud.

Vilayne was on first watch as the others hid from the rain under their blankets. The night was at its deepest, the grey clouds veiling the moon and stars completely. She practiced deep listening. There was a constant pattering of rain, which she thought was a lot for the beginning of summer. It was reputed there was stranger weather, close to the Sea of Dreams, which lay to the northwest.

She heard there were forests called "jungles" upon the Hucancha Peninsula, which the Spiderclaw clan called home.

Her thoughts were interrupted by a disturbance in the waters of the marsh. There were no tides, for the salted lands extended above sea level and far inland, but something sloshed through, slow and even. Though it was far away, it grew louder and louder.

She roused everyone quietly, shushing them the instant they awoke.

Sueda snored softly even as Vilayne shook her shoulders. She pinched a single hair of the woman's curls and yanked it from her head. Sueda jolted awake with a gasp, which Vilayne muffled with her palm.

The other goblins heard the sloshing, too. It was coming from multiple sources to the west. They armed themselves and fanned out among the tall reeds. Their clothes and skin were blotched with blue-grey mud, and in the darkness, no human would have been likely to see them.

Sueda crouched low where she had been sleeping, and strained to listen for what the goblins were concerned by.

Soon she heard it, too, like bodies stumbling through the marsh, crunching through the reeds, wading through the mud, splashing in the water. She took a sip of wine and whispered a chant to protect herself from evil.

Fumble drew his bowstring against his cheek, a hunting arrow ready to fly. Something emerged from the water in front of him, slowly, almost casually, and he strained his eyes to see what it was in the darkness. What he thought he saw was a human, and without a second thought, he released his arrow. It sunk into the figure's chest, but it did not react—not even a flinch. It just kept sloshing toward him.

"Zombies!" Fumble exclaimed. Instead of drawing another arrow, he plucked a firebomb from his satchel.

Vilayne shrieked a spell, sending green fire shooting from her torch, while Ezme used the brass wand she had claimed from Audrel, sending bright purple light streaking into the wet flesh of a nearing figure. With the bright but fleeting illumination, she could see the thing's white, unseeing eyes, its pale, rubbery hide, and the rotted remnants of what it once wore as clothes. Shelf mushrooms grew from its ribcage and from the side of its head.

It lunged, silently, up onto the mud above the water and reached for Fumble. Fumble looked determined to light the thing on fire with his firebomb, even with the risk that he might catch himself on fire, too, but just as he wheeled back his arm to smash the bottle into the thing's face, Trokar leapt from the reeds and sliced it clean in half at the waist. Its upper and lower halves fell into the mud.

"I had everything under control," Fumble said.

The upper half of the corpse suddenly grabbed Fumble's ankle, and he toppled onto his back, uttering a cry of surprise.

Trokar lopped off the zombie's hand at the wrist, then helped Fumble out of the mud, the hand still clutching his ankle.

"Let's get out of here!" Trokar exclaimed.

"Stand your ground!" Bonewise commanded. "I will send them away!"

Bonewise stretched his arms out, calling on the spirits of their ancestors for protection, asking for the evil spirits of the restless dead to be driven away, but the briny bodies kept advancing. He shook his staff and recited a different chant, but not one of the figures stopped advancing, lunging up out of the water.

"Nevermind," Bonewise said, "let's bolt!"

They tried to run through the mud, keeping to the highest ground there was, stepping on tufts of sedge where they could, but the going was slow. The mud gripped their every step.

"Have you lost your powers, Bonewise?" Ezme asked.

"It should have worked!" Bonewise grumbled.

"They're not undead!" Vilayne exclaimed.

"You mean they're alive?" Trokar asked in astonishment.

"It's the mushrooms! The fungus in them is alive, and it's controlling them!"

"Those mushrooms are about to get cooked!" Fumble exclaimed as he hurled a firebomb behind them at the gathering crowd of shambling bodies.

The glass bottle plunked intact into the mud in front of the half-decomposed figures.

"What a waste!" Fumble declared. "No, I can't allow it! Vilayne, do that thing again!"

"Make your own explosions, Fumble!" Vilayne called back as she forcefully slogged ahead.

"I can get it!" Ezme exclaimed. "Toss another one!"

Fumble tossed another firebomb toward the fungal zombies, and Ezme shot it with a blast from her brass wand. The resulting explosion splashed fire onto the wet bodies and the previous unexploded potion. It cracked from the heat, then burst, coating the zombies with more flame. The mushrooms on their flesh flushed red as the burning figures stumbled off the high ground and fell into the shallows.

Fumble grinned in triumph, but his smile vanished when the flames upon the mud and grass illuminated many, many more bog-zombies emerging from the reeds. The same figures he had just set alight stood in the water, flames extinguished.

"They're *learning*!" Fumble cried. "We have to outrun them!"

"I don't think that's an option," Vilayne said. She had stopped at a bend on the high ground, staring down at the mob of fungal zombies that had emerged from the marsh in front of them. There were more coming from everywhere. They were surrounded.

"I *told* you coming here was a bad idea!" Fumble cried.

They circled up, and Sueda drew the holy wine out of her bottle into a shield, though she didn't know what good it would do against these not-dead zombies.

Bonewise uttered a charm of blessing, if only for luck.

Ezme pulled out the wand The Wise Woman had given her, but Vilayne placed her hand on Ezme's wrist in restraint.

"Wait," Vilayne said, "they've stopped."

Sure enough, they'd stopped creeping forward, amassed in a circle just out of firebomb-throwing range.

"What are they doing?" Trokar asked.

"Maybe they're waiting for reinforcements," Fumble hypothesized.

"What do you want?!" Vilayne called out to the marsh.

The bodies began to gurgle, some expelling saltwater

from their mouths. They croaked and hummed, until sounds emerged from the mob that sounded like goblin words.

"Wwwwwhat . . . we . . . want . . . is the cycle . . . protected. We are . . . the mother . . . of the marsh. Whhhho . . . are . . . you?"

"We are goblins," Trokar answered. "Just passing through! We mean you no harm, Marsh Mother."

"There are . . . others . . . in the marsh. Humans and once-humans, rrrrobbers of the rot. Takers . . . of the dead. They corrupt the marsh . . . against the cycle."

"Takers of the dead?" Vilayne asked. "You mean necromancers?"

"Ennnemies of death . . . ennnemies of life."

"Sounds like the forces of the Witch Queen," Bonewise remarked.

"Weeeee sssense the ssscent and ssstride of a human . . . in your midst."

"Oh," Trokar said, "that's Sueda. She's like our pet."

"Excuse me?" Sueda frowned, scrunching her brow.

Trokar gestured vaguely to the bog-zombies and gave her an expression that seemed to ask if she had a better idea.

"I am nobody's pet," Sueda said loudly, addressing the Marsh Mother. "I am a servant of Mawwu and an enemy of the Witch Queen."

"Then we shall grant you sssafe passage . . ." the Marsh Mother said in a hundred dead voices, " . . . in exchange . . . for your help."

"How can we help you?" Sueda asked.

"The dead-takers mmmove . . . against the elves . . . of the forest. They do not know . . . we have told the elves . . .

of their coming. They do not know . . . they have awakened usss. Wwwe will ssstop them. You . . . will help."

"We shall aid you as best we can," Bonewise stated. "Lead us to the enemy."

"We mmmust mmmove quickly . . . to get you there . . . in time."

The bog-zombies turned to the northwest and shuffled through the shallows, then flopped down into the water and moved surprisingly fast, floating close to the surface. With no need to breathe, they simply glided along, face-down, in herds through the deeper channels between embankments. Sueda and the goblins had a difficult time matching their speed as they kept to the high, dry ground.

"What are we doing?" Fumble whispered.

"We either help the Marsh Mother willingly," Bonewise answered, "or become nutrients for her."

"Witches with the power to raise the dead scare me almost as much as this Marsh Mother does."

"I heard they fly around on brooms," Ezme remarked.

"I'm pretty sure that's just a metaphor," Fumble retorted.

"What are we going to do if they really do fly on brooms?" Trokar asked.

"Knock them down," Fumble declared. "We have magic, too—and arrows. Oh, I have magic arrows! I have three, so that's good for at least three witches."

"Never thought I'd be fighting against zombies alongside other zombies," Ezme said.

Fumble looked down at the water. "Our 'friends' here aren't technically zombies."

"Oh, whatever. Why do you always have to correct everyone?!"

"Quiet," Bonewise scolded softly. "We have the element of surprise, and I'd like to keep it."

CHAPTER NINE

THE DREAD MARSH

They slogged through the marsh until twilight, and a mist rose from the waters that became so thick, they couldn't tell which direction was east, unable to see the sun rise. Their muscles ached. Sueda's boots became heavy with caked mud and completely soaked through, so she carried them and went barefoot like the goblins.

The bog-zombies led them along an efficient route through the maze of marshland, and Bonewise knew they were covering ground much quicker than they would have been able to manage without the Marsh Mother's guidance. It was unsettling to see the long, rotted bodies floating through the waterways like alligators. As more converged upon them, not only were there human and elvish bodies but amorphous blobs of orange ooze as well.

"I'm sure glad we didn't need to fight our way out of this marsh," Trokar whispered.

Bonewise nodded but also shushed him.

Then they heard low, wet thud—rhythmic. Wood creaked, water splashed, and reeds bent. The outline of long, narrow ships appeared out of the mist. Sueda and the goblins crouched down in the tall grass. The ships were moving toward the northeast, and just as they were wondering how ships could traverse a marsh, they saw the creaking wooden legs, scorpion-like, with metal gears and cables, dragging the ships forward, scraping their bellies over the mud.

Instead of a mast, each ship had a wide, tall wheel in the center of the main deck, like a waterwheel, turned by dozens of animated skeletons that endlessly climbed the rungs on the inside and outside of the wheel's front end. They wore weighted backpacks to aid them in their tireless work. The great wheels turned gears that moved the legs of the ship up and down and side-to-side.

There seemed to be humans on the ships as well, muscle-bound warriors and scepter-wielding mages thin in frame, overseeing the undead. The goblins could only see two ships, but they heard dozens more. The bog-zombies of the Marsh Mother continued their silent advance.

"Well," Ezme said in a hushed tone, "how do we want to do this?"

"We can board one of those ships with my grappling hook," Trokar whispered, removing a coil of rope and a collapsible grappling hook from his pack to tie them together.

"We wait," Bonewise declared firmly and quietly, "then follow once they have passed."

"Attack from behind," Fumble agreed. "Good idea."

"How about from underneath?" Vilayne asked.

Passing silently overhead was another ship hovering about thirty feet above the ground, out of reach. It was smaller, built like a caravel, but it had buttressed beams hanging off the sides like two wings that supported enormous, wide brooms, a pair of them on each side. The bristles of the brooms were reed-like and half the length of the vessel. The curved ridge beam on the underside of the vessel was lapped in metal armor. The broomship's pace matched the crawl of its land-bound counterparts.

"They really do fly on brooms," Ezme whispered.

Trokar swung the grappling hook in a tight circle and tossed it up, trying to catch the broomship before it got too far away. He missed, but Vilayne whispered a spell and levitated the hook onto the back of the ship's aftcastle, securing it on the railing with only the slightest sound.

"I didn't know you could do that," Trokar whispered to her.

"There's a lot of things you don't know about me," she whispered back with a smile. "After you, muscle-head."

Trokar snapped his attention back to the rope, which was uncoiling at his feet. He jumped, caught the line and began to climb. His strength allowed him to ascend quickly, but the others had a harder time of it. Sueda was last to sneak up; she didn't have time to tuck away her boots so she dropped them and chased the end of the rope into the shallows. She was dragged through the mud of an embankment before she climbed higher, which was easier with bare feet.

Trokar climbed over the railing, leaving muddy streaks on the smooth, finely carved wood. There was a narrow walkway around the perimeter of the aftcastle, which was occupied in the center by a mound of green tent canvas secured to cleats by a net of rope. He didn't see anyone around, so he helped those behind him get over the railing when they reached it.

Once they were all on board, Trokar gave a hand signal for them to spread out.

Bonewise and Vilayne went on the walkway to the left, Ezme and Sueda went to the right, while Trokar and Fumble climbed the netted canvas. Fumble slipped and got his legs caught in the latticed rope a couple of times, but Trokar gave him a hand, yanking Fumble loose. Once they got to the top, they crawled forward on their bellies, seeing the others crouched near the narrow stairs on either side that led down to the main deck.

Vilayne held her torch in hand, ready to use it if need be.

On the balcony, at the front of the aftcastle, was a brown-haired woman with a tight bun-braid hugging the left side of her head. Voluminous bangs cascaded down to touch her cheek on the other. She stood about five and a half feet tall in a silk embroidered bodice, facing away from them. Her arms were tattooed with strange sigils and she wore leggings of black leather with matching boots. From her belt dangled a wide variety of components for spells, as well as a holster with a dark metal wand.

Instead of a steering wheel, she held a short broom with colorful, braided bristles pointed skyward, the end of the handle locked into some kind of gearbox on the deck. There were three other witches on the main deck, all with brooms. They were not household brooms, but long and thick at the end with braided reeds, the handles fitted with doweled footholds near the bottom and a red jewel set at the top. A fourth person stood on the forecastle, who wielded a staff with a bejeweled, metal dragon's head.

Unfortunately for the witches, they were focused on what lay in front of them, with no mind for what was behind.

Fumble tapped Trokar's shoulder, thumbed over his back at his quiver, then gestured for Trokar to pluck out one of the arrows, mouthing the words "magic arrow."

Trokar carefully did so, but before he handed it over, he smeared sticky marsh mud from his clothes onto the glass ball of the arrow, reaching into a side pocket on his pack for paprika. He sprinkled a pinch onto it from his spice bag, red dust sticking to the mud, then he presented it to Fumble with a wink.

Fumble grinned and notched the arrow. He hooked his feet under the rope netting and took aim at the broomship's pilot. She was only ten feet away, and he had a height advantage, but he aimed carefully, determined not to miss.

"Sidid lak!" One of the witches on the main deck called.

Suddenly, a fireball roared toward the prow from somewhere ahead, and the witch at the helm veered to the right to avoid it. The fireball streaked by the port side so close that Vilayne and Bonewise felt the heat of it on their faces. The pilot pulled up and gained altitude to rise above a volley of incoming fire. Bonewise thrust his staff through the rope netting next to him as an anchor while Vilayne and Sueda gripped the railing.

Fumble lost his balance, bumping into Trokar, almost losing his grip on the bowstring. He unintentionally pointed the arrow at Trokar, the crackling glass tip coming close to Trokar's eye; they both reflexively gasped in surprise and relief.

The witch at the helm craned her neck at the sound, spotting the two goblins.

"Ahwey weiev taen!" she cried, and pulled her wand from its holster, keeping one hand on the steering broom.

"Shoot!" Trokar shouted.

Fumble wobbled on one foot hooked under the rope, swinging his aim toward the woman. He plucked the string with a dainty tug, and the arrow plopped down onto the floorboards right where the witch was standing.

It shattered after a second of tense silence and confusion, a bright flash enveloping the witch. The space where she stood warped into a vortex with crackling paprika swirling and sparking . . . then she was gone, sucked into a single point of light that fizzled out of existence.

The steering broom fell against the railing, tilting the ship's nose downward; all the goblins grabbed hold of what they could as they felt sudden vertigo.

"Eov!" the witch with the dragon-staff shouted at the other three. The trio leapt onto their brooms and took flight, abandoning the ship. The one who remained pointed the metal dragon's head toward Fumble and Trokar, but then an explosion rocked the ship as a fireball struck the port side near the prow. The witch's aim was thrown off as the broomship pitched to the right in its downward spiral.

Bonewise did not wish to see what would come out of the dragon head of the staff, nor was he keen on crashing, so he let go of his rope-wedged staff and flung himself on the railing by the balcony, climbing the supports like the rungs of a ladder toward the steering broom.

Trokar and Fumble cried out together in terror as they gripped the netting.

Bonewise seized the steering broom and tugged it back, feeling a rush of magic shoot up his arms the moment he gripped it. On instinct, he directed the power back into the vessel and willed the ship to fly.

The broomship pulled up out of its slanted dive, and Bonewise tried to maintain his connection with the magic. The witch on the forecastle leveled the dragon staff at Trokar and Fumble, but Vilayne and Ezme pelted him with blasts of light and flame.

Fumble fired an arrow, ignorant that he had nocked one of the two remaining magical ones from Zalenthas.

One bright flash and explosion of lightning later, the witch was sent soaring overboard. The dragon staff however clattered across the deck and caught against the railing.

Bonewise oriented himself. He couldn't see much through the mist, though orange flashes and loud booms caught his attention. He steered the ship up and away from the explosions until they rose above the mist to see an expanse of tall, broad-leaved trees along the edge of the marsh, like green sea cliffs against the lazy surf of the fog. He tilted the ship so he could see the explosions below. Fireballs were being flung from both sides of the battleground, lighting up the mist sporadically in a swath stretching for leagues to the west.

"Check for anyone else on the ship!" Bonewise called out, loud enough for Sueda's smaller, human ears to hear.

Sueda went to a door on the main deck under the balcony below where Bonewise stood, placing a ready hand at the cork of her wine bottle. Trokar followed, his blade unsheathed, and gave her a nod. She opened the door and Trokar peeked inside. It was an armory, of sorts. Secure fixtures on the walls seemed to be where staffs and brooms could be stored safely—which were vacant, except for one black, twisted staff. Wooden gears and metal rods moved gingerly along the ceiling, and there was a stairwell in the center of the room going down to the lower deck. An oak door stood on the opposite end of the room.

While Trokar and Sueda swept the interior of the ship, Fumble scampered over to the dragon staff and picked it up. The staff itself was a lacquered wood, the head of dark metal was ornate, with red-jeweled eyes and a hole in the mouth. Judging by the scorch mark around the hole, Fumble had some idea of what it was for.

"Bonewise, do you want to crash this party?" Fumble asked with an appraising glance.

Bonewise could hear fighting on the Witch Queen's land-bound ships below. The servants of the Marsh Mother were rotting holes in the wooden hulls and tackling the undead within. Meanwhile, the elves launched volleys of flaming arrows and catapulted burning spheres from behind a palisade of thorns.

"Let's *wreck* it!" Bonewise declared with stoney resolve.

He steered the broomship to strafe the invading vessels, and Fumble ran to the front of the forecastle. He aimed the dragon-staff down at the ships of undead, but there wasn't a button or switch that he could find to activate it. He tried shaking it, then smacking it, but nothing happened.

"Hey, Vilayne?!" Fumble called across the main deck. "How does this thing work?!"

Vilayne focused her ears through the din of battle below them. They were flying over dozens of crawling land-ships, and more were lined up in the mist ahead. Between explosions, she heard voices reciting a word right before the whoosh of flame: *Dennhavix*.

She recited the word for Fumble, and Fumble shouted it with all the gusto of his certainty that it would work. A fireball burst out of the metal dragon's mouth with the nostril-curling scent of compressed chemical vapor. It hurtled into the turning wheel of one of the mechanical vessels, blasting the skeletons to bits and setting the wooden wheel on fire.

Fumble cried out in triumph, proceeding to rain down fireball after fireball on the chaos below.

"Incoming!" Vilayne warned, and Bonewise pulled up to avoid an elven volley of flaming artillery.

"Can't they see we're on their side?" Ezme complained.

"I don't think they're very perceptive," Vilayne replied.

A fireball suddenly exploded on their port side, opposite the elven front.

Bonewise felt a flickering power pulsing up the magic of the steering broom, and its colorful bristles quavered. The portside broomwing was on fire.

"There's no one down there!" Trokar announced as he and Sueda emerged from below deck. Trokar had sheathed his sword and instead held the twisted staff from the armory.

"The engines are on fire!" Fumble shouted.

"The brooms are on fire!!" Trokar cried, seeing the blazing inferno of what was keeping them in the sky. "Put it out!"

"Sure, I'll just spit on it," Fumble replied sarcastically.

Sueda waved her arms and recited a prayer to Mawwu, the River Goddess who was robed in the Mists of Mystery. The fog around her congealed into raindrops that she directed onto the burning wing. The flames hissed and died out, leaving it a singed and slightly smaller bundle of giant reeds.

Another broomship loomed above them, and another fireball soared down; Bonewise veered to the left, dodging it.

"Okay," Ezme said, "we helped, just like we promised. Now let's get out of here!"

Bolts of baleful magic peppered Bonewise's back, like needles of pure fire pricking his spine. He choked on the pain, but the Geostone thrummed in his blood, absorbing the power, guarding him against shock.

Sueda ran up the stairs and spun up a shield of her holy

wine, deflecting the next volley of magic from their pursuers.

Vilayne and Ezme fired back while gripping the railing, and Bonewise pulled up just out of the mist, skimming it with the broomship's underbelly.

The other broomship followed suit, and Bonewise veered to and fro as he dodged fireballs from the staff-wielder on its forecastle. He dipped the ship in and out of the fog, trying to throw off their pursuers.

Fumble arrived at the aftcastle and fired back with his dragon-staff, but the other ship dipped under it. He fumed with frustration at his slim chances of landing a hit. He grabbed the netting over the tent canvas to steady himself as Bonewise dodged another fireball; the woven nettle fibers bit into his hand, and he had an idea.

"Trokar?!" Fumble called.

"Yeah?" Trokar grunted as he tried to twist the staff with all his might, as if he might wring the magic out of it.

"Did you find any flammable liquids down there?"

Trokar's eyes lit up.

"Maybe! I'll be right back!"

Trokar tossed the twisted staff to Ezme as he slid down the railing of the stairs from the aftcastle, and she barely caught it. Before she could hurl an insult at him, he was below deck. He quickly returned with his arms full of two clay jugs with waxed stoppers on top. Both jugs were painted with a series of symbols, one of which resembled flames.

"I don't know what these are," Trokar said, "but they look flammable!"

Fumble took one of them and twisted the stopper off, sniffing. "Excellent! Pour it onto the canvas!"

"You want to light *our* ship on fire?!"

"No! Trust me, I have a plan!"

Trokar thought that Fumble's plans usually went well, so he climbed onto the heap of netted canvas, stumbling back and forth as Bonewise dodged incoming fire. Trokar poured the fluid all over the top of the canvas while Fumble did the same all around the edges. It reeked of alcohol, fuming oil, and other volatile scents they could only guess at.

"Bonewise," Fumble said, "get us right over them!"

Bonewise nodded and dipped the broomship down into the mist, gaining speed. Their pursuers followed, and when he could hear the clashing battle below them, he pulled up sharply.

"Hang on!" Bonewise called, and he strained as he channeled his own magic into the ship, urging it up, up, up, propelling them almost vertically into the sky. He recited a chant, calling on his ancestors to aid him, and he felt the pebble in his pocket weighing him down, yet, at the same time, securing his conduit to the Power Below. He knew he wouldn't be able to keep it up for long.

"Release the canvas!" Fumble commanded, clutching the railing so he wouldn't fall.

Trokar blinked in sudden understanding. He barked with frustration, because the canvas was not easily untied from the cleats. Resolved, he leapt onto the canvas slope from above, sliding down it toward the enemy broomship below. He hooked his sword underneath the rope net and opened it like a zipper, grabbing the railing at the back of the aftcastle. The soaked tent canvas spilled out and flared open as it fell.

Fumble was ready. With his legs wrapped around the railing, he spat out *"Dennhavix"* and launched a fireball from the dragon-staff. The streak of fire flowered against the spreading canvas, flaring aflame. The broomship following them could not turn fast enough, and it was caught in the trap. It was wrapped by the burning canvas, careening back toward the fog.

They cheered with relief. Even Sueda laughed, her melodic voice threading between the louder goblin voices, but one voice was absent. Bonewise could not hold the power any longer; he fell backwards, exhausted of all spiritual energy, and for a moment, all became weightless.

They were in free-fall, the air whistling around them in gale force, twisting in vortices of mist as they dropped back into the fog.

Trokar saw Bonewise tumble like a rag doll as the broomship's nose swung toward the marsh below. He grabbed the sliced netting with one hand and kicked off the railing, colliding with Bonewise, quickly wrapping his arm under the elder goblin's shoulder as he reached for something to grab. He clutched the shaman to his chest with all his might, hyperventilating with the anticipation of a sticky death only a few breaths away, and there was nothing he could do to stop it.

Vilayne climbed over the balcony from the main deck, and, still hugging the railing, reached out to grab the engraved wood of the broom handle. She didn't understand the meaning of the runes on its surface, but she knew that they held power, and if Bonewise could bend it to his will, then so could she.

Letting go of the railing, she grabbed the broom handle with both hands and planted her feet firmly on the deck. She closed her eyes and felt the wind in her nostrils, imagining herself riding the streams of air rattling the reeds of the brooms.

Her feet pressed hard into the floorboards as the

broomship swooped up out of its nosedive, and there was a loud crash as the armored underbelly of the vessel smashed across the deck of a marsh crawler, sending several figures flying overboard.

Far to the west, a series of green flares shot up over the fog and illuminated the landscape in neon bursts. Those of the crawling ships that had not yet smashed into the wall of thorns at the forest's edge reversed their skeleton-powered wheels and began to crawl back the way they had come, still fending off bog creatures. Flaming arrows chased after them, but they quickly disappeared into the fog.

"We did it!" Fumble declared.

"*Now* can we get out of here?" Ezme asked. "There's nothing left for the elves to shoot at but *us*!"

Vilayne pulled the ship up out of the fog, veering around a flaming artillery bolt that was lobbed at them. She muttered a spell under her breath as she tried to cement her connection to the mysterious power of the broom in her hands. She looked around the horizon, seeing nothing but rolling fog to her left and misty treetops to her right. The sun burned orange on the horizon behind her.

"Soon as we cross into the forest," Vilayne said, "we could get a lot of arrows coming at us."

"Fly higher!" Fumble said.

The higher Vilayne tried to steer the ship, the thinner her connection to the magic stretched, and she began to shake as though she were fevered from sudden windchill. She did not want to suffer the same fate as Bonewise, so she dipped lower over the marsh, keeping her distance from the elvish lines.

"Is Bonewise breathing?" Sueda asked, half-stumbling up the stairs with muddy feet to the aftcastle as the ship pitched and swayed. Trokar was kneeling at the shaman's side and bent his ear to the crinkled face.

Trokar nodded to Sueda as she knelt at his other side. She flicked a drip of holy wine onto Bonewise's tongue and said a prayer, but he did not stir. She felt his chest and neck, then lifted his eyelids, one by one, and saw they were dilated but otherwise unmoving.

Knowledge from every class she had ever attended about the healing arts bubbled to the surface of her mind, and she felt a gentle tingle at her forehead where the Skystone was strapped.

"He's stuck in some kind of torpor," Sueda said.

"You mean he's stricken with laziness?" Fumble asked skeptically.

"A severe form of it," she answered. "He must have given everything to fly us so high. I don't know how to heal this."

"I could shove some fully-reacted salts up his nose?" Fumble suggested. "I have three different flavors!"

"We need rest," Sueda said, feeling the ache in her muscles deepen from their sprint through the marshland, then she looked to Trokar. "We can travel quickly with this flying ship, but we might not be able to find a place to land in the Glyphwood."

"We also don't know where in the forest we need to go," Ezme added as she came up onto the aftcastle. "Bonewise usually knows that kind of thing."

"Perhaps the Marsh Mother can tell us something?"

"What about the elves?" Trokar asked. "They probably know everything about the forest!"

"Are you crazy?!" Fumble cried. "I dunno if you noticed, but those earless bastards were shooting at us!"

"They just didn't know we were helping," Trokar reasoned.

"And you think that if we politely explain to them that we are *goblins*, they will welcome us?"

"No—but maybe we could make a trade?"

"The last time we made a trade we were *betrayed*!"

"Technically, it was *us* who went back on that deal, but it wasn't a fair deal."

"Yeah," Fumble agreed thoughtfully, "five hundred silver for a powerful, ancient artifact is insulting. That human had no honor!"

"Elves are very into honor! The leader of their warriors surely won't go back on his word?"

"Yes, Trokar!" Fumble clutched his scalp. "*Especially* if they hate goblins! We can't trust *anyone* who hates goblins!"

Trokar thought about this for a moment.

"You know what elves don't hate?" Trokar asked.

"What?" Fumble crossed his arms.

"Their hair." Trokar waggled his eyebrows.

Fumble's ears perked up. Fumble knew that Trokar had packed extra jars of their hair-care concoctions.

"If there's one thing people say about elves," Trokar said, "it's that they love being beautiful. If we can show them how good our beauty products are, they'll have to respect us!"

"You make a good point . . ." Fumble frowned. "I never pass up an opportunity to break into a new market. But we can't talk to them if they keep shooting at us!"

"We need to signal them!" Trokar bolted down the stairs and disappeared below deck. He returned with a white bedsheet from the captain's cabin. "Take us down!"

He told Vilayne, then he waved the sheet around from the fore of the broomship.

Vilayne wanted to ignore Trokar's unbearable optimism and hightail it over the forest; he wouldn't be able to stop her. She turned the ship so the sunrise was on her right, the forest somewhere through the fog to the north. She gripped the broomstick and prepared to rush the elvish lines, but a chill ran up her spine. They might get shot down, she thought, and they needed Bonewise to guide them. Begrudgingly, she also admitted to herself that she was as worn-out as the others. Perhaps meeting with the elves was worth the risk.

With a weary sigh, she let the ship float languidly toward the north.

"Fumble, make sure they see that bedsheet," Vilayne said.

"Aye-aye!" Fumble answered, and he conjured sparks above Trokar, illuminating the sheet.

"Sueda," Vilayne said with a turn of her head, "clear the mist."

Commander Erolith Aefaren of the Southern Glyphwood dismounted from his two-legged, feathered riding lizard to parley with the enemy ship that had signaled surrender to his battalion. The unnatural craft had settled its armored keel atop the wall of thorns the druids had grown for the defense.

The enemy was not known to seek negotiations after losing a battle, so he expected a trap. The battalion was on high alert, arrows nocked and artillery primed. A dark-skinned woman appeared on the deck. Beautiful, despite the mud caked to her robe and cloak. He was certain that she was human, despite her ears being hidden behind frizzy curls, for he could not imagine any elf serving the unholy folly of the Witch Queen.

He nodded to the druids perched in the branches of the swamp oak nearby. The women spoke to the vines that entangled the tree, and from the roots in the ground, more vines grew and wove themselves into a ramp that connected to the front of the broomship.

A short figure behind the woman seemed to nudge her forward, and she walked barefoot out onto the ramp with a nervous chuckle. Erolith spotted bat-like ears poking up from behind the railing. He cursed under his breath when he saw not one but *three* goblins follow the woman down. Such ugly creatures! One of them flashed a white sheet half-bunched up in his hand, smiling like a fool. Now Erolith was *sure* it was a trick. All his long life he had been told that only a fool would ever trust a goblin.

CHAPTER

TEN

ENEMY OF MY ENEMY

Sueda gave her best diplomatic smile as the elvish commander removed his helmet, uncovering his red braids. He did not smile back.

"Shardae," Sueda greeted in Elvish before introducing herself in the common tongue. "I am Sueda, priestess of Mawwu, friend to the Glyphwood and its protectors."

"Commissaire Erolith Aefaren, Glyphwyrda arn," the commander said in Elvish with an incline of his head. "Sal col haren ath mara cerlica Mawwu surnar tel' Cor'Etriel versa?"

Sueda understood that he was questioning how a priestess of Mawwu could serve the unholy forces of the Witch Queen. She thought that even though he seemed to understand her language, she should answer in Elvish as a show of respect.

She explained that she and her allies had taken the enemy ship by force and had aided the defenders of the forest, a spectacle that had surely been witnessed by some of his officers.

"What are you saying to him?" Fumble asked Sueda suspiciously.

"Tell him we are emissaries of the Marsh Mother," Trokar said.

Sueda gestured for them to be patient, keeping her attention on Erolith.

"Jen goblien alet lythari lor nae viaren ebrath?" the elf asked with all the edge of authority in his rigid stance.

Trokar, Fumble, and Ezme, keenly aware that the word "goblien" had been spoken, waited as Sueda explained in Elvish that she had saved their lives as they had saved hers, and that the Goddess of the Sacred Waters gave life to all without price.

Pretty words, he replied, but he went on to say that it did not explain how they came to be there at the precise time of the invasion. Sueda told him about their deal with the Marsh Mother, and that his druids could confirm their allegiance if they communed with the fungal wardens.

Erolith gestured to one of the druids in the oak, who promptly swung down on a vine to receive his quiet command.

The druid nodded and walked through the bramble wall toward the marsh, vines curling out of her way to admit her through.

In the silence that followed, Trokar cleared his throat and stepped forward; Erolith frowned at him.

"Tell him we want to make a trade," Trokar said to Sueda.

"Var deslara saille escomalie," Sueda translated.

"Kesa denos vara ysele," Erolith answered with a renewed frown.

"He says it depends on if what we said is true."

Trokar nodded with a smile and turned to give a wink to Ezme and Fumble.

Soon after, the elf druid returned through the bramble tunnel, which wove itself shut behind her. She whispered something to Erolith and the commander's brow arched up in apparent surprise, then he gestured for her to return to her post. He slowly turned to face Sueda and the goblins again.

"Va kaweh avae," Erolith stated.

"He recognizes we spoke true," Sueda translated with a smile.

"Good!" Trokar said. "Tell him that first, we present a gift of goodwill, a sample of our highly-refined cosmetic oil, which strengthens one's hair and gives it a most beautiful shine!"

Sueda translated, and Trokar extended to him a fist-sized bottle of moth oil, putting on his most charismatic smile.

"Wait, you're just giving it away?" Ezme protested.

"First one is free," Fumble assured her quietly. "Once they see the results, then we charge them for more."

The elf frowned and eyed the bottle suspiciously.

Trokar ran his hand through his finely-sculpted hair and gave a couple encouraging nods to the commander.

Erolith motioned for a junior officer standing at attention nearby to inspect the contents of the bottle. Trokar didn't understand what was said, but he graciously handed the bottle over to her.

"Var escomalie?" Erolith asked as the bottle was taken away.

"He wants to know what trade you propose," Sueda said.

"Tell him that they can inspect the ship, to help them

against our common enemy, if he promises to let us leave in the same way that we came."

Sueda nodded and related Trokar's words in Elvish.

"Va var salen ysele," Erolith responded after a brief, thoughtful silence.

"He gives his word," Sueda said.

The goblins grinned and chatted among one another for a moment, then Trokar turned back to Erolith with a plaintive gesture and asked: "May we rest in your camp while you make your inspection? One of our number was injured during the battle."

Sueda relayed his question to Erolith, who frowned again but nodded.

"Ernath guarde," Erolith stipulated.

"We will be under guard," Sueda translated.

"He wants to make us his prisoners!" Fumble declared.

"No, it's fine," Trokar said calmly. "He gave his word."

"We'll see about that," Fumble commented sourly.

The goblins returned to the broomship and told Vilayne what had transpired. She had been watching over Bonewise on the aftcastle, ready to get the ship airborne again if something went wrong. Though she was not completely assured of their safety, she helped them carry Bonewise down to a campfire encircled by guards positioned at a respectable distance.

They toasted rations over the flames and rested. Fumble insisted they keep watch on their watchers, so they slept in shifts. All through the morning and early afternoon they dozed, and though Sueda was still unused to sleep during the day, she slept for hours with her mud-heavy cloak wrapped around her, head against her scroll case.

Meanwhile, the broomship was scrutinized by elves with pen and parchment. They took meticulous notes and measurements, copying runic inscriptions and sketching out its interior.

In the late afternoon, their mages and scribes finally departed the broomship, making their way to commander Erolith's round command tent.

Bonewise regained consciousness, grumbling at the brightness of the sun through the trees. His back ached from the burns he had suffered and he felt hungover as he cast a withering gaze around at the elves that surrounded them.

"Trokar," Bonewise groaned, "what have you done?"

"We cut a deal!" Trokar happily reported.

"Why?"

"Because you yakked out, Bone-dome," Ezme teased.

"Fumble," Bonewise addressed, "I'm surprised you went along with this."

"Yeah, me too," Fumble admitted. "Maybe a part of me wanted Trokar to prove himself wrong."

"But I wasn't wrong!" Trokar announced cheerfully. "A deal was made and now we get to leave in our new flying ship! Warface is going to be picking his jaw off the ground!"

"It is . . . unseemly luck," Bonewise commented cautiously.

"It's destiny!" Trokar declared. "We seized it with both hands for goblin glory!"

"We don't want to hear about your double-fisted glory, Trokar," Vilayne said.

"That glory is a bit premature, too," Ezme added. "We're not even back in the saddle!"

"You should have listened to me, Trokar," Fumble said. "These elves are about to betray us any moment now, you'll see!"

Erolith emerged from his tent, followed by an elf

woman in mage's robes. The warriors guarding the area stepped aside as he strode up to his guests. His expression was strangely pleasant.

"Sar miir var," Erolith said with an open gesture, "nesh yn feer bren wihylo. Sal thro millentu viaren scient, ent sal am aniq lor var Raun esk."

"He thanks you for delivering this artifact into their care," Sueda translated. "He says your kind is known to covet gold, and he is prepared to offer you a large amount."

"Whoa, whoa, whoa"—Trokar put up his hands—"the ship is not for sale. We said you could inspect it, not take it!"

Sueda translated, and the commander's expression was one of confusion for a moment, then he became very serious.

"Bren vess nha alles Mah wihylo aleth magnafara ik," the elf lectured. "Nelien nae *goblien*, quin op annela, nesh siilen, lor nae ik nesh fiaen sienen."

"This vessel is a magical artifact of extraordinary power," Sueda translated. "It would be irresponsible to allow goblins, or anyone, for that matter, to use its power for their whims."

Fumble elbowed Trokar and gave him a wide-eyed stare.

"You gave us your word!" Trokar accused, ignoring Fumble.

"Va feer vian ysele," Sueda translated for Erolith.

"Avavaen," the elf responded with a shake of his head, "siilen var denarlen. Va tela bhen ha lor nae shan."

"He says that he promised that you could leave, nothing more."

"No," Trokar asserted. "Tell him that he promised we

could leave in the same way that we came. That is how you translated it, right?"

Sueda nodded.

"And we came in this ship!" Trokar pointed.

"This pompous schmuck thinks we're nothing more than mercenaries," Ezme commented as Sueda translated Trokar's statement.

Bonewise shook his head in distaste.

"Siilen nha—nha reconselliqua!" The elf huffed in outrage. "Va twellen ysele! Tel braar nha jen var sehan, col tel' ya durr var sehan!"

"He says that is ridiculous and that you twist his words," Sueda said. "He says the ship is *how* you came, not the *way* you came."

"You can't decide what I meant in a way that is convenient for you," Trokar pressed. "That would be a dirty trick!"

Sueda translated Trokar's words in a quieter voice and the commander's eyes widened even more.

Trokar took a step forward and spoke again in a more measured tone. "We came by way of this ship," he said. "We *risked our lives*."

Ezme stepped forward, said: "We didn't have to land! We allowed you to examine it! We did you a big favor!"

"Yeah," Fumble added, "and this is how you treat us?! I thought the elves were supposed to be all noble and *honorable* and shit!"

Sueda put up her hand before anyone else could chime in, quickly translating for Erolith most of what the goblins had said.

Erolith looked aghast, turning his gaze from the goblins, to the ship, then back to Sueda; he seemed to be at a loss for words. He turned his head to lock eyes with the mage that had accompanied him from the command tent. They remained still for a long moment, as if they were communicating their very thoughts.

During the tense silence, the elf woman who had taken the Oil of Moth returned and bowed with a quiet word of greeting or apology. Erolith looked to her and saw the sheen of her dark-red hair, with flecks of iridescent silver glittering in the sun. She spoke a dozen words in a low voice, then offered the bottle, still mostly full, to her commander.

He took the bottle and nodded to her. As she withdrew, he seemed to consider the gift in his hand and grunted softly in a thoughtful manner.

"Uann goblien," Erloith muttered.

Crafty goblins, Sueda translated for herself.

"Desha," he said, looking up. "Var shan."

"He says we can go!" Sueda grinned.

"With the ship?" Bonewise asked.

"He said 'so be it,' so, yes!"

"I told you it would work!" Trokar shoved Fumble teasingly.

"Thanks to *my* formula!" Fumble shoved back. "Now we need to talk about pricing and distribution. Sueda, tell him we can have fifty bottles ready in a month for half a pound of gold, not including delivery—"

Bonewise smacked Fumble lightly on the head with his staff and grabbed him by the ear, tugging him toward the broomship.

"Say nothing but our thanks," Bonewise said to Sueda over Fumble's complaints.

"Let's go before he changes his mind!" Vilayne exclaimed as she grabbed Trokar's ear, giving him the same treatment before he could launch into pleasantries.

"Sali Alus," Sueda said in Elvish with a reverent bow. In her own language, the phrase was said in parting among followers of Mawwu meaning "sweet water." She didn't know what gods Erolith worshiped, but she felt the words would be appreciated.

Erolith turned up the corners of his mouth in a small smile, bowing his head in return. Sueda turned to follow her companions, but she paused; Erolith could see that she wanted to say something else, and he tilted his head in curiosity.

"What is the Crown of the Glyphwood?"

"Al shesh col n' salen Akhura dor lor nae trodae," he replied with grim forbearance. *A place not even my warriors dare to tread.*

So, it is a place, Sueda thought.

"Why?"

"Tel kiein lor Tel' brambis Cor'Quessir."

"The Briar King? From children's stories?"

"Hinal azae bren veris shesh." *The truth of the stories lives there.*

"He is not of your people?"

"Su nha eldar salen quessir. Thas siilen viaren ou' auren ent quaratri viaren faen."

Far older than my people, he had said. *They that would whisk away your wits and dance away your life.*

She locked eyes with Erolith, seeing that he was dancing around her questions. He was giving her a warning.

"Sueda," Erolith addressed as the woman turned away to follow her party, and she halted to look at him. "Dance with goblins at your peril."

He said it in her own language, and before she could

respond, he turned away and vanished into his command tent with his advisors.

CHAPTER
ELEVEN
CROWN OF THE GLYPHWOOD

Bonewise stood at the broomstick, keeping the morning sun on the starboard side, using his best guess at their direction when it rose slowly overhead. It glided over the tops of oaks and towering cottonwoods, their green and silver leaves rustling in the breeze. Flocks of colorful birds fluttered from the treetops at their passing.

What he was looking for, Bonewise didn't know, but he reasoned that heading toward the heart of the forest might reveal some sign. He trusted that the ancestors would guide him, for long before the elves claimed the Glyphwood as their own, goblins had roamed it in the time of the Goblin King.

Ezme stood at the prow, the twisted staff Trokar had tossed her in hand. She felt it flicker with electric energy and knew—somehow—she could command its power if the need arose. She watched for anything that might catch her eye between the branches, but all she could see below the canopy were darting feathers and tangled green.

Meanwhile, Sueda thumbed through scrolls in the

captain's cabin, trying to interpret northern script and coded symbols. Around the corner, Fumble was overjoyed to find a small alchemist's laboratory across from the galley, busying himself with sniffing various jars and vials, disregarding the writing on the labels.

Vilayne, somewhere in the ship's belly, opened a door to find a room filled with crystals, beams of multicolored light bouncing off mirrors that were connected to gears and rods. There were small drawers on the inside wall beside the door, labeled with script she couldn't read. She rummaged through them, finding an assortment of polished gemstones, likely kept as spares in case any components needed to be replaced. One had a single sunstone—which she pocketed—and another was full of chalk. She used a piece to write the goblin symbol for "keep out" on the chamber door.

Further down the corridor, Trokar attempted to open a copper vault inscribed with runes, but failed, finding no way to open it. He pressed an ear to its surface, only to hear what sounded like wind whirling around inside, even though it was in the center of the ship. Odd, he thought, deciding to leave it alone.

Around the bend and up a narrow hallway, he came to what seemed to be a dead end near the fore of the ship, but upon closer inspection, he noticed a small door in the hull, like a cupboard space. He opened the door and peered inside.

He got a glimpse of a small dim room with tiny furnishings—a bed and a table, each no bigger than his own head. Suddenly, he was blinded as a wet rag slapped against his face, thrown by something hiding behind a moldy curtain draped around a battered bucket opposite the door.

"What the—" Trokar exclaimed as a tiny foot collided with his nose.

A small, rotund toad-skinned creature with pointed ears scampered over his head and hopped down onto the floor, sprinting down the corridor.

Vilayne stood at the other end of the corridor, firing two bolts of green flame from her torch to scorch the wood in front of the yellow-skinned thing, startling it to a halt.

Trokar threw down the filthy rag and reached for his sword, but stopped himself from drawing it when he saw how the creature cowered.

"Stop!" Trokar called, both to Vilayne and the creature.

"No kill me!" the creature pleaded in goblin-speech.

"You speak our language?" Vilayne asked, keeping her torch raised and ready.

"Yes! I know many! Long time out of practice, but know many things! Number one useful!"

"What are you?" Vilayne interrogated as Trokar stepped closer to it.

"Name is Gret! Gret is gremlin called. Gret knows Moonbeam, keep fixed, keep clean!" Gret made a scrubbing motion with one hand.

"What is the Moonbeam?" Trokar asked.

"Name of ship!"

"And you're the janitor?"

Gret shrugged.

"Why are you working for the witches of Vorn?" Vilayne asked.

"Why?" Gret echoed with a perplexed look. "There is no 'why!' Only do! Gret not get political."

"That's good. You work for us now." Vilayne relaxed her stance.

"I do?"

"Gret," Trokar interjected, "does the Moonbeam have any rum?"

"One jug in galley. Gret not take!"

"Do you like rum?"

"Number one like!" Gret gave a sharp, toothy grin.

"We will pay you with rum and other booze if you work for us."

"Wow! Witches never paid Gret, especially not booze! What job Gret need do?"

"Same as before," Vilayne answered. "Keep the ship fixed and clean."

"You got!" Gret gave a little salute. "Gret have rum now?"

"Show me where it is and we can drink it together," Trokar said with a smile.

Gret led Trokar to the galley, showing him where the jugs were and which contained rum. Half a cup was poured for the gremlin, and a full one for Trokar.

Vilayne called everyone above deck to introduce Gret. Sueda was fascinated by the creature, for they were very rare, and their great intellect baffled scholars to such a degree that many denied they even existed.

"Can you fix that?" Vilayne asked Gret, pointing to the partially burned, giant broom on the port side.

"No do—no got tower-grass," Gret answered with a wince.

"There's no extra on board?" Ezme asked.

"No got," Gret answered. "Need special way to dry, special way to bind with crystals in ship. Only grow one place!"

"There will be time for that later," Bonewise said from the steering broomstick. "We approach a place of power. Behold!" He pointed in the direction they flew, and a broad section of the forest seemed to reach thrice as high as the treetops surrounding it. They walked to the railings to get a better view, seeing a rocky plateau gripped by roots on all sides, with meadows between crowning crags around the edges. A tall, thick forest populated the interior, many leagues wide. Against all reason, a waterfall poured over the edge, fed from some inexhaustible source hidden from view.

"The Crown of the Glyphwood!" Sueda exclaimed. "That must be it!"

"Bonewise, can you set us down there?" Vilayne asked.

"I have not yet landed this thing," Bonewise answered. "How did you do it"

"I dropped it onto a pile of brambles."

"Aiie!" Gret grimaced. "So *that* why there thorns in wings! Gret have to pull all out!"

"There will be more rum for you when it's done," Trokar assured him.

"At least put brooms up when land this time?"

"Huh?"

"Landing gear!" Gret scampered over the deck by the aftcastle and opened a floor hatch, revealing a turning wheel. "I get comb for brooms!" He hopped down through the open hatch, vanishing from sight.

Bonewise steered the ship to the lip of the plateau, where windblown grasses clung to the rocky soil. Trokar muscled the wheel into motion, slowly hinging the broomwings into an upright position; simultaneously, a tripod of curved legs unfolded from the bottom of the hull. Bonewise huffed and grunted with effort as he set the ship down against the buffeting winds, resting at last on the iron-capped legs.

The moment Bonewise let go of the broomstick, he felt

the weight of his years and an overwhelming need to lie down.

"We have traveled further in one morning than we could have hoped to travel in three nights on foot," Bonewise announced. "Yet I feel as though I have indeed walked for that long! We shall make camp here for the afternoon."

"But the rest of us aren't tired!" Ezme protested.

"I've been keeping us aloft all day!" Bonewise grumbled.

"Perhaps we should scout around before we get too comfortable," Vilayne suggested.

"I agree," Fumble said. "You can rest, Bonewise. We'll make sure the area is safe."

"Very well," Bonewise said. "Stay together!"

"I am still translating scrolls," Sueda announced. "I'll stay here."

"You'd rather look at filthy scribbles than explore a 'Place of Power?'" Fumble asked with disdain.

"Oh, so now you *want* the human to tag along?" Ezme jeered.

"Those scribbles don't even look anything like the things they represent! It's *wrong*!" Fumble stomped his foot.

"Enough!" Bonewise growled. "Give me a few hours of peace! Just don't fall off a cliff or eat anything poisonous."

A DISTANT SCREECHING sound pierced through the birdsong of the forest, and the squish of peat under goblin feet stopped as they turned their ears.

"What was that?" Trokar asked, clutching his sword.

"Maybe it's a bird?" Ezme suggested.

"Maybe it's your mom," Fumble teased.

"I don't know my mom, and neither do you!"

"My mother is dead," Vilayne interjected, deadpan.

Fumble frowned. "Well, now I feel like a butt."

"You'll feel dead like my mother if you don't shut up," she said, matter-of-factly.

"Holy grub! Vilayne just made a joke! Or, wait, was that a threat? Or both?"

"It's a fact that you're making noise in a forest filled with unknown creatures that might be hungry. Shut your mouth and open your ears."

"You sound just like Bonewise," Fumble muttered.

Vilayne walked on, followed by Trokar with his sword, Ezme with her twisted staff, and Fumble with his fireball launcher.

Grey stones loomed tall and smooth around them, some half-swallowed by trees and vines. The bark of the trees grew in such a way that seemed to swirl, meandering in strange and diverse shapes—like magic symbols.

"Look!" Ezme whispered, pointing at one of the tall stones that looked like a face.

Vilayne brushed some vines aside to reveal the face of a goblin. It was so encrusted with moss, it was difficult to tell at first, but the distinctive curl of a bat-like nose was visible.

"Our ancestors built this," Vilayne said softly. "We must be close." She had paid attention to The Wise Woman's long, rambling stories. There was something captivating about these Source Stones, as Sueda called them. Something about them being the Goblin King's source of power, the key to his god-like abilities and, ultimately, the keys to his undoing. She touched the stone, wondering—

"Twenty-foreheads!" Fumble declared in front of the

stone face, but nothing happened. Vilayne slanted her ears in annoyance.

"Does this look like a doorway to you?" Ezme chided.

"It worked the last time we found goblin ruins!" Fumble replied.

As Fumble and Ezme argued, Trokar's gaze wandered along a row of similar stones nearby, seemingly tossed about by old tree roots. Between the trees and the stones, he was stunned to see a metal contraption with spiked wheels. The metal was bronze-like, similar to his sword, and like his sword, it was mostly unblemished by age, though there was thick moss draped over the body of it.

Spellbound by the bizarre thing, he walked toward it. The wide spoked wheels were made of the same metal, half sunk into the forest floor. There were red crystals protruding from a cylinder on the back of the wagon-like contraption.

"Ho, there, wayward wander'r."

Trokar almost dropped his sword as he jerked, jumping at the sound of an unfamiliar voice. Standing near the front of the wagon, casual as could be, was a male-presenting goblin. His skin tone and manner of dress was unlike anything Trokar had ever seen.

The fellow's skin was golden yellow, and his tunic was of fine woven wool, dyed cochineal red with a checkerboard pattern. On his feet were woven sandals of yellow fiber, and his sharp toenails and fingernails were gold as well. His spiny, golden hair was banded in bronze clasps.

"Hello!" Trokar greeted, relieved and amazed to find one of his own kind living in such a place. "I am Trokar, of Kol'grathu. Who are—"

"Cometh nay farth'r, or beest thou lost!" the odd goblin said.

"Come again?" Trokar asked. The golden goblin's speech was a strange dialect Trokar had never heard before.

"Nay," the golden goblin replied, "never again shall I cometh. Mine own cart is broke, and it has't been here a fortnight since forever. Turneth ye 'round!"

"Do you need help? My friends and I could assist you."

"But wayward wander'r, the road goeth nowhere! I has't been here a fortnight, and it has't been a fortnight since, and more! Turneth 'round!"

"What the grub?!" Ezme exclaimed as she approached behind Trokar, followed by the others.

"You see him too?" Trokar asked Ezme, for he had begun to wonder if he was seeing a ghost.

"What is that thing?" Vilayne asked, eyeing the wheeled machine.

"The wheels turneth nay m're!" the golden goblin exclaimed. "We has't languished a fortnight, and the road goeth nowhere! Turneth 'round!"

"That cart looks like it's been here longer than a fortnight," Fumble observed.

"Where are you from?" Trokar asked the odd goblin. "Tell us of your people?"

"We art lost!" the golden goblin exclaimed, his eyebrows slanting at curious angles. "The most wondrous compass is bootless!"

"How long, exactly, have you been here?" Ezme asked skeptically.

He seemed to consider the question for a moment, and as he did so, a clicking sound began to emanate from the machine. "A fortnight we has't languished," he said, "and has't been a fortnight since, and a fortnight since! And a . . ." He paused, gasping silently.

"Let us help you!" Trokar said, and he stepped closer.

"Nowhere!" the goblin suddenly cried. "It goes *nowhere*!"

The machine began to rattle, and the red crystals on the cylinder began to glow.

"Get back!" Vilayne called, and she grabbed Trokar's backpack, yanking him backwards as Fumble and Ezme darted behind trees.

The image of the golden goblin fizzled, vanishing from sight. At once, the machine burst with a loud crack and a spray of sparks. White electricity zigzagged between the red crystals on the split cylinder for a moment, then nothing. A puff of grey smoke wafted from the singed moss on top, but it was too damp to catch flame.

The hair on Trokar's forearms stood on end, and he stood with his mouth agape.

"What just happened?!" Ezme asked, peeking from behind her tree.

"A ghost," Vilayne answered.

"Well, that was confusing," Fumble said. "He was talking like we were supposed to know where the road goes."

"He told us," Ezme asserted. "He said it goes nowhere."

"How am I supposed to know where?"

"No, I mean, a place that isn't anywhere!"

"That's not a real place," Fumble said dismissively.

"It was a grubbin' metaphor," Vilayne insisted, "and *clearly* a warning from the ancestors."

"We must be getting close!" Trokar said with delight.

"To *danger*," Vilayne stressed.

"We should head back to camp," Ezme said.

"I agree," Vilayne added. "We should tell Bonewise what we have seen."

"Right, right," Trokar said, then they trudged back to the cliffs.

CHAPTER
TWELVE
THE BRIAR KING

Stones were gathered around in a circle, dry branches were bundled, and grubs were snatched from a broken, rotting log. No one had been eager to wake Bonewise from his sleep, so the goblins prepared to get comfortable, and Trokar insisted that a ghost story required a campfire. Sueda kept asking everyone what had happened, but all she could get from anybody was: "We saw a ghost and a thing blew up."

When Bonewise emerged from the Moonbeam, dusk was upon them, the perfect time for goblins to begin their day. A small fire cast orange light on the faces of his company, and he went to ask them what story they had to tell.

"Well, did anyone die?" he asked as he took his place at the fire.

"Once, long ago . . ." Trokar began, "there was a goblin who died. His ghost lingered beside his broken cart on the lonely forest road . . ."

After Trokar recounted the story of their encounter, there was much debate over what it meant.

"The Lady of Mystery weaves in mysterious ways," Sueda said after many theories had been voiced.

"I wouldn't have guessed," Fumble commented slyly.

As the debate continued, night closed in, and the goblins got off track. Their rebukes turned into a game, and as they got more wildly outlandish in their comebacks, the mood shifted to enjoyment, kicking back and toasting the grubs they had gathered.

Bonewise unpacked his flute-pipe, stuffing blue cave lichen into its bowl from his medicine pouch. He lit the herb and started playing a mash-up of a few tunes he knew while the others shared rum from the galley around the fire. By the time all had taken a swig, Bonewise and his flute were warmed up. He played in circles—scraps of old songs looped together like the fabric Sueda was tying around her bootless feet.

"These grubs make the empty feeling in my stomach go away," Fumble said, rubbing his belly, "but what I wouldn't give for some fluffy, baked stuff."

"You mean like—" Ezme began with a big grin.

Right on queue, Bonewise switched his tune to a familiar riff, and Fumble sounded the beat with clapping hands. "Who remembers the words?"

"Yak-yak yah!" Trokar answered with the beat, and everyone smiled as they joined in clapping and stomping. Trokar sang:

"Rumbling gut and aching head
　What we need is bug butt bread
　Mashed and baked when they're freshly dead
　Sticks in your teeth that bug-butt-bread!
　Bug butt bread, bug butt bread!"

. . .

Bonewise improvised a tune that sprang into the space between the first stanza and the second, and after running with it for a short while, he returned to the familiar riff for Trokar to pick up on.

"Strung-out, beat-down, thoughts of dread
    What you need is bug butt bread
    Snap them butts when they've bred
    Feast all night on bug-butt-bread
    Bug butt bread, bug butt bread!"

Bonewise plugged the hole that allowed air to be drawn into the pipe through the smoking bowl, puffing a great cloud as he took off with a new improvisation that climbed into the heights of the trees. Fumble cheered him on as the music flowed, and after a joyful melody, Bonewise returned to the familiar notes so Trokar could sing the final part.

"Next generation will take its stead
    Mash those butts to get us fed
    Crusty foods no more to-night
    Give us an end to our buttless plight!
    Loaf in mouth for teeth to shred
    Love that sweet—bug butt bread!"

The goblins clapped double-time after the pause in the last line, and Bonewise accentuated it with a final note on his flute. Everyone took a breath and laughed, including Sueda, who found the goblin's music delightful.

"That was nothing like the strict, formal music played in the temples and courts of House Meklar," Sueda declared with a grin.

"Being strict about music is no fun!" Ezme declared.

As their banter continued, Trokar wandered to the edge of the dark forest and relieved himself against a red berry-laden bush. Some of the berries seemed to hide from him. Trokar tilted his head, wondering what was gently rustling so close to his ears.

At first glance, he thought they were spiders, but to his relief, he noticed they weren't exactly spider-shaped. He peered closer, curiosity getting the better of him. They weren't entirely un-bug-like, but they were wearing berries on their heads, like little helmets, and their little faces were remarkably emotive, watching him with great interest.

"Hello?" Trokar said.

Whatever the small creatures were, they scattered to the four winds at the rumble of his voice.

Trokar shrugged, stepping away from the bush as he straightened his tunic and adjusted his trousers. Something drew his attention upward, into the shadows of the towering trees above. Another face—feathered and enormous—bent to greet him, though the only thing the face conveyed was "sharp teeth."

Trokar blanched, turning sharply on his heel back toward camp. "Hungry beast!" he cried in terror as he sprinted back to the campfire to grab his sword.

The goblins moved at his call: Fumble and Ezme reached for their staffs. Bonewise placed a stone in his leather sling. Sueda uncorked her holy wine and uttered a prayer of protection, while Vilayne grabbed her torch.

The beast hopped over the tall brush and bushes, shaking the meadow with its scaly three-toed feet. White feathers flared forward from the nape of its neck, contrasting the dark brown feathers along its back, narrow and thick like quills along its spine. It let out a long ear-splitting screech, then warbled with excitement at finding such conveniently-sized morsels.

"Begone!" Bonewise shouted, whirling his staff to loose the jagged stone loaded in its sling. It bonked the feathered beast's nose.

The bird screeched its disapproval, then lunged for Bonewise. It was faster than any of them expected, and with the uncanny precision of a rooster plucking up a single grain of wheat, Bonewise was in its jaws.

Each of the goblins gasped, and so did Sueda. "Bonewise!"

Bonewise twisted his head as the jaws came down around him, shoving the large femur bone in his headdress into the corner of its mouth so its jaw could not close. As the huge predator tried to shake the boney goblin and roll him loose with its tongue, Trokar slashed the tip of his sword down the creature's underside with a two-handed strike, drawing blood.

The beast shrieked, tossing its head up and throwing Bonewise into the bushes.

"*Dennhavix!*" Fumble cried, and fire burst out of the metal mouth of his dragon staff.

Trokar ducked, barely dodging the roaring flames.

Ezme thumped her twisted staff on the ground between her feet, and a bright lightning bolt flashed out from its charred tip. The feathered beast shrieked unbearably and leapt backwards, tormented by lightning and searing flame. Vilayne sent green firebolts forth to add to the destructive forces. Ezme kept lightning arcing from her staff until its power was spent, and Fumble emptied the dragon staff of its last inferno.

Crispy on the outside and sizzling, the great beast collapsed, dead.

All around the meadow, tiny faces smiled in the bushes and trees, erupting into applause, clapping their jointed hands together and singing.

Bonewise stepped from the bushes with the little people riding his slobbered headdress. "Seems we are their entertainment tonight," Bonewise said.

Ezme leaned closer, peering with amazement. "Are these fey creatures?"

"They look like bugs," Fumble commented, "but we probably shouldn't eat them."

Hundreds of the little people fluttered on crystalline insect wings in a circle around the smoldering carcass of the beast, dancing in the air around it. A sparkling glow grew around the body and it floated up into the air, hovering a few handspans above the ground. The fey creatures danced the body into the forest, and where they passed, the trunks of trees lit up with multicolored glyphs.

"We should follow them," Bonewise said, and without waiting for agreement, he picked up his staff and walked along after the promenade, following the trail of glowing glyphs. The others followed after him, and as they marched deeper into the forested plateau, horse-like figures appeared, walking parallel to them around the periphery.

Sueda gasped as she beheld the beings known as centaurs, with humanoid upper bodies sat atop the front of long four-legged lower bodies. Fur covered them from head to toe, and the only clothing seen were wool-woven breast binders on the females. Their cloven feet thunked against wood and clacked against stone, their eyes peering cautiously between the trees at Sueda and the goblins.

The roasted beast was placed upon a large woven mat of ferns in a bright glade, and the centaurs began carving into the flesh with sharp stones, harvesting all they could.

Illuminated, despite the darkness of the night above, the bright glade was surrounded by the oldest, most gnarled trees any of them had ever seen. The glade was a bowl in the landscape, with flowering moss growing along grooves in the exposed bedrock which formed a spiral down to a shallow pool of water. Twenty feet directly above the center of the pool floated a shining yellow gem glowing with the light of day, like a shard of the sun. The branches of the trees all around reached into the clearing, stretching toward the constant source of light. Sueda shielded her eyes, uttering a prayer of respect to Utu as she beheld it, and the Skystone strapped to her forehead shimmered bright blue.

On the opposite side of the glade was a tree, resembling the shape of a man, seated upon a throne formed by the first fork of a fat, squat oak. It seemed to be a tree, until it smiled and turned its leafy head to look at the newcomers. The tree had a masculine face with a beard of deep green conifer needles and long trailing branches of spiny foliage draped down around his knotted shoulders. He was gigantic, even for being hunched in his seat. A long skirt of purple petals adorned his body below the waist.

"Welcome, guests," he said with a soft-wooded voice in perfect goblin-speech. "My people tell me you struck down the feathered tyrant with sky-fire and flame. It must have been quite a spectacle!"

"Are you the Briar King?" Sueda asked.

"That is what they call me," he answered.

"King Briar," Trokar addressed with a bow. "We are goblins of Kol'grathu."

"Emissaries of the Marsh Mother," Fumble added.

"Lord King," Bonewise said, stepping to the front, "what power shines the light of day upon us even while under the shadow of the world?"

"Ahh . . ." the Briar King mused with a rustling of his leaves, "my party stone? It has graced my court with eternal light since the springtime of my realm. Truth be told, I've quite forgotten how it came to be mine! I made a bargain with someone, I think." He stroked his evergreen needles with a four-jointed, branchy finger, deep in thought.

Bonewise could feel the resonance of the Geostone thrumming in his bones. He plucked it from his pocket and held it up, framing it against the floating gem of light. It vibrated between his thumb and forefinger, then, quick as a dart, shot toward his head. With a clack, it struck his bony headdress, holding firm against the union of many tiny bones that converged at the rim across his forehead. Like the Skystone on Sueda's headband, it now sat over his proverbial third eye.

Bonewise blinked in confusion, feeling the Geostone's new location with his finger. The resonance precipitated more clearly, and he felt a triangle of forces strung between the Geostone, the Skystone, and the bright gem before them.

"Do you feel it?" Bonewise asked Sueda, to which she nodded.

The Briar King seemed to shake himself from his reverie.

"Auspicious guests," the King addressed with a welcoming gesture, "The occasion is ripe for a feast! My people shall prepare the nutrients of the feathered tyrant, and we shall share the fruits of the forest!"

"It would be our most sacred honor to feast with you, King!" Trokar declared with glee.

Carved wooden bowls of berries, nuts, and honeyed meat were brought by centaurs, and a vine-haired green woman wearing a dress of pink rose petals delivered a wooden vase of sweet mead.

The small winged fey sang in chorus as the centaurs played flutes, creating a symphony as intoxicating as the drinks. The glowing gem above them flashed with dancing sunbeams, and when the beat dropped, the trees themselves seemed to creak and crack in rhythm.

They danced and reveled all night, and through the course of it all, the goblins sang all the traditional songs of Kol'grathu for the King's pleasure. The King was delighted, and said they were welcome to stay as his guests for as long as they liked.

Bonewise could not remember the last time he had been in such a good mood, free of worry and caution. It unnerved him. He stepped away from the party to ground himself, happening upon a life-sized statue of a goblin, pitted with age and covered in lichen. It held in one hand a stringless crossbow of a slightly tarnished bronze-like metal, the same kind of metal as Trokar's ancient sword. He brushed some of the lichen from the statue's face.

The stone goblin was stocky, but had feminine features. She seemed to be frozen in an expression of surprise. The Geostone pulsed silently upon his headdress. There was something odd about the substance of the statue, and somehow Bonewise knew the statue had once been a real person.

The pleasantness of their host concealed the danger of

lingering too long, Bonewise realized. They needed to obtain the third Source Stone, but how? It was too high to jump, and there was no way to take it without being seen. They would need to bargain for it, he thought, but what did they have that the King might want? He looked into the statue's grey eyes and wondered what risk there would be in the asking.

Bonewise headed back to the bright clearing, where birds sang the morning chorus in tune with the other music being played, a salutation to the rising sun. Ezme and Vilayne dozed against a tree, and Fumble was laying across a branch above them, smoking something from a hollow fruit. Trokar was trying to show stretching aerobics to the green-skinned woman in the petal dress, who, true to her vine-like nature, was far more successful at the poses than he himself.

"Where is Sueda?" Bonewise asked, gazing about.

"Uh," Trokar began as he collapsed from his pose, "I think she followed the furry people somewhere, but that was a while ago."

"Find her at once! We must conclude our business here."

"But it's almost bedtime!" Trokar protested. "What's the rush?"

"We must not overstay our welcome. Retrieve Sueda and we shall make our case to the King."

Trokar found Sueda asleep by a smoldering fire, laying against the belly of a sleeping male centaur.

"What's this?" Trokar asked with curiosity. "Sueda, are you awake?"

"H-Huh?" Sueda responded.

"Sueda, we need to speak to the King. Bonewise wants you there."

Sueda offered a quiet good-bye to the centaur, who seemed to be sleeping. On the short walk to the glade, Trokar studied her.

"Just what happened between you and that centaur?" Trokar asked inquisitively.

"Nothing!" Sueda said with a blush. "We just slept together."

"Slept together, you say?" Trokar waggled his eyebrows.

"Yes, sleeping. He was warm."

"I'll bet he was!"

"Oh, stop it! Nothing happened!"

"What didn't happen?" Ezme asked as they entered the clearing.

"Sueda slept with a centaur!" Trokar announced.

"It wasn't like that!" Sueda insisted, cheeks burning.

"Who cares?" Vilayne said. "What you do in the bushes with another consenting, sentient being is your own business, sleeping or otherwise. The business at hand now is that someone needs to wake up the King."

"Are you sure he's asleep?" Fumble asked.

The Briar King sat on his living throne, where he had been since they arrived. His head was bowed down against his bark-crusted chest, eyes closed.

"Is he dead?" Trokar asked. "He's not breathing!"

"Trees breathe through their leaves," Fumble commented.

"Good morning, Your Majesty!" Trokar called.

The Briar King creaked awake, the knots of his eyes flexing open; he smiled pleasantly at his guests. "Good morning, my friends."

"Lord King," Bonewise said, "we have traveled far and through much danger in search of what you call 'the party stone.' We beseech you to place it into our care, that we may return to our people with it."

"Well, now!" the Briar King exclaimed, his eyebrows creaking high. "You would ask such a boon? It is the crown jewel of my court!"

"Your court is beautiful," Trokar proclaimed, "and it will be just as beautiful under moonlight, wise king."

"That is true," the King admitted. "And yet, this place just wouldn't be the same without my party stone. Why do you need it?"

"We believe it is a sacred relic of our ancestors," Bonewise said.

"You lay claim to it as your own?" The Briar King frowned in scrutiny.

"Actually," Trokar said as he stepped in front of Bonewise, "the reason we need it, Majesty, is that it is very dark in our home . . ."

"Yes," Fumble chimed in, "we live in caves, you see, deep underground!"

"And the soot of torches stings our eyes!" Ezme added.

"My potted plants will not grow in the dark," Vilayne said truthfully.

"So many of our problems would be solved if we had this glowing rock," Trokar implored, "and it would always remind us of you and the fine time we had in your company, Lord King!"

"Hmmmm . . ." the Briar King rumbled thoughtfully, "perhaps it is time for a change in decor, but it cannot be that easy. I shall play you for it!"

"A game?" Bonewise asked.

"Yes, a game of questions and answers. If you win, you get my party stone. If you lose, you stay here forever!"

"That doesn't sound so bad," Ezme said, picking up a half-empty cup of mead.

"I accept your terms!" Trokar announced.

"Excellent! First question: When you walk on them living, they don't even mumble. Walk on them dead, they mutter and grumble. What are they?"

"Oh!" Trokar said with a snap of his fingers. "We ran into these recently! Zombies!"

The Briar King crackled with laughter, and Trokar chuckled along, a sinking feeling growing in the pit of his stomach.

"Very funny!" the King exclaimed. "A very funny answer indeed!"

"So, did I win?"

"I'm afraid not."

With that, the Briar King snapped his fingers with a loud clack. At once, Trokar and everything he wore, save for his sword, was turned to stone. He stood a statue, a confused look locked onto his face.

"What the *grub*?!" Ezme exclaimed.

"Oh," Fumble said, "So *that's* how we stay here forever."

"Lord King," Vilayne spoke up, "Our loud companion spoke out of turn. He answered for only himself, and not the rest of us."

"Well," the Briar King said with a smile, "he shall be silent now, if you wish to try again!"

"We do," Bonewise said.

"What is your answer, then?"

Sueda crouched down as the goblins huddled beside her, and they discussed how they might answer, but they couldn't get the thought of the living dead out of their minds.

"May we have a different question, Lord King?" Bonewise asked.

"Certainly! The answer was right under your feet, by the way. Leaves!"

Looking down at scattered leaves on the ground—some soft and green, others dead and dry—they groaned that they missed such an obvious answer.

"Second question," the King began. "If you get this one right, your friend shall be restored. What always runs but never walks, often murmurs, never talks, has a bed but never sleeps, has a mouth but never eats?"

The goblins huddled, but a word had not yet been spoken between them when Sueda's face lit up.

"I know the answer!" Sueda exclaimed.

"Are you sure?" Bonewise asked.

"The wisdom of the goddess guides me." She nodded with a smile. "A river runs, murmurs, has a river bed, and has a mouth where it meets the sea."

"Seems like a good answer to me," Ezmo said.

The others nodded agreement and Sueda stood up, facing the king.

"A river," she answered with confidence in her squared shoulders.

"Correct!" the King chimed, and he snapped his fingers.

Trokar heaved a breath and coughed, spewing dust as stone flaked from his body. He felt his chest, then his crotch, making sure all his parts had returned to flesh.

"What was the answer?" he croaked.

"Leaves," the others said in unison.

"Did we win, then?"

"No," they all answered.

"You could give up the game," the King offered, "and all will be as it was before it began."

"Ask us a third question," Bonewise said, "but if we win, in addition to the gem, anyone that you turned to stone will be restored. Deal?"

"Very well! If you get it correct, you shall have the gem of light, and all that I have turned to stone shall be set right. It shall not be so easy as the first two, however!"

"Bring it!" Fumble exclaimed confidently.

"You see a boat filled with people. You look again, but this time you don't see a single person on the boat! Why?"

They huddled and puzzled over the question, agreeing that the boat was the key to understanding the riddle; Ezme was confident she knew the answer.

"The boat tipped over!" Ezme declared.

"It did not," the King replied, and with a snap of his fingers, Ezme became a statue.

"The people jumped off the boat!" Trokar exclaimed.

"The people are still on the boat," the King contradicted, and with another snap, Trokar was once again turned to stone.

"The people turned invisible," Vilayne answered.

"They are not invisible," the King countered with a shake of his head, and he snapped Vilayne into a statue. For her, like Ezme and Trokar, time stopped, and their spirits drifted through a timeless realm of unremembered dreams.

"We're running out of ammo," Fumble muttered.

"It doesn't make any sense," Sueda complained. "How can we not see anyone if the boat and all the people are still there?"

"And they are not invisible," Bonewise added with a perplexed expression.

"We're missing the trick," Fumble said, rubbing his head. "The boat might be a distraction . . . it's too conspicuous."

"What do you mean?" Bonewise asked. "The element of the boat is the only thing we know aside from the presence of people on it."

"We also know that nothing happens to the boat. It's a static element. The only thing that changes is that when we look again, 'we don't see a single person on it.'"

"But the King said the people are still there!" Sueda exclaimed. "It's not possible!"

"Exactly! We need to think about it from a different angle, just like with the foreheads riddle!" He tapped his temple, then his eyes widened. "That's it!"

"What?" Bonewise asked.

"It's not about the people physically being there or not . . . it's not a number puzzle, it's a word puzzle! We don't see a *single* person on the boat because they aren't *single*."

"Are you suggesting they . . . fused together?" Sueda asked.

"Metaphorically, yes! They all got married!"

The Briar King smiled and gave a clap of applause.

"Well done!" the King said. "Our bargain you have won!"

The King snapped both his fingers with all the strength of two falling trees and the crust of stone flaked off Trokar, Ezme, and Vilayne as they gasped, drawing in fresh air.

"And the other one you turned to stone," Bonewise said.

"There is another?" the Briar King asked.

"Yes, the one just there," he pointed, "in the forest. You vowed to restore anyone you had turned to stone."

"So I did," the King admitted with good humor. "A thorough change in decor, it shall be!"

He snapped his fingers again.

"Who are we talking about?" Ezme asked, looking around.

"We shall soon find out," Bonewise answered, and he turned toward the edge of the glade where a figure approached.

CHAPTER

THIRTEEN

OLD BATTLES

A middle-aged, muscular goblin squinted against the light, stepping into the clearing. She holstered her stringless crossbow and scratched lichen from her arms. Her ears were tattered from where stone had weathered, and her olive-green skin was pockmarked, too, like from a thousand old wounds—likely from the same. The flare of her nose was stubby from erosion, and her earthy hair was thin. She wore a segmented, copper-colored corselet, tarnished green in places. Her checkered pants were reinforced over the thighs by banded mail, and a leather bandolier held metallic crossbow bolts and pouches. She scanned the assembly.

"Thou art not . . ." she said, her voice hoarse.

"You drink once more from the river of Time," the King said to the stranger, "as was foretold in my people's nursery rhymes."

"Thou fusty snag!" the stranger cursed, drawing her crossbow. She simply gripped it in anger, realizing it had no drawstring. "Thou couldst has't rest'r'd me at any hour! How longeth wast I ston'd?"

"I did not count the days, as that is not my way. T'was a bargain that bound you, so t'was a bargain that unbound you. These cunning revelers broke your spell!"

"Tav . . . he did betray me." She seemed to shake with fury, then fell to her knees.

Trokar approached but stopped a respectable distance away. "I'm Trokar," he said, "of Kol'grathu. Do you know of Kol'grathu?"

"Silvermoth," she mused morosely. "Means naught to me."

Trokar's shoulders slumped. He had hoped their warren would be known to a goblin from the past.

"What is your name?" Sueda asked, bending over to try to meet the stranger's eyes.

"*Fie*! A plaited *huuer*? Bid me thine name, lassie, and I'll bid thee mine."

"Such an interesting dialect! I am Sueda, priestess of Mawwu, and this is Ezme, Vilayne, Fumble, and Bonewise."

The stranger pushed herself to her feet and gave each one of them a long, hard look, studying their tools and attire.

"Koryphaios Elisiadora Shacklespurf, Lady o' the House of Grektelfarch. They calleth me Shacklespurf in ease. For what reason didst thou rest're me?"

"We came here to reclaim the power of our ancestors," Vilayne explained. "What can you tell us about the Source Stones?"

The stranger blinked, and looked as if she had just been asked an absurd question. She looked down and stared at the back of her hands, which were strangely weathered from her long internment as a statue.

"Vile ruin . . ." she cursed, "I has't been h're time beyond mem'ry. After all that wast sacrificed to hideth the accursed things hence . . ." Her eyes darted up, then flicked across the other goblins. "Doth thou serve the Goblin King?"

"Well," Trokar began diplomatically, "we all serve the Goblin King, in our own—"

Shacklespurf socked Trokar in the chin with a cross punch, sending him toppling over and down into the pool of water in the center of the king's court. Hundreds of fey creatures gathered in the trees to watch.

Trokar lurched out of the water only to meet Shacklespurf's fist again, which pummeled him back down with a splash.

"Bloody fascists!" She grabbed the neck of his leather cuirass and yanked him up, punched him back into the water, and repeated the process.

"In our own way!" Trokar gasped between water and fist, gurgling and sputtering in his plea to calm her. "*Ambiguity*! I'm neutral!"

Bonewise, Vilayne, Ezme, and Fumble each grabbed a limb and pulled Shacklespurf away from Trokar.

"Th're is nay 'neutral' stand'n at which hour it cometh to choose life or death f'r our people!"

"No, you're right!" Trokar said as he stood from the water. "The Goblin King was a jerk! Er, what did he do again?"

"Thou doth not knoweth? Truly?"

"You must excuse him," Vilayne said from Shacklespurf's left shoulder, "he's a muscle-head. The rest of us know the Goblin King turned his back on death and betrayed the ancestors."

"We are no servants of his," Bonewise inserted.

Shacklespurf tugged her arms and legs to free herself from their grasp, and they willingly let go.

"He didst not just reject death f'r himself . . . He didst try to impose it upon us all! Sev'r us from our ancestors!"

"How did you defeat him?" Vilayne asked.

"T'was not I. I knoweth not how, only that he wast fopped, and that he, 'long with all of his follow'rs, w're banished from the w'rld. The rest o' us had to crisp up the leavings an' make sure he never returned! Yet now, ye seekest to restore the power of the Source Stones? Be ye warned! Their pow'r combin'd is the single thing that can giveth the mad king a way back from the realm beyond death!"

"Are you saying . . ." Fumble asked, "that he's locked in some cage just waiting for someone to open the door from the outside?"

"One way to putteth it, aye."

"Then we have nothing to worry about!" Fumble beamed. "We just won't get all of the stones! Leave one or two buried, and reap the benefit of the others, right?"

"T's not so simple! Otherwise I wouldst has't dropped the Daystone in a hole and been done with it!"

"That's the Daystone, I presume?" Ezme asked, pointing to the shining gem.

"The 'party stone' is a much better name!" the Briar King said. "But it is now yours, and you may call it what you will."

"Lord King," Vilayne addressed, "How about this as a replacement?" She fished out the sunstone gem she had found on the Moonbeam, and with an underhand toss, sent it flying across the court to him.

The Briar King nimbly snatched it out of the air with his branchy fingers. "Ah," he said, examining it closely, "this will do nicely!"

With a gesture of his other hand, the Daystone floated

down to Vilayne, and she let it fall into her open hand. The Briar King then tossed up the mundane gem, and it floated to the place above the pool where the Daystone had been. With a snap of his fingers, it lit up with yellow light, not as close to daylight as the Daystone had been, but enough to dazzle the cheering fey folk.

Vilayne turned to Bonewise, presenting the warm, smooth gem. Bonewise did not reach for it. He seemed to consider it for a moment, then shook his head, said: "You are the torch-bearer, Vilayne. This one is for you to carry."

Vilayne's ears fell half-back, but she nodded, squinting at the small stone. "I wonder if I can—" Vilayne began, and she lifted the gem to get a better look at it against the sky.

It darted from her grasp and planted itself against her forehead. The stone was warm and gave her a pleasant feeling of calm that radiated through her body. Colors were sharper, and she could even make out some hues of light that she had never seen before. Her pupils became dots as she stood still, dumbfounded by the beauty of the light all around her.

"It likes you," Ezme said to Vilayne.

"Shacklespurf," Bonewise addressed. "Will you do us the honor of accompanying us back to our warren?"

"Thy quaint w'rds art wasteth. If't be true th're is aught left for me in this time, 'twill beest in Zalenthas."

"Zalenthas?" Ezme asked. "That's where we found the Geostone!"

"Thou found it?" Shacklespurf asked, then she looked to where Bonewise was pointing on his headdress. "So thou didst. Thou were not crushed?"

"I was, a little," Trokar said.

"Remorse congeals within me," she said dryly.

"We fly south," Bonewise said. "You are welcome to

travel with us on your way to Zalenthas, though you should know that it is a tomb."

"It might beest I shalt findeth answ'rs there, nonetheless. Didst thee say 'fly?'"

"We have a flying ship."

"P'rhaps thou art not as primitive as I took thee for. In that case, I'll taketh thee up on thy off'r to travel togeth'r."

THE BRIAR KING bid them farewell, and all the fey folk waved goodbye as the goblins and Sueda left his court and made their way to the Moonbeam.

"Dost thou *sweep* the skies?" Shacklespurf asked dubiously when she saw the broomship.

"For adventure!" Trokar answered.

She spat. "Fie! *Adventurers*."

"Hey," Fumble interjected, "weren't you on a bold and perilous quest to hide powerful relics? 'Cause that seems awfully adventurous!"

"I'm a *soldier*," Shacklespurf countered. "I did what were requir'd so that thou couldst be born!"

"Thanks for that," Vilayne said. "Please, will you help us recover some of the other Source Stones?"

"Absolute *nay*!" Shacklespurf spat.

CHAPTER

FOURTEEN

THE CHALLENGE

They took flight once again, leaving the Glyphwood and the Briar King's court behind as they passed over the marsh without stopping. Bonewise and Vilayne took turns piloting the broomship, switching whenever one of them got tired.

The rest of them did not have much to do. Fumble finally, begrudgingly asked for Sueda's help in updating labels in the alchemy room with goblin pictographs, while above deck, the others gazed at the landscape passing beneath them from the railing.

"Hey, Shucklespurf?" Trokar inquired across the deck.

"Shacklespurf," she corrected.

"Right, sorry. Um, are there any moves you can show me?"

"'Moves?'" she asked in the same exasperated tone.

"Yeah, you know, fighting moves from the time of goblin greatness? You're a soldier, right?"

"I suppose I oweth thee f'r freeing me from a timeless stone prison. Aye, I shall teachest thee a thing or two."

Trokar smiled and drew his sword, ready for instruction.

"First," Shacklespurf said, "tell me what thee knoweth about the twelve guards."

"Uhh . . ." Trokar began. It had been at least five years since he had received any training. "I don't remember?"

"Fie! Alloweth us to wend with three of them, then."

Shacklespurf took hold of the spent dragon-headed staff as a stand-in for a sword, drilling Trokar in essential fighting stances. She started with the basic stance and the passing step to change position. Trokar learned names for fighting moves he had seen countless times in the sparring room but had not been distilled into named techniques. For two nights, Shacklespurf taught him the first three stances and their related maneuvers: the Warg's Tooth, the Horn, the Roof.

On the third day, they landed to let both Bonewise and Vilayne rest at the edge of the Quaking Hills until late afternoon, then they took off again and flew all night until they came upon the Duskfen River. From there, they followed it west to Shipwreck Bay; it was mid-afternoon when they reached the sea.

Trokar smelled the salt on the wind and excitedly spread the word, so that everyone came above deck.

"Where are we going to land?" Ezme asked.

"I can set it down on a plateau by the cliffs," Bonewise answered from the broomstick.

"Why would we *walk* to the warren," Trokar asked, "when we could arrive in this badass flying ship?"

"We would have to land in the brambles," Bonewise cautioned. "It would break tradition!"

"There's *a tradition* of not flying ships into the brambles??"

"It's tradition to keep the entrance to the warren *secret*!"

"I agree with Trokar," Vilayne announced.

"You do?" Trokar asked, blinking.

Bonewise looked at her like he had just swallowed a bug down the wrong tube.

"Normally, I would agree with you, Bonewise," Vilayne explained, "but I think we have an opportunity here. Anything we give Warface just helps him gain standing at the Moot. He might win leadership with the magic javelin we already gave him!"

"Hmmm . . ." Bonewise grumbled, "that's actually a good point. All the more reason to keep this ship a secret."

"If Warface leads the summer raids, all it will accomplish is more of the same. If we present *this ship* to the Moot, *we* can lead the other clans. This is how we can help Sueda. We could use the summer raids to coordinate with her rebellion."

"Vilayne," Trokar said, "you're a genius! We could change everything!"

"Only the war-chief can present an offering to the Moot!" Bonewise argued. "Even if we *did* take it there, it is no guarantee that our clan would be chosen to lead."

"I'm not an expert on Moots or relics," Ezme chimed in, "but I think a flying ship is the most magnificent thing our warren has ever seen or could ever hope to see, and the same is probably true for the other clans. I think this thing will blow away any other offering!"

"You heard Bonewise," Fumble said. "Only the war-chief is eligible to be elected. Do you want to hand that kind of power over to *Warface*?"

"I'm *through* suffering the abuse of bullies like Warface!" Trokar exclaimed. "If we show the warren what we've scored, we can challenge him!"

"Bef're the war," Shacklespurf growled, "th're w're nay war-chiefs. Who doth thee war with?"

"Humans, mostly," Ezme told her.

"How couldst huuers possibly stand against thee?" She gestured to Sueda. "Are they not primitives?"

"Oh, they are," Fumble informed her, "except they generally have better weapons, and better armor, and bigger cities—plus they have armies and navies—though they mostly fight each other with those!"

"They claim our land," Vilayne added, "yet they call *us* thieves and hunt us down for sport." She glanced at Sueda, wondering if the human felt offended that they were generalizing the behavior of her species. Sueda hung her head and made no attempt to defend her people.

"Right!" Trokar said, "and this is our chance to *change* all that! To take back our right to be here! To be respected!" There was a fire in his heart that he had never felt before. All the suppressed rage of being belittled and shoved aside by Warface and his goons, the rage of his entire species being belittled and shoved aside by more powerful civilizations, it bolstered his resolve.

"And you want Warface out of your way?" Bonewise asked.

"We could stage a coup!" Fumble said excitedly.

Bonewise frowned. "The warren would be bathed in blood!"

"Only his!" Trokar asserted. "Or *mine*."

"*You* would challenge him, Trokar?"

Bonewise had taken little part in raising Warface, so stricken was he with the grief of Creamfoot's death. He regretted not being there to teach Warface to be a leader, the better ways to be one, before he had earned his name. Back then, he had no way to know the sprat would grow up to become the next war-chief. If he had taken a more active role in Warface's upbringing instead of avoiding him, leaving him to become a bully amongst the other sprats, perhaps things could have been different. Bonewise had been endlessly patient with Warface's cruelty, but perhaps, he thought, it was time for a *change*.

Trokar had a lot to learn, but if he could summon the courage to make the challenge, then perhaps he *was* worthy of the ancestors.

"I'll do it!" Trokar announced impetuously. "I invoke the right of Shal'draaken!"

Bonewise inhaled sharply. "So be it."

THEY RAISED the broomwings and lowered the landing legs so Bonewise could set the Moonbeam down on top of the bramble maze surrounding the leaning stones of the warren's entrance. The goblins stood against the railing, facing the stones as Sueda hid herself below deck, safe in the belly of the ship.

Killgap raised the alarm as soon as the ship was in sight, warriors came rushing up from the caves to meet the unknown threat. Trokar called out telling of his triumphant return, with a flying ship wondrous to behold, and as the message spread down to the caves, it rippled through the tunnels in waves that woke sleeping goblins, and a groggy but excited mob grew.

Warface could not stop the droves of goblins that raced to the surface to see for themselves.

By the time he himself arrived, there were over a hundred goblins gathered throughout the bramble tunnels; some peeked between the thorns to get a glimpse of the strange ship, while others streamed out, climbing atop the leaning stones to get a better view.

"And then I cut open the feathered tyrant's innards with this sword of our ancient ancestors!" Trokar regaled loudly from the ship's railing, lifting the blade. "With fire and lightning, the spell-singers of our clan finished it off, and we feasted on its roasted carcass!"

"What is this madness?!" Warface roared, trudging out of the tunnel.

Everyone turned toward him, ears erect and alert as whispers of anticipation skittered between the thorns.

"You think you can just parade in here," Warface fumed, "and expose our warren like this in the light of day, with a plumed *boat*?!"

"No longer will we need to hide from the humans!" Trokar called out to everyone, his heart pounding. "Your reign of fear and rage is *over*, Warface! I invoke Shal'draaken!"

Warface stopped in his tracks.

His wide-eyed expression changed quickly to a grin, accompanied by his cruel laughter.

"*You*?!" Warface barked. "You dare to challenge me?!"

"Kol'grathu has languished under your leadership! I would see our clan embrace transformative change!"

"You are a *fool*, Trokar!" Warface bellowed. "You are a liar and a stain upon our clan! Come down into the thorns and meet your death!" He unsheathed his barbed sword.

"Still your tooth!" The Wise Woman shouted, emerging from the leaning stones with an entourage of furry spiders.

Warface whirled around, but remained where he was, silent in his rage, knowing that he could not defy the mediation of the clan elder.

"We do not allow Shal'draaken to become a spectacle,"

The Wise Woman said in her gravely voice. "The tradition of our ancestors shall be upheld! Gather the sprats! Put up the bramble camp! At sundown, Shal'draaken shall commence!"

THE WARREN WAS EVACUATED, and camp was set up in the bramble maze to accommodate the entire clan for the night. There were no fires, for everyone understood that the risks of brushfire were too great to entertain. Warface chattered and chuckled snidely with his two most loyal friends, Kneecap and Shivsalt. Vilayne couldn't see him from the deck of the Moonbeam, but she could hear Warface through the sea of soft voices.

Trokar fretted, pacing up and down the main deck, hand on the hilt of his sword. He didn't know if he could beat Warface, but he had to try, because he was sure nobody else would. He never dreamed he could be warchief, and he never wanted to be. All he wanted to do was lift, have a strong body, flirt with Cavesong, win her heart, and be a successful mascot of goblin-made beauty products.

"It's been nice knowing you, Trokar," Ezme said.

"Have a little faith, Ezme!" Trokar pleaded.

"I would, but Warface is a seasoned warrior, and you're, well . . . not."

"True enough," Trokar admitted, "but I've watched that earless asshole in the sparring room a thousand times! I can beat him."

"And if you do not," Bonewise said, placing a hand on his shoulder, "know that the ancestors will welcome you into their company."

"Thanks, Bonewise." Tears welled up in Trokar's eyes. It was the most affection the old goblin had ever shown to him. He was embarrassed to start crying, and he didn't want anyone to think he was crying out of fear, so he shoved it down. He certainly was afraid, but there was no backing out.

Shacklespurf saw the goblin's jitteriness, and she grumbled a sigh, filled with empathy for him despite herself.

"Thou art drilled in the first three guards," Shacklespurf told Trokar. "I shalt now teachest thee the fourth guard."

Trokar's ears perked up, and he drew his sword, waiting for instruction.

"The fourth guard is 'the Fool,'" Shacklespurf said, at last.

"Why is it called 'the Fool?'"

"Pointeth the tip of thy sw'rd f'rward and down toward the grind. This guard gives the extern' appearance thou art ope' to attack, and thee can persuade thy opponent into attacking. Th're art many things thee can do from this position, such as lifting the tip into a thrust, 'r stepping aside and cutting up into the arms of thy opponent's downward strike." She demonstrated how to counter downward strikes from the Fool's guard.

As Trokar practiced, Vilayne kept her ears turned toward the part of the brambles where the hunters and warriors had set up camp. Warface's usual boasting and laughter grew faint alongside the voices of his friends as he moved farther away. She walked up to the aftcastle to get more height, and from that vantage, she could listen over the other sounds and focus on Warface's voice as it skipped off the leaning stones from the far side.

She couldn't quite make it out. She thought they might even be whispering, but then, Warface spoke loudly about needing meat for his victory. He ordered Kneecap and Shivsalt to go hunting, and to return in time for the midnight feast.

So that's your game, Vilayne thought. "Classy," she muttered to herself. She descended the stairs to the main deck.

"Hey, Trokar," Vilayne said as she approached. "You may have a problem."

"I got several!" Trokar half-joked as he failed to counter a diagonal swing from Shacklespurf.

"There's treachery afoot," she said quietly.

Trokar gasped in shock.

"Treachery?!" Fumble blurted. Bonewise smacked him lightly in the back of the head with his staff.

"Teach-ery," Fumble said, "There's teaching going on! *That's* what I said, if anybody was eavesdropping."

"Sundown is soon," Bonewise said. "Let us talk in the ship."

"Wend on," Shacklespurf said. "I'll stayeth topside and keep an ear out."

They filed down below deck, and Bonewise told Sueda through the door to unlock the captain's cabin. Vilayne and Ezme sat on the bed, Fumble on the desk, while Sueda and Trokar were in the middle, sitting comfortably on the floor; Bonewise put his back against the door, sinking to the floor.

"Warface is up to something," Vilayne said at last. "He sent his two best hunters to make a kill."

"Well," Trokar said, "that's good, right? If they're away—"

"What if they're not away? What if they sneak into the warren to make sure Warface wins?"

"Cheating!" Trokar gasped.

"I expected this!" Fumble declared. "I say that if they can cheat, then *we* can cheat!"

"I thought he would be too proud to cheat," Ezme admitted.

"That's what everyone will think," Vilayne said. "I don't know it for certain, but I bet Warface is counting on it."

Trokar bristled. "Just when I thought I couldn't hate him any more than I already do!"

"Perhaps you can expose this treachery?" Sueda suggested.

"Nobody is allowed in the warren except the challenged and the challenger," Bonewise said. "We cannot interrupt it, and we cannot prove anything until after the struggle is already over."

"You mean we cannot be *seen* interrupting it," Fumble corrected.

"Yes," Bonewise grumbled. "I agree that there is too much at stake to trust to honor. Some of us will have to get inside unseen to counter an ambush, if there is one. However, Trokar must be the one to defeat Warface, or our clan shall be disgraced in the eyes of the ancestors!"

"I'll go!" Fumble exclaimed. "There's a drainage tunnel that goes down to the beach. We can get into the warren through there, and I can grab some useful stuff from my laboratory."

"I better come along to make sure you don't blow yourself up," Ezme said.

Vilayne nodded. "I'm coming too."

"What about ol' Shacklesmack?" Trokar asked. "She's a great warrior!"

"She does not know the warren," Bonewise mused. "Better that she guard the ship. We don't want anyone to find Sueda."

Sueda gave Bonewise a grateful look. "Thank you."

"What about you, Bonedome?" Trokar asked.

"I must report to The Wise Woman," Bonewise answered. "We will need a plan, in case you fall."

Trokar's ears drooped.

"Take heart, Trokar." Bonewise reassured him. "Warface is overconfident and quick to anger. You may draw him into a rash attack with that silver tongue of yours."

CHAPTER
FIFTEEN
THE WARRIOR'S FATE

The familiar sound of the river echoing through the tunnels was louder than Trokar could ever remember it. Absent were the voices of more goblins than he could count, the clatter of their work, and the muffling scuff of their comings and goings, only the river—clear and constant.

Warface, being the incumbent war-chief, had entered the warren first. After the last drop of beer fell from a three-foot cask, Trokar was allowed inside. It had not taken long for it to be emptied, and Trokar was heartened to see so many goblins taking a drink, even two, on his behalf. Had he been widely disliked, few would drink, giving the incumbent more time to prepare.

Trokar stepped lightly, peeking around every corner, sword in hand. Everything in the warren was normal: lanterns lit at crossways, craft projects and food scraps abandoned on the tables.

He knew his friends would be entering from the west side of the warren, and on the bottom level. He had entered from the east side, on the top level, using the main entrance. He hoped they would reach the enemy in the middle at the same time, together. He kept his ears stiff and alert, turning them from side to side as he moved across open spaces. Without his heavy pack and all his gear, he was light on his feet, and he was used to sneaking around the warren to avoid Warface anyway. But now there was no crowd to blend in with, no distractions, and Warface and his friends could be waiting silently in ambush just around the next corner.

He quickly pranced across the central crossway toward the main gathering chamber. He thought it might be the most likely place for a confrontation. He passed the kitchen on his left, a pot of "forever stew" still simmering over red coals on a stove of cobbled stone. On his right, the windy blackness of the garbage pit whispered through an archway.

In the silence, the sharp twang of a bow echoed.

Trokar reflexively dropped, rolling backwards as an arrow from the end of the corridor shot over him. It was Kneecap, bow in hand, already notching another arrow.

Something that looked like a brown wine bottle tumbled down from a balcony of the gathering chamber, breaking on the stone floor right behind Kneecap. He tumbled forward, further into the corridor, propelled by the fiery explosion, glass shards tinkling.

Suddenly, a spear jabbed at Trokar from the kitchen doorway, aiming for his armpit, where there was a gap in his leather armor. He twisted toward the attacker, catching the tip of the spear in his boiled leather cuirass. Trokar yowled in pain as it pierced through the stiff layers, biting into his pectoral muscle.

Shivsalt grinned triumphantly, shoving forward from his crouched position to drive Trokar backwards toward the garbage pit. Though Shivsalt's advance faltered as green bolts of fire splashed into him from the end of the hallway. Vilayne shrieked another barrage of fire from her green torch, and the Daystone at her forehead winked like a glimpse of the sun.

A blinding beam of yellow light shot out from the Daystone, passing over the hazel shaft of the spear, burning it to charcoal. Vilayne blinked in surprise, for she had not known she'd activated the gem's power. Trokar broke through the burned spear shaft with a swing of his sword, then yanked the spear head out of his chest.

Ezme flung flashes of energy at Kneecap from her brass wand, and he pressed himself against a natural niche in the wall. He strung an arrow, shooting it in her direction, but she ducked back around the corner. Vilayne continued her barrage of green fire against Shivsalt, and Trokar took the opportunity to land a decisive strike, sweeping his blade under Shivsalt's chin. Blood spilled over the wiry warrior's chest and Trokar stared into his eyes with shock, an expression mirrored by Shivsalt, who clutched his gushing neck then collapsed to the floor.

The hairs on the back of Trokar's neck stood on end, adrenaline pumping. He had never killed another goblin before; he had surely meant to do it, but the reality of it was much heavier than he could have imagined. For one goblin to kill another . . . it was a rare, meaningful event, but he had no time to grieve the loss of his innocence, for Warface entered the corridor from the main crossway, javelin in hand.

~

Bonewise gripped the broom handle of the ship and lifted off the brambles, wowing the crowd of goblins peering between the woven vines. Shacklespurf turned the gearbox and brought down the broomwings. The Wise Woman and her apprentice had agreed that moving it was a priority, lest it draw unwanted attention to the warren. So he steered north along the coastal plateau, looking for a clear, flat spot.

He worried about Trokar. Warface was ruthless—and dangerous enough with any weapon—but if the javelin Trokar had given him truly contained power, Trokar may have sealed his own doom.

"Shacklespurf," Bonewise said, "in your time, did you have Javelins of Lightning?"

Shacklespurf snorted a laugh.

"Only one," she answered, "and only in story. Twas the weapon of a popular hero of picture books. Imitations w're oft sold at market."

"Enchanted?"

"Aye, to miss! Twas a toy."

"Ancestors be praised."

The javelin whizzed past Trokar's ear and clattered against the wall. Warface looked furious that he had missed, and that no lightning had sparked from the weapon. Trokar barked a laugh as he ran to grab up the javelin. He hurled it back at Warface, who side-stepped its path, but it also seemed like the javelin veered more than it should have.

Warface ran after it, plucking it up off the ground, then he ran down the corridor toward Trokar, growling with determination.

"You're a liar," Warface cursed, "and your javelin is *garbage!*" He threw it as he came closer, watching it veer once again.

"You're just not using it right!" Trokar countered as he chased it down. He turned, throwing it with all his might before Warface could charge him.

He was sure it should have struck, but it seemed to bend over Warface's head as it vanished into the endless darkness of the pit behind. Warface retreated to the wooden walkway around the mouth of the tunnel, and Trokar glanced toward the gathering chamber. Vilayne and Ezme continued to fire on Kneecap, who was pinned behind a crevice in the stone wall. Fumble prepared another bottle, and Trokar felt it was wise to not be in the same hallway.

Reaching for his courage, he stepped through the archway, sword held in "the Roof" guard. The wide pit seemed to drop into the depths of the world. Warface lunged from the shadows with a jab of his steel sword, and Trokar deflected it with his own, swatting the strike away. Sharp grey metal pinged against brown, and they both backed off to face each other again. Trokar took the Warg's Tooth posture, while Warface shifted into the Horn guard. An explosion sounded nearby, but neither of them budged.

"You're not a warrior," Warface scoffed. "You're a clown."

"Maybe I am," Trokar said, and he let the tip of his blade drop into the Fool. "But we need joy, and the beauty it brings to—"

"You are *weak!*" Warface wheeled a diagonal overhand cut.

Trokar lunged forward and tried to cut up into Warface's arms, as he had practiced, but his blade sparked against the iron bands of his opponent's vambraces.

Warface smashed the pommel of his sword into Trokar's face, sending him staggering back with a bruise that would soon welt. Trokar had almost no room to maneuver on the walkway, and Warface pressed his advantage.

Trokar instinctually brought his sword up into a hanging guard, deflecting the swift strike aimed for his head. He tried to strike for his opponent's exposed side, but Warface jerked the hilt of his sword up to catch Trokar's counter swing in the crossguard. The brass guard chipped from the impact, and Warface pressed forward into the bind of blades.

"You're the real coward," Trokar accused. "You were going to have your friends kill me and then take the credit! You're a cheater!"

"I only cheated because I knew *you* would cheat!" Warface blurted.

"Well, *I* only cheated because *you* cheated!"

"There was too much at stake! I will not allow you to bring *shame* to our clan with your blind obsession with *appearances*!"

Too late, Trokar felt a trip cord press into the back of his ankle as he gave ground, and he fell onto his back. The wooden boards of the walkway creaked under the impact.

"*Ah-ha*! I have dreamt of this moment!" Warface crowed, and he brought his blade down in a wrathful strike.

Trokar braced his sword with both hands, deflecting the deadly blow into the floorboards as he rolled onto his side, but there was no room on the walkway. He rolled under the guardrail and grabbed the edge of the walkway with one hand, dangling above the endless darkness below. If he let go, he would fall for a very long time. In desperation, he swung his sword up for Warface's ankle, but Warface disarmed him with a sweep of his barbed steel blade.

Trokar watched as his sword clattered across the planks of the walkway.

"Your luck has run out, Trokar!" Warface chopped at Trokar's hands, but he shuffled, switching hands. With each chop, Trokar shimmied, climbing up onto the outside of the roundwood railing and down to the end of the walkway.

"I'm going to dispose of you like the garbage you are!" Warface growled.

The war-chief thrust his blade under the railing, aiming for Trokar's belly. Trokar stuck his butt out and sucked in his gut, his skin barely avoiding the tip as it bit into the leather of his cuirass.

Trokar let go of the railing, and as he began to fall backward, he grabbed Warface's sword arm with both hands. With his weight, he pulled Warface forward, the war-chief's scarred face smashing against the handrail.

Warface barked in surprise, and Trokar pulled, clambering over him, both feet back on the walkway.

Warface yanked his sword back and swept it furiously in an arc, but Trokar was right there to move in close and catch his wrist. With his other hand, Warface drew a dagger from his belt and shoved it into Trokar's side with a snarl, the blade biting between the lacing of his armor. Trokar gasped in pain but maintained his hold.

"You never even tried my hair cream, you *jerk*!" Trokar cried. He went low, grabbing the war-chief's ankle and lifting with all his might. Warface was flipped over backwards, toppling over the railing with a shout of panic, tumbling into the darkness below. His roar of anguish echoed for a very long time, then it was silent.

Trokar fell to his knees, grunting as a burn in his side bubbled where the dagger was still planted. He pulled it out and let it fall from his hand, blood burning hot. He thought he heard Fumble's voice as his vision of the dim cave faded to black, and he fell face-down onto the old rough-hewn planks. A rushing fever took him, and he was enclosed by oblivion.

CHAPTER

SIXTEEN

THE VETERAN

Trokar awoke on a soft bed in a cavernous room, lit dimly by a single oil lamp on a round wooden table. There were hunting trophies mounted on the walls, racks full of weapons, and the bed was overflowing with fine furs that spilled out across the floor, blending with faded ornate rugs. A quilted banner hung on the wall behind the bed, proudly displaying the moth motif emblem of Kol'grathu, bordered with pictographs of its history. He had never seen the room before, but he knew where he was: the war-chief's chamber.

Trokar was wearing only drawstring breeches. He carefully felt the stab wound at his side. It was bandaged, as was the gash on his chest. Fog filled his head, and his temple ached from the welt left by the pommel strike.

"Bloodburn poison," The Wise Woman said from across the room. Trokar was startled by her voice, and he cringed at the pain of his wounds when he jolted. She was seated in a high-backed chair against the wall, petting a spider crouched in her lap.

"Your friend Fumble actually kept you alive long

enough for me to tend to you," she continued conversationally. "Warface missed your kidney, otherwise you'd be dead."

"I killed him," Trokar stated plainly. The memory of it all came rushing back to the forefront of his mind. He felt no glory, only numbness.

"Are you sure?" The Wise Woman asked, narrowing her eyes. "We could not find his body."

"I tossed him into the garbage pit," Trokar answered, the howl of anguish echoing in his mind.

"So it is true. A shame his body cannot join the halls of the hallowed dead."

"Hallowed?" Trokar scoffed. "For *him*?"

"It is not for us to pass judgment!" she snapped harshly. "Without the guidance of the ancestor spirits, he will wander lost on the byroads of Fate, consumed by the anger that poisoned him in life. This will bring bad dreams to *us all*." She shook her head low.

"I did what I had to do," Trokar said defensively.

"Hrmph! Well, since you are so certain of yourself, perhaps you don't need my guidance about what happens next." She rose stiffly from her seat; her spider skittered down her robes as she turned toward the door.

"No, wait! What happens next?"

"There will be a party . . ."

"Good!" He grinned, eager to drown the recent past in revelry.

"There will be danger for you there, Trokar."

"Huh? But I won. Aren't I the war-chief now?"

"The circumstances of your victory complicate matters. Tradition was broken. Shal'draaken was corrupted by the involvement of others. There will be those who will question your legitimacy. This is your first test as war-chief!

Many in the clan will celebrate the death of Warface, but others will see an opportunity. You may be challenged."

"Ugh! Another Shal'draaken?"

"No. It cannot be invoked again until the next moon, but they may poison your drinks."

"Not more poison?!"

"Fire-top mushrooms, most likely. Very easy to mix with drink. It can cause extreme rage, which they can exploit to provoke you into a fight, giving them an excuse to kill you."

"Well, I just won't drink anything!"

"If you drink nothing, you will be seen as weak and cowardly."

"Ugh! When is the party?"

"Now."

"Now?!"

"It has already begun. You are late."

"But I'm wounded!"

"If you do not attend—"

"I know, I know! I will be seen as *weak*! I'll get dressed and be out in a few drips."

Layers of bluish smoke drifted gently across the gathering chamber as pipes puffed and the music flowed as freely as the grog. The great chamber was packed, and Cavesong called for several more casks to be brought up from the reserves. The hunters and warriors huddled in small groups, sharing stories about Warface; they boasted of hunting expeditions and successful raids he'd led them on.

Not everyone had such fond memories of the former war-chief, even if they respected his service to the warren.

Even so, there were whisperings of anxiety about broken tradition. An ill omen, some said, that both parties in Shal'draaken had cheated by involving others.

"They're talking smack about us," Vilayne commented from her seat at the table beside Bonewise and Ezme.

Fumble smoked from the other side, turning his ears about. "Who?"

"That group of oldsters over there"—Vilayne flicked her ears forward at the huddle of lined faces a stone's throw away—"and others, I'm sure."

"What are they saying?" Ezme asked.

"They fret about omens, and about how Shal'draaken was not done proper."

"How is that our fault?"

"Those moldy old farts wouldn't know a good omen if it flew in on a flying ship!" Fumble declared.

"Speaking of old farts," Ezme said, "here comes the moldiest." She pointed to The Wise Woman, who had just emerged from the corridor that connected to the sparring room and the war-chief's chamber.

"Trokar must be awake," Bonewise stated.

Trokar entered the gathering chamber behind The Wise Woman, and she peeled off to ascend to her balcony. Trokar wore his leather armor, over which he had a cape of rabbit furs that hung about his shoulders. His hair was curled over with moth oil in an attempt to hide the welt on his temple, and a golden, bejeweled ring circled his left forefinger, the one he had taken from Audrel. He thought it fit him surprisingly well. Goblins eagerly greeted him, competing with each other for a moment of his attention. Trokar smiled graciously, accepting compliments and deflecting questions as he pressed on through the crowd toward the speaking stone.

"Pardon me," Fumble said as he wedged between bodies. He thought he should tell Trokar about the mood of the assembly, but the crowd soon became packed tight and was too stubborn to make space for him.

Trokar, on the other hand, was granted space wherever he wanted to step. He walked through a haze of his own bewilderment, for he was used to being ignored. Now, he was the center of attention for the entire clan. His bare feet gripped the slope of the speaking stone, smooth from the use of generations.

He had climbed its gentle summit many times when the chamber was empty, imagining what it would be like to speak his truth with power. He felt it then—a palpable energy holding the center, as if it radiated from the many ears that turned toward him.

"Kol'grathu!" Trokar called from atop the stone, seizing the attention. "Kol'grathu, let me hear you!"

The chamber rang with a mosaic of voices singing their own names, as dissonant and beautiful as Trokar had ever heard. As the voices receded, he bowed his head and raised his arms with his palms up—a gesture of uplifting thanks.

"It is an honor to be your war-chief! A time of change is upon us! A time of opportunity!"

Words of excitement blended with grumbles around the chamber.

"The reign of Warface is over! He hated me so dearly that he disgraced our traditions and had his goons try to kill me!"

Many in the crowd booed, but Trokar couldn't honestly tell if they were booing him or Warface; some of the warriors shouted angrily in disgust, others in disbelief.

"It is true!" Trokar continued. "Shivsalt and Kneecap should have known better! Our wise spell-singers uncovered their treachery and came to defend our clan's honor! As they did battle, I crossed blades with Warface alone!"

"Where is his body?!" a rough voice demanded from a group of hunters. It sounded like Pepperbolt, one of the senior warriors.

"I threw him down into the deep below!" Trokar answered, heart pounding as gasps of disbelief and outrage rippled around the chamber. He immediately regretted telling the truth, but it was too late. "Warface tried to do the same to me! He left me no choice!"

Sweat beaded on Trokar's forehead, his eyes darting desperately to The Wise Woman seated on her stone slab balcony against the cave wall. She gazed back at him harshly; her resentment for burdening the clan with murder and tragedy burned a hole through him. His heart sank, paralyzed by the disappointment of many. The moment dragged on as the murmuring voices grew in intensity to loud arguments, rippling with dissonance. Trokar teetered on the brink of panic. He fought back tears of sudden despair, using every speck of willpower he had left to keep his ears up. He felt himself unworthy.

Clack. A sling-staff struck the bottom of the speaking stone. Clack. Bonewise ascended, the bone headdress towering over Trokar as the elder practically pressed up against him at the top of the speaking stone. When Trokar realized he should move, Bonewise placed a hand on the soft rabbit fur that covered his shoulder.

The chamber had grown silent, shushed by the final clack of Bonewise's staff against the stone.

"The bodies of Kneecap and Shivsalt prove the treachery of the old war-chief!" Bonewise declared. "The spirits guided our spell-singers to salvage the honor of our clan by removing the interference from our most deadly tradition. The fall of Warface is a bad dream we shall carry forever, but the succession is true! Trokar is our war-chief, and the Moot is in less than a ten-night!"

Bonewise turned an eye to Trokar, giving him a subtle cue.

"That's right!" Trokar mustered, gripping the glimmer of hope given to him. "Our delegation to the Moot," Trokar continued, "guided by our wise elders, will direct the strength of all goblin-kin! The humans underestimate us. They only pay attention to us when we make trouble for them, so I'm going to make some trouble they'll never forget!"

Enthusiastic words echoed in the chamber, drowning out worried mutterings. Bonewise stepped away, giving Trokar the stone once more.

"With our fantastic flying ship," Trokar said, "I am absolutely *certain* we will win the position of leading clan at the Moot!"

Ears perked up at that. Whispers about the flying ship rippled back and forth, and even those who resented Warface's death could not deny the benefit of leading the summer raids.

And soon, many goblins chanted, "Loot! Loot! Loot!"

"The Moot is for *more* than loot!" Trokar announced. "We will break the very foundations of the human empire!"

Confused looks populated the faces of the crowd, and scoffs emanated from the warriors. Too much, too soon, Trokar thought.

"And . . . with a flying ship, we can take swag like never before! From the very heart of the empire, or at least, its stomach!"

"Loot! Loot! Loot!"

"Let us celebrate!" Trokar concluded, and he stepped off

the speaking stone to head for the bar. Friendly banter filled the chamber, along with renewed arguments, but the mood had shifted to a more festive foundation.

Cavesong served drinks, assisted by Slinger, the moth rancher who poured for her on busy occasions such as this. Trokar was boxed in by curious goblins who demanded to know more about the flying ship, the witches, the feathered beast, and everything else Trokar had mentioned in his earlier telling of their journey. He omitted the Source Stones, telling instead of seeking clues to a mysterious treasure, which was part of the truth.

Nothing he said would satisfy the crowd, however, and they persisted with their questions. Many offered him drinks, but he remembered The Wise Woman's warning and bided his time. He felt trapped, closed in, and he hoped Bonewise would return, or for Fumble to appear in a puff of smoke, but his friends were nowhere to be seen.

"If you're going to keep crowding my bar," Cavesong butted in, "then you had better order a drink!"

The sound of her silken voice gave him bird bumps, his ears hot. He turned to the bar and placed his hands wide on the polished driftwood, smiling. She held an empty drinking horn in one hand, the other tumbling a thick coin of solid gold about her nimble fingers. She wore a black strapless top that showcased her spotted shoulders, but he kept his eyes on hers, ignoring everything else.

"Is there some kind of special drink traditionally offered to a new war-chief?" Trokar asked, jokingly.

"As a matter of fact, there is," Cavesong quipped.

His ears perked up, trying—and perhaps failing—to be playful. "Is it grog?"

She smiles. "Wine is a much more traditional drink for special occasions, don't you think?"

"There's wine?" Trokar asked in genuine surprise.

"Unopened," she replied, and with a smooth sleight-of-hand, the gold coin was gone. "It's not free, though."

"We can't afford any more breaks in tradition." Trokar reached under his rabbit-fur mantle to an inner pocket, pulling out a roughly-hammered scrap of silver. He had found three of them in his quick rummage through the war-chief's chamber, and he gauged it more than a good trade for a bottle of wine.

"It's spiced mog-berry wine." She leaned forward on the bar. "I brewed it myself."

Trokar didn't dare turn his eyes from her, but he could feel others watching them. His ears burned from the attention. He couldn't back down now, pulling out the other two pieces of silver to extend all three in one hand.

A shiver went up his spine as she scooped them up, letting her filed claw-tips lightly scrape across his palm.

Cavesong then produced a bottle, set it on the bar, singing a high note that rose in perfect pitch with a jut of her chin. At once, the green glass vibrated from bottom to top, and the cork shot up out of the neck with a pop. Gasps of awe whispered from those gathered around the bar, some even swooned.

She poured the dark purple liquid into the horn, then placed it on the bar in front of Trokar.

Trokar swelled with pride, relieved, too, that he could drink from a trusted source. He brought the cup to his lips, closing his eyes as he inhaled its peculiar, peppery scent. The crisp, fruity flavor glided over his tongue with a spicy, robust aftertaste, reminding him of mog-berry cobbler in autumn.

When Trokar opened his eyes, Cavesong was already serving grog to others down the bar, but the open bottle of wine was left on the counter for him. Trokar resolved to nurse his cup, for he needed to keep his wits about him. Already voices around him were competing for his attention. He did not want to seem aloof, so he turned to face those speaking to him.

A grey-streaked, rusty-bearded goblin of bluish complexion stepped forward with grim conviction, his scarred nose scrunched in agitation. He had been waiting behind a pair of warriors, Strong-Mouth the Silent and Gleatlugs the Spear-hunter. Trokar recognized the grey-streaked goblin at once as Pepperbolt, outfitted in a quilted gambeson.

"I'd like to see what kind of warrior you are without the help of spell-singers and mystics," Pepperbolt said loudly, so that others could hear; nearby chatter ceased.

"I defeated Warface alone," Trokar stated resolutely.

"Says who?" Pepperbolt jabbed. "You and the same spell-singers and mystics? I've never seen you on a hunt. I've never seen you in battle. No one has!"

Trokar's heart pounded in his chest and against his neck. A part of him knew that if he tried to argue, it would only play into Pepperbolt's game. A diminishing part of him wanted to avoid confrontation, to just walk away.

But a fire burned in Trokar's blood, reminding him of the feverish sting of poison from Warface's blade, and rage boiled up.

"We have only your word?" Pepperbolt scoffed when Trokar gave no answer. "What if Kneecap and Shivsalt were the ones trying to stop an ambush? What if *you* are the one who cheated, with your gaggle of conspirators, those apprentices and your huckster?! Schemers! Tricksters! And *you*? Everyone knows you're a coward and a liar!"

Trokar slanted his ears back with a grimace, gripping

the hilt of his sword. Feet scuffed as the crowd opened up space around them, and attentive silence spread across the great chamber. Musical smoking implements smoldered gently in the sudden quiet, bluish smoke wafting in trails above ears that turned toward the commotion.

"You want to see how I fight?" Trokar asked, nose flared. "I'll show you! Right now!"

"Let's have it then!" Pepperbolt replied, gripping the hilt of his own sword.

Goblins scooted back and others flipped tables on their sides all around, which scattered wooden plates and drinking horns across the floor, spilling their contents. Soon, a horseshoe barricade formed, butting up against the bar to separate the duelists from the crowd.

It took all of Trokar's willpower to patiently wait for the arena to be completed. He felt almost dizzy from anger. Was he drugged, he wondered? Had fire-top mushrooms been snuck into something? The thoughts spun across his mind, but he refused to believe that Cavesong would betray him in such a way. No, his frustration, his anger, he decided, were true.

He drew his sword, the bronze blade catching the light of mirrored oil lamps hanging from chains over the bar. Pepperbolt answered by unsheathing his down-curving, single-edged, fullered blade of polished steel. It was heavy near the tip, making it an ideal tool for chopping through vegetation—or limbs.

The precious moments of preparation gave Trokar time to think. He struggled against the fog of rage simmering inside him. He knew Pepperbolt was more skilled at fighting, but he didn't care. He wasn't interested in trying to be more skillful, he only needed to make a point. He raised his sword into "the Roof" guard, mindful that his blade was longer than his opponent's. From that position, his bicep bulged near his cheek, reminding him that his many years of weighted exercises had given him exceptional strength of body. Maybe that made him a "muscle-head," but there was beauty and power in that strength, he believed, and he could use it to his advantage.

He lunged forward, bringing his blade down and thrusting out to clash against Pepperbolt's reactionary, deflective move. Just as quickly, Trokar retracted his blade and thrust again before Pepperbolt could maneuver closer to reach with his shorter sword. Trokar lunged back, then forward again, wheeled his sword left, then right, then over and under, delivering a rain of blows that Pepperbolt skillfully parried, but it denied the senior fighter an opportunity to strike. Trokar's healing wounds ached, but the pain seemed distant.

Pepperbolt's single-edged sword swirled around in graceful, looping movements, continually pushing Trokar's strikes to the outside, but Trokar's double-edged blade could repel with such force that it kept Pepperbolt on the defensive.

They wrangled around their makeshift enclosure, shouts of encouragement sporadically shouted for both of them. Wagers were made in the crowd. Pepperbolt lost his smugness as chips appeared in his sword under the onslaught of the stronger metal, and more and more, he ducked and dodged away instead of trying to maneuver in close.

Both were soaked with sweat and breathing heavily, but Trokar judged he could last longer by sheer endurance. He kept up his attacks, pivoting and switching his stance often, imagining it like a randomized workout routine. The anger was less overpowering as he channeled it into his muscles, remembering he did not want to kill Pepperbolt for voicing his thoughts. He would not be like Warface.

Trokar relented for a moment, lowering the tip of his sword into the Fool's Guard.

Pepperbolt took the bait, eager to seize an opportunity to go on the offensive. He struck aside Trokar's blade and dashed in close, but Trokar dashed forward at the same time, drawing close his blade to guard against the steel, then jerked it across Pepperbolt's forearms. The quilted gambeson was sliced open, but the cut was all speed and little power, not even grazing the flesh beneath.

They both pivoted, frozen in place.

The edge of Trokar's blade pressed against the red stubble under Pepperbolt's trimmed beard. In the stillness, Trokar felt the tip of Pepperbolt's sword poised at the inside of his meaty thigh, ready to pierce through his breeches and carve into the major artery there.

"So," Pepperbolt whispered, "you *can* fight, after all."

"Shall we both die here," Trokar huffed, "or shall we work together for the strength of Kol'grathu?"

Pepperbolt smirked, then grumbled a begrudging chuckle.

"For Kol'grathu then," Pepperbolt said at last, and he withdrew his blade; Trokar did the same.

"I need a true warrior at my side," Trokar said, sheathing his blade and trying to control his shaking muscles. "Will you join me in representing our clan at the Moot?"

Pepperbolt turned his arm, looking at the damage to his gambeson. He took a thoughtful breath before sheathing his weapon. "We should leave soon," Pepperbolt said nonchalantly. "How fast does that ship fly?"

"Fast," Trokar said with a smile. "But you are right, we should leave soon."

"But not before we *party*!" Fumble cried as he jumped up onto the bar from a puff of smoke. Sparkling streamers flew from his hands and soared over the crowd.

The goblins cheered, and the tables were turned back onto their feet. Trokar went back to the bar, to his cup of wine, the bottle, and Fumble's feet.

"Get off my bar!" Cavesong cried as she strode over. "Shoo!"

"Uh-oh!" Fumble exclaimed, leaping down onto a barstool.

Laughter barked from onlookers.

"Stick around," Cavesong said to Trokar as she passed, winking over her shoulder.

Fumble started talking, but Trokar barely paid attention to his friend as the story of the duel was told from Fumble's perspective behind the crowd.

The more of the wine he sipped, the stronger his feelings became, and the weaker his inhibitions. Throughout the night, he played games and sang songs, periodically glancing back to the bar to see if Cavesong was still serving —or looking his way.

A couple hours before dawn, Fumble grinned as he watched Trokar swagger out of the great chamber with Cavesong. Fumble took the half-full bottle of wine that Trokar had left behind and uncorked it for a sample.

"I know that smell!" Fumble declared to Ezme as he sniffed the contents. "Fire-top mushrooms!"

"What do those do?" Ezme asked sleepily.

"They make you hot! Hot with anger, or desire!"

"Are you telling me that there is an aphrodisiac in that wine?"

He gave her a wide grin.

CHAPTER
SEVENTEEN
PREJUDICE AND PRIDE

Vilayne rubbed her eyes as she hiked at the back of the group to the place where Bonewise had hidden the broomship. They took a game trail that was occasionally maintained by hunters to travel up the coastal plateau. It had been two nights since the celebration, and she felt rested enough, but as the moonlight slanted in from the east, strange things kept moving at the edges of her vision, like waking dreams.

She looked out into the jacaranda forest, hoping to see nothing but silvery, shaggy bark and purple petals, but there was more than that. Wherever she looked, in the trail of her field of vision, she thought she saw translucent, worm-like creatures with wide, flapping filaments gliding around the trunks of the trees, appearing in moonlight and disappearing in shadow.

There were also blobs of color, like glowing jellyfish, flapping above the fallen petals on the forest floor. In a nearby clearing, she caught a glimpse of a shadowy bipedal figure with an octopus for a head step through a circle of light. She blinked, and it was gone.

Then there were no creatures, just the trees.

"Bonewise," Vilayne said, catching up to him, "do you see anything unusual about the forest tonight?"

Bonewise scanned the ground, the trunks, the canopy. "Trees are flowering late this year, I suppose," he finally said. "Why do you ask?"

"You don't see them?"

"What?" Bonewise turned and planted his staff, suddenly eyeing the trees behind Vilayne with diligence. "What do you see?"

"I thought I saw . . . jellies," Vilayne tested the word, feeling out if she herself believed it.

"Jelly mushrooms?" Bonewise asked with a more hopeful glance about the forest. "What color are they?"

"Not mushrooms."

"What then?"

"Actually, never mind." She walked past Bonewise. *Maybe I just ate a bad bug*, Vilayne thought. *Or a misplaced odd mushroom in my trail ration, perhaps. It will pass.*

Bonewise cast his gaze back to the forest, letting his thoughts settle. He listened deeply, but nature filled the space with sights and sounds that seemed ordinary. After a beat or two, he turned to catch up with her. "Vilayne," Bonewise began quietly, "we must ensure our new warrior escort gets along with the rest of the crew."

"What would you bet that Trokar forgot all about Sueda?" She jutted her chin toward the front of the group. Her ears slanted back, fearful that Pepperbolt might be eavesdropping, but he showed no sign of having overheard.

"I would not bet," he grumbled.

"I'll get a sound on it."

She pressed on past Ezme, Fumble, catching up to Pepperbolt, who walked behind Trokar.

"Hey, Pepperbolt," she said. "What do you think of humans?"

"What do you *mean* what do I think?" Pepperbolt asked in an agitated tone.

"Have you ever met one?"

"Killed my fair share," he muttered, turning his eyes back to the trail.

"But you wouldn't kill every human you saw?"

"I kill every human I can, and so should you! The only good human is a dead one."

"Reality is more complicated, Pepperbolt. Say there were two groups of humans who were enemies, and the smaller group wanted to work with us to defeat the more powerful one. Would you make a trade?"

"*Trade*?" He sneered. "We don't *trade* with those sprat-killers, those land-grabbers, flag-planters! We raid them!"

"Would you rather raid a palace or a hovel?"

Pepperbolt glowered. "What are you getting at?"

"The people living in the hovels aren't the ones putting bounties on goblin heads."

"But they would *collect*, wouldn't they?" he asked rhetorically. "If we show weakness, there will be forays, and settlers will encroach on our land. We must constantly remind them to fear us!"

"If you want better odds at claiming a big prize, you need cunning. You need to play all the angles."

"The only *angle* you'll get *trading* with humans is the *knife* angled down into your back when they betray you, or track you back to the warren and kill us all!"

"If we do nothing but raid them, then that's inevitable."

"Zah!" He hissed indignantly. "They can't track our warriors, but they would sure as bones have an easier time tracking a bunch of empty-headed traders! *Traitors*, more like!"

"Can't track something that flies."

"What are you getting at, *witch*?"

"I'm just curious how smart you are." Vilayne walked around him, ignoring his snarl as she came up alongside Trokar. She gave him a sidelong glance, noticing he was profusely sweating. He was overburdened with an overstuffed backpack, trying to take some of the weight off his shoulders with his thumbs hooked under the straps.

She gleaned that he had not gotten much rest since the celebration. Cavesong had her way, which she guessed took precedence over sleep. At all other times, she saw him harried by petitioners, swept into impromptu meetings, always wearing a smile, but she saw the weary look in his eyes. He was not smiling now.

"Your tongue up to the task?" she asked him. The furtive glance he cast her way confirmed that he knew what she was referring to. He had been listening, after all; he breathed a heavy sigh.

"Not yet," she cautioned. "When we get off the ground."

"You taking orders from this witch, War-chief?" Pepperbolt jibed from behind.

"I'm advising our wise and cunning leader," Vilayne said bitingly over her shoulder, then gave Trokar a knowing look.

"I know what I'm doing," Trokar muttered. Vilayne could tell Trokar was indignant, and she could *see* it exuding from him like a dull red light that smoldered on his face.

She blinked, looked again, but the light vanished if she *tried* to see it. The thought occurred to her that there was magic at work. Could she *see* emotions? Were there indeed invisible creatures in the forest, or was she losing her grasp on reality?

"I know," Trokar said, noticing her reaction, "you probably thought I was just blundering my way from one foot to the next, but I've got everything under control."

He picked up his pace with the broomship in view. Sueda and Shacklespurf had apparently put some effort into hiding it with branches and woody brush; greenery up against the hull, draped all around it and over the top on pole lashings. There was a fire pit with cold charcoal on the ground near a makeshift ladder that leaned up against the railing. The fire pit had a spit of hazel branches propped over it, the green wood charred from cooking. *Shacklespurf must have hunted something*, Vilayne thought.

As the first of their number climbed aboard, Bonewise vocalized a simple contact call of two barks, as old as goblin-kind, which were repeated back to them from the camouflaged aftcastle. Shacklespurf stepped down to the main deck, bayoneted crossbow in hand. Vilayne noticed she had replaced the drawstring with what looked like braided sinew, probably from whatever she had hunted. The crossbow was not loaded, but a newly-made pouch of quarrels hung from her hip.

"Where did you get those?" Vilayne asked, pointing to the crossbow bolts.

"Did carve them," Shacklespurf answered. "Bone-tipped. Salted some o' the meat."

Vilayne peered at the eroded features of the ancient soldier, wondering if she could detect Shacklespurf's feelings. As Vilayne let her eyes relax, unfocused, a steely blue color seemed to vent from Shacklespurf's nostrils. Her aura was tinged with grief.

"How are you feeling, Shacklespurf?" Vilayne asked.

Shacklespurf gave her a long look, and that same dull red light that had been on Trokar's face bloomed on hers.

"Bored," Shacklespurf said curtly. "Two long nights." She flicked her gaze to Pepperbolt. "I see a new face be among ye."

"This is Pepperbolt!" Trokar said grandly. "He is a skilled and loyal warrior of our clan!"

"Excellent!" Shacklespurf said with relief in her voice. "Then I will be fain to take my leave."

"Wait, you're leaving?"

"Aye. Ye has't my gratitude, but there is unfinish'd business I must attendeth."

"What business?" Ezme asked.

"Tis a private matter."

"Where will you go?" Vilayne asked.

"Zalenthas."

"We would be happy to take you there!" Trokar exclaimed graciously. "But we have to go to the Moot first. It's a very important meeting of all the war-leaders of goblin-kin."

"I has't had enow o' war." She hung her crossbow on a leather-fastened bone hook at her shoulder.

"All you will find in Zalenthas are the bones of the restless dead," Bonewise said.

"They were *very* restless," Fumble added.

"Yeah," Ezme chimed in, "don't open the entrance unless you're ready to fight an army!"

"I has't dealt with dead ones before," Shacklespurf countered. "There is one 'mongst them I must has't words with."

"Goblins need to stick together," Trokar said. "After the Moot, we will take you there, I promise."

"The land has changed a lot since you were there," Fumble said. "If you go on foot, you might get lost!"

Shacklespurf sighed, a breath of deeper blue visible to Vilayne.

"I s'pose a few more days riding this cork-carved tinder boat won't maketh any difference. So be it."

"Great!" Trokar said. "Let's get all these branches off and get underway!"

Trokar hurried himself to the door that went below deck, which began to open from the inside. "Ah!" He shouted, slamming it shut again to stop Sueda from being seen. "Look lively, now!"

Pepperbolt grunted and got to work with the others, dragging the branches down while Trokar squeezed himself below deck to talk to Sueda. Vilayne saw Fumble thrumming with frustration as he tried to untie one of the firm lashings holding the pole frame together. She drew her knife and sliced through the ropes at each joint, causing the frame to lean to one side and collapse.

"Hey, that was good rope!" Fumble complained as he dodged the falling branches.

"Maybe you can make a concoction to glue it back together," Vilayne teased. She muttered a spell, twirling her finger, and all the rope she had cut slithered across the deck like snakes, curling themselves up in a heap.

"I'll glue your sassy mouth shut," Fumble muttered as he threw poles and branches overboard.

Once the broomship was freed from its cover, Bonewise took hold of the broomstick and began a chant to connect himself with its magic. They floated up off the landing legs, and Fumble directed Pepperbolt to turn the crank to retract the legs and put the broomwings down into flying position.

The warrior burned red, scowling at being ordered around by the likes of Fumble, but he did as he was told.

Vilayne then saw a mist of warm, orange wonderment exude from Pepperbolt's mouth as he placed his hands on the railing, the trees falling beneath them. Bonewise hummed a long note as he mustered the reeds of the broomwings, which rattled and quivered, and then they were soaring over the sinkholes that defined clearings in the forest. Trokar emerged from below deck and approached Pepperbolt.

"We scored big-time with this thing," Trokar said, "wouldn't you say?"

"Yes," Pepperbolt replied in a half-whisper. "Quite a thing."

Vilayne watched Trokar stand quiet for a moment, his breath almost white, tinged with yellow. *Anxious*, she thought.

Sueda then stepped cautiously from the doorway, but Pepperbolt did not notice. Vilayne placed herself near the priestess, whose breath was coming out a similar white-yellow color. The human nodded to her in greeting, offering a reassuring smile, as if Vilayne was the one who needed assurance. Vilayne inclined her head in the direction of Pepperbolt, and Sueda faced that way, clasping her hands loosely on the front of her purple robes, which had been scrubbed of mud.

"So . . . Pep,'" Trokar began casually, "I forgot to mention, we have a human aboard!"

A small spasm jolted Pepperbolt for an instant, then he whirled to look at Trokar, but his gaze diverted at once to Sueda.

"Human!" Pepperbolt exclaimed, as if to confirm for

himself what he saw. "Have you lost your rotted mind, Trokar?!"

"She's not a danger to us," Trokar assured him. "She's like a pet!"

Sueda's passive demeanor cracked. Vilayne saw a ruby red light flare over the human's heart, and with her next breath, an electric purple mist vented from her nostrils. She stamped toward Trokar, and Pepperbolt seized the handle of his sword, ready to draw. Trokar stepped in front of Pepperbolt to restrain him.

"I am not a pet!" Sueda declared to Trokar's back, standing tall. "I am not your slave, nor am I here for your amusement!"

"It speaks," Pepperbolt said in astonishment at her fluency in goblin speech.

Trokar swiveled his head to Sueda and made a frustrated gesture toward Pepperbolt, as if to make plain the reason he had spoken thusly.

"I will not be treated as lesser," Sueda said to Trokar, "not by you, nor anyone! I deserve the same respect I have shown you. Have I not earned that?"

"Cease this babbling!" Pepperbolt ordered, yanking his blade from its scabbard.

Trokar snapped his head back to Pepperbolt, pointing a harsh finger at him; Vilayne saw a flurry of yellow and purple colors dance in Trokar's aura.

"You draw that sword against her," Trokar declared, "you draw it against me!"

Pepperbolt gaped at him, and for a moment, only the wind made a sound as it flowed over the carved wood of the craft. Bonewise kept an eye on the standoff as he held their easterly course, and the others watched as well, waiting to see what would happen. Vilayne softened her gaze, and saw Pepperbolt's aura shift from red to a deep purple.

"Sueda is a water witch," Vilayne said. "She could boil your blood with a word."

"Why is it here?" Peperbolt growled.

"She wants to help us!" Ezme said, taking a step closer.

"The humans are playing you for a fool!" Pepperbolt shot back.

"What do *you* know, Pepperbolt? You can't see past your loathing."

"I can see she's a witch! Unnatural speech—she's put a spell on you all! This rotted ship is her doing, isn't it?"

Fumble interjected, "Wrong, Pepperbutt! She helped us steal this ship from witches. She's a priestess!"

"Ancestor's bones! Priesters are even *worse*! Their kind and their profane gods take joy in exterminating us!"

"It is true that the rulers of my people have sought to wipe you out," Sueda admitted.

All eyes turned to Sueda, and Vilayne saw wind-snakes dancing around the towering human as they swept by; Sueda paused to take a breath.

"People who thought themselves holy and right were guided only by hatred and greed," Sueda continued, "and made it law. I do not follow those laws. I know your people have suffered because of my kind, and continue to suffer, and it must stop. That is why I am here. The rebellion against the Republic can only grow stronger if we help each other."

Pepperbolt's breath came out hot pink to Vilayne's sight, much to her bewilderment, and the burning red color undulated over his face.

"Pretty words, *human*," Pepperbolt said with spite. "You might even believe them. But I don't believe that you came here to help us out of *guilt*. No, you came to serve your own cause, not ours."

Vilayne saw Sueda's aura plunge into a swirl of misty whites and deep blue, like the sea on a cloudy day. Sueda cast her eyes down. *A touch of truth there*, Vilayne thought.

"This fool has't made up his mind," Shacklespurf said from across the deck where she leaned against the railing. "Ye will not sway him."

"Who asked *you*, stranger?" Pepperbolt shot back. "You a human-lover?"

"The huuer and I hads't time to talk. 'Hast caught up on some hist'ry. Plenty o' deeds lacking in valor between goblin and huuer, but t'was not always that way. One thing I knoweth ... things change."

"Trokar," Vilayne said, "it's not your responsibility to change his mind."

"You're right," Trokar said with a sigh. "But I'm still war-chief, and I say having Sueda on the crew is part of the war-plan. You gotta accept that, Pepperbolt. That's an order!"

Ears flat in outrage, Pepperbolt growled under his breath. He shifted his eyes across the deck, eyeing everyone as they waited to see what he would do, but he sheathed his sword.

CHAPTER
EIGHTEEN
THE HERMIT

They found where the river flowed over the surface and followed it upstream. By mid-morning, they had left the jacaranda forest behind and flew over the borderlands of almost impenetrable bramble and thorny scrub, which soon vanished under a rising ocean of reedy grass. The land was a sea of lime green, each blade of grass standing thirty feet tall, though it might have been more accurate to say that they floated, anchored to their roots. The slightest breeze made them weave and bob, creating rippling waves in the canopy.

"Can this thing go any faster?" Pepperbolt asked Bonewise from his post at the rear of the aftcastle.

Vilayne and Ezme sat with their backs to the railing, splicing back together the three-weave rope that Vilayne had cut earlier. Vilayne found that if she focused on some task, the distracting visions went away. She glanced between the railing columns and looked down, the broomship's shadow sweeping over the willows that hugged the riverbank, which held the space between grass and water. They were gliding along four or five times faster than any goblin could run, by her reckoning.

"I'm sorry," Bonewise grumbled sarcastically. "Is this not fast enough for you?" He had been chanting for hours to keep a steady speed, and Ezme and Vilayne had been chanting along for support while they worked.

"Not fast enough to escape a *thunderbird*."

"Wait," Ezme said, her ears perking up. "Thunderbirds are *real*?"

"They're not just tall tales," Pepperbolt said. "Everyone who attends a Moot is sworn to secrecy, including all the things they see on the way there and back, but there are always stories. The thunderbirds are the most unbelievable, and the most true."

"Is it true that they are big enough to carry a whale?" Vilayne asked.

"How else do you think *that* got here?" Pepperbolt pointed ahead.

Sun-bleached bones curved up out of the willows on the left bank, a whale's rib cage.

"Have you ever seen one?" Ezme asked.

"No," Pepperbolt admitted. "But it is said they travel within storms. Perhaps they create the storms? No one knows. When we traveled on foot, we stayed hidden when one blew over, but we were always more concerned with the other dangers of the tower-grass. With this flying thing, though . . . a thunderbird might see it as a challenger in its territory."

"Wait," Ezme said, "*what* other dangers?"

"Beetles, snakes, spiders, wyverns, mantises, rats."

"How big are they?"

"*Everything* is big in the tower-grass."

"How did you not get eaten, then, traveling on foot?"

"We stayed alert, moved fast, and stayed on the trails."

"There's a trail down there?" Vilayne asked.

"Many! The rats keep their own, but we maintain one to get across. Tower-grass takes years to grow tall, see, and if you cut it close to the ground in a narrow strip that runs west-east, not enough light gets down for new shoots to come out. It doesn't even try. It's all one plant, hear?"

"What do you mean it's all one?" Ezme asked.

"The roots are all connected," Bonewise answered, pausing his chanting.

"That's what I was gonna say," Pepperbolt remarked. "Anyway, there are markers showing the shortest way. The river wobbles and curves, so we cut through the grass between the bends. T'grass just . . . floats away on the air when cut." He flicked his hand skyward.

"This ship uses tower-grass to fly," Vilayne said thoughtfully. "Gret said something about a special way to dry it."

"Who's Gret?" Pepperbolt asked with severely angled brows. "Not another human?!"

"I don't know *what* Gret is," Ezme said with a shake of her head. "Did he run away? I haven't seen him since the Glyphwood."

"Gret!" Bonewise called.

A board bent up in the decking beside where Bonewise stood, and the bumpy, yellow face of Gret appeared as he poked his head out.

"Yes, boss?" Gret asked.

Pepperbolt jolted and his eyes went wide.

"Oh good," Bonewise said, "you're still here. If we cut some tower-grass, would you be able to repair the damaged wing?"

"Sorry, boss, no-can-do! No dry on the fly! Need more alchemy stuff than ship got! No tuning crystals, no—"

"Never you mind, then. As you were."

"Aye-aye!" The board snapped back down into place.

"Seems we're stuck with this limp," Bonewise grumbled, shifting his grip on the steering broom and adjusting the ship's tilt.

"Perhaps we should fly low over the river," Vilayne suggested, "so we don't stick out above the grass."

"Not a bad idea."

"That will take twice as long!" Pepperbolt protested, shaking off his flabbergast. "Didn't you hear what I said about wobbles and curves?"

"I'm not going to sprint this thing all the way to the mountains," Bonewise asserted. "We take the long way, keep a low profile. Vilayne, you swap with me. I need a break."

Vilayne had to concentrate extra hard on maintaining her bond with the magic of the ship. Instead of coasting along in a straight line, she had to follow the meander of the river, sometimes dipping so low that their keel skimmed the water.

They passed an expanse of rock from an old lava flow, littered with a chaotic array of bones and smashed serpentine skulls that in life could have swallowed her whole. In the midst of the bones was a half-rotted, three-masted seafaring ship with a broken spine. The only way it could have gotten there, she thought, was if it had been dropped from above.

Vilayne was glad Trokar was below deck, or he might

want to search the wreck for treasure. She was sure it was a graveyard crawling with bone beetles, which, though small, a large number could strip flesh from a body in minutes.

A little further up the river, a beaked leather-wing bolted from its willow perch as the Moonbeam approached, and in a flash, it was grabbed out of the air by a green mantis halfway-up the tower-grass along the riverbank. Its powerful jaws crunched the leather-wing before it even had time to shriek. Its compound eyes, each as big as a boulder, seemed to follow her as she passed. She gave it a wide berth.

The etheric energies flowing through the rune-carved wood supercharged her second sight, and she saw will-o'-the-wisps dancing in the shade of the willows, and colorful jellies floating between the swaying tower-grass.

She was awake and alert, more than she had ever felt at midday. Maybe more than she had felt, ever. The Daystone was warm against her forehead, and she wondered if the gem of power was feeding her the sun's energy. She also wondered if it had caused these visions she was seeing. She had already tested the theory earlier by removing it, but the invisible creatures were still there, in the periphery of her sight. Still, the gem's power might have been the catalyst.

She looked again toward the dancing lights amongst the willow, and they vanished when she focused on them, but something else caught her eye. The willows looked different than those she had seen downstream, in the way that they grew. They seemed denser, more angled and knobby at the joints.

She didn't know much about above-ground rivers, but she knew someone who did.

"Gret!" Vilayne called.

"Yeah, boss?" Gret said as a board creaked up.

"Tell Sueda to get up here." She glanced down to Gret. He radiated golden-green joyfulness, his skin-tone and toothy grin matching his aura. "Please," she added.

"Aye-aye!" Gret saluted, and the board snapped down on him.

Sueda soon hurried out onto the main deck and looked up at Vilayne.

Vilayne then motioned to the passing riverbank. "What's with these willows?"

Sueda walked to the railing and studied the willows with darting eyes.

"They've been coppiced!" Sueda declared. "They've been harvested from many times, but it looks like not for several years."

"Are you sure?"

"Yes, I spent a lot of time working a willow copse at a Mawwu temple. It looks like these trees have several years growth from the most recent joints."

"Huh," Vilayne huffed. Who would live in the middle of the tower-grass plains, she wondered. She had heard stories of tall insect people with four arms living in the most inhospitable places. Whoever had been here, she hoped they were long gone.

Then, around the next bend, there was a break in the willows and a hill of stone loomed; like from the heart of a volcano, half-buried in the silt of the floodplain. The river flowed around it to the right, polishing the stone on that side. Vilayne saw it even before they had rounded the bend, for it glowed with a rainbow of colors.

"What is that?" Vilayne asked in awe.

"It is . . . very round," Sueda said, appraising the stone formation, which appeared to her as regular stone.

Vilayne tightened her grip on the broom-handle and

pulled back a little, tilting the fore upward. The broomship glided to a halt, the broomwings rustling restlessly to keep them afloat.

"This place is . . . amazing." Vilayne stared softly at the dome of rock, its colors bleeding out into the sky. "This is a place of power. Get everyone up!"

THEY FOLDED up the broomwings and set the ship down in the river, anchoring it to the trunk of an old willow. They then climbed down using a makeshift ladder they'd brought, and trekked through the willow thicket on the shore, searching the stoney clearing between the dome and the tower-grass.

Right away, they found the remains of an old campfire. Bonewise stirred it with the foot of his staff and remarked on its age, evident by the moss creeping onto the charcoal from the ring of stones. There were also bundles of rotted willow sticks and the remains of a willow-woven fish trap.

"Looks like a ranger's camp," Pepperbolt said. "Whoever was here is long gone."

"I've found something!" Ezme called from behind some willows.

Everyone hurried over and gazed at a green, coppery metal frame forming an inverted pyramid; the point was fused to the top of a tarnished bronze-like box, which Ezme revealed by kicking off a woven willow screen, evidently placed to block view of it from the river. The sticks crumbled apart from rot. Atop one of the lofty corners of the frame was a little cross of spoons which twirled around in the breeze.

"What in a human hell is *that*?" Pepperbolt asked.

"Looketh like an antenna," Shacklespurf said.

"Like moth's ears?" Trokar asked.

"Aye, some-like."

"Maybe it's a puzzle?" Ezme said, stopping the spinner of spoons with a long willow stick, then pushed so it spun the opposite direction.

"Maybe it will blow up!" Fumble cautioned, at which Ezme backed away.

"Shacklespurf," Vilayne said, "have you seen something like this before?"

Shacklespurf nodded. "Aye. We did use them for far and festinate communication, and t' sense things yond that cannot beest seen." She jutted her chin up sharply.

Vilayne gazed at the contraption softly, but did not see anything otherworldly about it, besides a trio of jellies circling around the spoon spinner playfully.

"Can we take it with us?" Fumble asked eagerly. "I want to understand it! With this kind of power, we could—"

"Perhaps," Bonewise interrupted, "we should seek to understand its purpose here before tampering with it."

"That's just what I was going to suggest!" Fumble said as he set down his pack, and he got out his crowbar. "We might find a clue if we look inside of it."

As Fumble and Bonewise argued, Vilayne walked to the top of the dome. Even from that high vantage, she could not see anything beyond the surrounding expanse of towergrass. But she could see down into the clearing, and the light seemed to refract sharply around something at the base of the dome.

She walked down to it, and what had been invisible became visible to her as an archway of glass, a tunnel that, when she gazed at it from a forward-facing angle, vanished into the rock.

A floating eye the size of her own head blinked open in the archway.

"Boo!" the eye said in a deep, echoing voice.

Vilayne stumbled backward, adrenaline spiking. The eye seemed to smile, and a gravely laughter emanated.

"Hey!" Vilayne shouted so the others would hear. "Why did you do that?!"

"I've waited a long time to do that," the voice said. "You should have seen the look on your face! I can show you!" The eye blinked closed and a silent recreation of Vilayne stumbling back played out in the archway. Then it was gone, and the eye opened again.

"Who are you?" Vilayne asked as she regained her poise.

"Maddus, but everyone calls me Dreadfault—or they used to."

The others came running over, and Vilayne gestured to the eye.

"Can you see this?" Vilayne asked with a tint of worry in her voice.

"We apologize for our trespass, o' spirit," Bonewise said as he planted his sling-staff. A wash of relief swept over Vilayne; she was not losing her mind.

"I ain't dead, sprat!" Maddus rebuked. "Now stop messing with my instruments and clear off!" The eye closed and the glass archway vanished.

"Sprat?" Bonewise asked.

"It needs its eye checked," Ezme commented.

"Wait!" Fumble cried, pointing toward where the eye had been. "Please, eye thing, I want to learn about your instruments! I can trade!"

Nothing happened.

"Its name is Dreadfault," Vilayne reported.

"Dreadfault!" Fumble called. Still nothing. He called it three times.

"Maybe it can't hear us?" Ezme asked.

"Let's get its attention again!"

Fumble and Ezme ran back to the device and swatted at the spinning spoons with willow whips, making it spin erratically. Bonewise shrugged and stood waiting with the others to see if the eye came back.

It wasn't long until the archway and the eye popped back into being.

"Don't make me come out there!" Maddus growled in its strange, deep voice.

Bonewise bowed slightly. "We are a delegation from Kol'grathu—"

"And emissaries of the Marsh Mother!" Fumble shouted as he ran back from the machine.

"We would like to offer a trade," Bonewise continued. "Your instruments are poorly hidden. Allow us to weave you a new screen of willow to conceal them. In return, we ask only information."

"I'll do it myself, thanks," the eye answered curtly.

"Ah," Fumble chimed in, "but I see you have not had time to fish in a long while, since your fish trap is broken. We have *barrels* of salted fish!"

"Hrmph. I get plenty of fish here. Easy work."

"What about carru meat?" Shacklespurf asked. "Doth thou have that?"

"Oh," the eye said, a change in its tone. "Red meat. That would be nice. Is it fresh?"

"Smoked yesternight."

"Backstrap?"

"Aye."

"Hmm. Wait, is that a huuer?" The eye got bigger, staring at Sueda.

"Yes," Sueda answered in goblin speech.

"Well now. Times have changed! Alright, you can come in. Bring the backstrap!"

CHAPTER
NINETEEN
CHRONOSTONES AND WONDROUS THINGS

The glass tunnel whisked them through the dark stone to an archway of deep red crystal in a black void. On the other side was the interior of a massive geode, the crystals swimming with a rainbow of colors. More than that, Vilayne could see a languid blue energy flowing up the walls to an opalescent stalactite hanging from the center of the dome ceiling.

Beneath their feet was a metal floor, the same color as Trokar's sword, spanning the chamber at its widest latitude, and heaped all about were machines, shelves, and tables cluttered with oddities. They walked down a ramp that abutted the crystal archway, glowing with light focused onto it from a huge hinged array of mirrors and lenses splitting and bending a light beam from a whirring machine overhead.

"Don't touch anything!" a gruff goblin voice called from the center of the chamber.

They walked between cluttered tables and shelves, passing a glass terrarium containing an undulating cube of goo that had several fish skeletons inside it.

At the center, a series of wide, hollow rings of glass, suspended by welded gold, which in turn was held by a bronze-like frame that stopped near the ceiling, was positioned beneath the strange stalactite.

An elderly brown-skinned goblin stood next to a squat cushioned stool, white beard braided tightly, lacking hair anywhere else besides his long eyebrows and huge floppy ears. A gold stud poked from his wide leaf-shaped nose. He removed a cylinder made of metal and glass from over his right eye and placed it in his vest pocket.

Across the room, a small stage held a pair of goblin-like puppets jabbering and whacking each other with little clubs.

"Cut it!" the old goblin barked toward the puppets, and they went limp.

"I know thine face . . ." Shacklespurf said, pushing to the front with the smoked meat slung over her shoulder. "Thou art Maddus! Thou didst serve the Goblin King!"

Everyone froze in place at that.

"Is that malarkey still going on?" Dreadfault asked in annoyance. "That was a long time ago, even for *me*. And I didn't *serve* him, I just worked for him!"

"Same difference!"

"Look, I made some mistakes, but I don't work for anyone anymore. 'Cept for myself, o'course. So I'm not taking any crap—and no commissions! Let's see that backstrap, eh?"

Shacklespurf threw down the meat on the metal floor, teeth clenched with bitterness.

"Joke's on you!" Dreadfault said. "That floor is clean enough to eat off of."

Shacklespurf looked like she was about to move toward him. Vilayne could see the red rage climbing, so she placed a hand on Shacklespurf's shoulder, and the soldier remembered herself, shrugging away from Vilayne's touch as she turned.

Vilayne stepped forward. "How is it possible you are still alive after ten thousand years?"

"Ten thousand years?!" Dreadfault's eyes bulged under an arched brow. "Gadzooks! *That's* how long it's been out there? No wonder no one's called! My own offspring are surely dead by now. Grandkids too. Surely . . ."

Vilayne could see the blue swirls of grief held back behind the old goblin's eyes, recognizing it was a grief he already knew well; what she saw was but an echo. She felt sorrow for the old goblin.

"How come you don't talk like Shacklespurf, here?" Fumble asked of Dreadfault, thumbing at Shacklespurf.

"I ain't no gob-town bonker," Dreadfault said dismissively. "I grew up running with spacers."

"Ah, that makes sense," Fumble said, looking at Trokar with a shrug.

"Are you immortal?" Trokar asked innocently.

"Thankfully not! Just been skipping along faster than the rest of you, relatively speaking."

"How is that even possible?" Vilayne asked again.

"Time dilation," Dreadfault answered plainly. "This here is a crystal node." He then gestured widely. "It's connected to a network that directs etheric energy around the whole planet—"

"What's a planet?" Trokar asked.

Dreadfault blinked and gave him a disbelieving look.

"Thou dost not have to explain it to *me*," Shacklespurf said, crossing her arms.

"I know what planets are," Ezme said. "They're stars

that move different from all the other stars in the sky, right?"

"I was taught they are part of a celestial network that influences our thoughts and feelings," Sueda added.

"I think they're great big burning balls of gas!" Fumble proclaimed.

"That's all . . . somewhat correct," Dreadfault groaned. "What I meant was the world, the whole world under us, it has these currents of energy, and it condenses in places like this, right there"—he pointed to the ceiling—"just enough so that I can draw it into corporeal form, collect it once every one hundred years or so, most reliably on the night of the fourth full moon. I built a machine that uses chronostones to dilate time by about a factor of twenty in this place, so I only have to wait about five years, understand?"

"That would still make you very old," Vilayne said.

"I ain't no spring lizard!"

"Are we dilated right now?" Fumble asked. "The Moot! We might be late!"

"No, no, I turned it off. I'm running low on chronostones, actually. Speaking of which . . . you might be able to help me."

"Are we talking trade?" Fumble asked.

"If you bring me more chronostones, I'll trade you some of my inventions! You want weapons? I got plenty!" He looked at Shacklespurf. "How about it, soldier? Want something with more punch than that crossbow?"

"It's reliable enough," she answered tersely.

"What about this?" Ezme asked, pointing to an upright machine that held a shimmering, semi-translucent circle like a stretched animal hide.

"Good eye!" Dreadfault exclaimed. "I call it a portable

hole! Wove it from space-spider silk. Not easy to get, let me tell you!"

"What does it do?" Trokar asked, peering closer at the wavering threads along the edge.

"Makes a hole through any physical matter," he answered proudly.

"That sounds . . . *super* useful."

While the others discussed it, Vilayne swept her gaze across the area, softening her vision and letting the cacophony of energy auras flood her otherworldly sense. Something small and bright caught her attention. Wedged between two dusty cabinets was a metal pedestal with a glass cover on it, with the small thing inside resting on a metal plate, winking chromatic light.

She approached it and let her vision come into focus again. To her mundane eyes, it was a small, translucent, geometric shape—round with triangular facets that seemed to flip and shift around on its surface and even inside of it.

"Don't touch that!" Dreadfault called to her.

She turned, holding up her empty hands. "This seems special."

"One of my special *mistakes*," Dreadfault said wearily as he walked over, gazing at the thing. "I call it the infinity die, 'cause it can kill you in an infinite number of ways."

"How?"

"Truth be, I don't know. Made it in an adamantine pressure cooker with a good chronostone."

"But what does it do?"

"Anything! Far as I can tell, it alters the probability of something happening when it strikes something hard enough. No telling what it might do! I saw some weird stuff happen, and most of it wasn't good."

Vilayne couldn't stop looking at it; it tickled the edges of her second sight with incomprehensible possibility. "Would you trade for it?"

"*Blood and thunders*, are you *crazy*?"

Vilayne shot him a withering glare at the word *crazy*, and the old goblin sucked in his lips for a moment.

"It's too dangerous to let loose," Dreadfault said, assertive but gentle.

"Before we settle on what we are trading for," Bonewise said, "where can we find these stones you need?"

"I usually find them near thunderbird nests."

"Thunderbird nests?!" Pepperbolt blurted.

"Chances are you can walk right up and grab them. They discard them, understand? They form in their crazy gizzards and get spit up every few hundred years."

"If it's so easy, why don't *you* do it?" Pepperbolt asked.

"Well, I could, and I will, if you don't take the job, but I don't get around quite so smooth as I used to! Besides, there hasn't been a thunderstorm in these parts for three years, which either means the beastie is dead or has moved on to elsewhere."

"How are we to find a nest?" Bonewise asked.

"It's northeast of here, in the mountains. I've got it marked on a map I can give you!" He began rummaging through a stack of papers on a writing desk.

"Wait," Ezme said to Bonewise, "you're not thinking of actually going, are you?"

"We haven't agreed to anything," Bonewise answered calmly. "I am only seeking information."

"You can help yourself to any treasure you find," Dreadfault added, flipping through maps. "Thunderbirds like to collect shiny things."

"Shiny things, you say?" Ezme asked with intrigue in her voice.

"This floppy old sorcerer is trying to toss us into a suicide mission," Pepperbolt whispered behind Trokar.

"This old fart is a powerful ancestor," Trokar whispered back, "show some respect!"

"This job," Fumble began, "there is substantial risk involved. Perhaps there is some incentive you could offer, some payment up front?"

"Ha!" Dreadfault barked. "This opportunity is once in a lifetime! Once in a thousand! First ones to comb an abandoned thunderbird nest become very wealthy! I'll give you its location for free! You could even run off with the chronostones, and I'd never be the wiser. But you won't find anybody else who knows what they are or how to use them."

"We need to talk about it," Bonewise said.

Dreadfault did not respond, only muttered to himself as he checked another stack of papers. The goblins huddled in the biggest expanse of open floor available, by the puppet stage.

Sueda hovered, peering at the lifeless puppets. Vilayne could see the echoing specters of the spirits that had animated the meticulously sewn characters—they unsettled her.

"You gobs," Trokar said, "that portable hole is a game-changer! No castle could keep us out!"

"I say we do it," Ezme said. "We have a few nights before the moon is full, don't we?"

"Yeah," Fumble said, "we can be there and back again in a day! If there's no thunderbirds around, we don't need to keep low!"

"Or there *are*," Pepperbolt countered, "and we all *die* for this crazy weirdo's private hobby!"

"What if we stayed low to be safe," Fumble reasoned, "and still check it out?"

"I think it's worth the risk," Vilayne said. She chanced a glance back to the chromatic sparkle in the glass display. She felt drawn to it, but she tore her eyes back to the circle. "If we don't find anything, we don't come back here."

"Sounds good to me," Ezme said.

"Thunderbirds are mighty beings," Bonewise said, "very old and very wise. It would be a wonder to see one, but I'll settle for an abandoned nest."

"Stuffed with treasure!" Trokar added.

"Bethinks me you shouldst not aid this fascist-enabling profit'r," Shacklespurf stated.

"What about you, Sueda? What do you think?"

"The human gets a vote?!" Pepperbolt fumed.

"She's on our crew, so she gets a vote!"

Sueda looked around at the confounding devices, then down at Trokar and smiled. "This is an astonishing place." She paused to glance up at the shining crystals above. "I have never seen magic like this. If this Maddus can help us, I think we should help him."

"Then that settles it," Trokar said, turning back to the old goblin. "We'll take the job!"

CHAPTER TWENTY
THE THUNDERBIRD

Sleep was blissful. Vilayne swam through beautiful music, rivers of choruses like a warren-wide song on a long winter's night. She sang with them, dancing around pillars of chromatic flame. Never had her dreams been so vivid.

She awoke suddenly, tears streaming. She trembled as she sat up, touching her wet cheeks. The power and emotion of the dream had overwhelmed her.

She peeked from her shelter of fresh-cut willow branches, squinting at the afternoon light that streamed between distant rain clouds. The campfire smoldered with a gentle trickle of smoke, some coal having survived the quench.

Bonewise had insisted they make camp in the clearing outside the geode, for many practical reasons. For one, the willows scraped against the hull of the Moonbeam, making the interior unpleasant for rest. Vilayne was due for next watch, but Bonewise had not yet come to rouse her so she could relieve him. Her unfocused eyes squinted at the colorful aura of the geode dome like a second sun. She could see a Bonewise-shaped blur seated atop it, facing away from the clearing. She turned her ears toward him and heard the murmuring of the song she'd heard in her dream.

She wiped her wet cheeks with the back of her hand, then impulsively touched the Daystone on her forehead. It gently pressed against her skin, by some queer force of attraction, and she pulled it into her palm. She did not ask for this power, she thought to herself. It dissolved the boundaries of her mind, yet she was enthralled by its beauty. She enclosed the gem in her hand.

Vilayne decided she would sleep with it in a pouch tied around her neck, from then on; she needed to limit her connection to it.

Her ears turned at some rustling sound, but when she looked, it was only Trokar, thrashing under his blanket in his shelter nearby. She began to look away, but something in the edge of her vision brought her back. A purple aura hovered beside his shelter, but Trokar's was dark orange, wobbling over his heart, and flashes of red sliced across him like blades. His ears were back, and his face writhed in panic as his body trembled.

She rose and carefully crossed the silt-packed rocks, gazing obliquely to the side. As she drew near Trokar's shelter, she could hear something besides Trokar's own stiff breaths, like something letting out a sigh that didn't stop to catch its wind. As with looking at auras, if she tried to listen to it, to focus on the sound, it vanished.

She was standing right next to the goblin-sized presence.

"Warface," Vilayne said, naming it.

The aura turned toward her with a sneer, then vanished into thin air.

Trokar lurched awake, gasping, and Vilayne knelt down beside him, placing her hand firmly against his chest.

"You're alright, Trokar," Vilayne assured him. "It was just a dream."

"It was—" he gasped, "I was—" His eyes to Vilayne, then he looked away, swallowing his next word. "It was . . . just a dream."

"It was just a dream," Vilayne reassured, gently pushing him back down. "Go back to sleep." She drew a soft breath, then sang:

"The surf of the bay comes sweeping in—
    A companion to the hush of noon.
    Rest we keep until we've been—
    Brushed by the light of the moon."

Trokar's eyes fluttered shut, and an overwhelming fatigue came over him, covering him like a heavy blanket, and he slept.

Vilayne cut a sprig of willow and quickly wove it into a star. She held it close to her lips, whispering a spell of warding, then stuck it in the ground in front of Trokar's shelter.

It would work for at least the first day.

∽

Bonewise guided the Moonbeam over the river, which narrowed the further east they traveled. He dared to glide on a level with the canopy of the tower-grass as the sun dipped over the horizon behind them, illuminating only the swaying tips, creating a golden-green line between land and sky.

He slowed the Moonbeam to a hovering stop. The tower-grass ended abruptly ahead, as did the willows, leaving an empty expanse of barren silt on either side of the river.

"Pepperbolt," Bonewise called over his shoulder.

"Yeah?" Pepperbolt answered from his post.

"What is this opening up ahead?"

Pepperbolt walked to the edge of the stairs that went down to the main deck and peered past the forecastle.

"I'm not sure," Pepperbolt said. "Never seen that before."

"Will you have a look for us? I do not yet want to fly us into the open."

"Fine," Pepperbolt grumbled. He leapt from the portside railing into the tower-grass canopy, hooking a bundle of fat reeds in his arms. They slowed his descent, offering more and more resistance the more of their length he pulled down with him, until his feet touched the ground, vanishing into the thicket.

Others wandered up from below deck, wondering why they had stopped. Bonewise pointed to what lay ahead, and asked Trokar to raise the broomwings. Once they were up, Bonewise set the Moonbeam down in the river, keeping just enough magical pressure on to keep them stationary in the current. Pepperbolt soon returned, giving a contact call from the willows. They threw him a rope and pulled him aboard.

"Looks like an encampment," Pepperbolt said. "A big one. They've cut everything down to the ground for leagues!"

"Why?" Ezme asked. "Who would be out here?"

"I think I know," Vilayne said.

"The forces of the Witch Queen," Bonewise said; Vilayne nodded.

"We could double back, go far around, skim the grass?"

"They might patrol the skies. We would have no cover."

"If only ol' Dreadfart had given us some way to be invisible," Trokar lamented.

"Maybe we can be," Emze said. "Like how we got away from the ravenous gibberers."

"What, pray tell," Shacklespurf asked, "is a 'gibberling?'"

"Spiny flesh eaters," Fumble answered.

"How didst thou get away?"

"Sueda whipped up a fog," Ezme said.

"A huuer deity aided goblins?"

"Mawwu is not human," Sueda interjected. "Her compassion extends to all."

"Spare us the sermon," Pepperbolt began, "you earless—"

"Enough!" Bonewise declared. "Even now we risk being discovered. Sueda, can you call up a fog thick enough?"

"I will beseech the goddess," she said.

Sueda stood at the fore of the Moonbeam and sang her water song with uplifted arms. A mist arose from the river, spilling over the banks and creeping out over the desecrated land. It was not unusual for there to be some mist over the river at dawn, but seldom at dusk. Its density was conspicuous, and they hoped they would cross to the other side of the clearing before anyone from the encampment had time to get curious and investigate.

Bonewise had to glide along slowly, taking cues from the others placed on each side of the ship when he strayed too far from the middle of the water. They kept their voices down, and time stretched on, with no way to tell how much farther the clearing went.

Bonewise wasn't sure if it was stress wetting his skin or condensation, and he fretted about what they would do if they were seen. He'd bet there were enemy broomships in that encampment, not to mention witches on individual brooms, with powerful staves of destruction, like the dragon staff the goblins no longer had.

But the clearing came to an end, and once more, they were in the canyon-like shelter of the tower-grass on either side of the water. Bonewise hurried then, skimming their armored keel in the water, until the river split more and more into tributaries and the willows closed in, brushing the tips of the broomwings.

"There they are!" Trokar exclaimed as they rounded another bend. On the horizon, the last rays of sunlight graced the snow-capped peaks of the Nargunul Mountains. Glints of red adorned the snowy heights, like specks of blood.

Bonewise chanted under his breath, channeling his own power into the ship. They rose up through the air, and the wind from their passing bent the tower-grass behind them like a sweeping gale. The grass diminished in height as the soil became rockier, until only bunches flapped in the wind between creeping kinnikinnick bushes on the steepening slope of the mountains. The Duskfen River, fed by snowmelt, swerved, crashing over and around great boulders and shelves of dark stone, very unlike the sedimentary limestone of the coast.

Bonewise thought he might get tired, but his connection to the Moonbeam was solid, and something about the mountains gave him strength. He pushed the Moonbeam on over the rubble-strewn slopes.

"Shacklespurf," Bonewise called, "where does that map say we will find the nest?"

"North," she answered whilst gripping the map in both hands against the thrashing wind, "about thirty leagues."

Flying north along the edge of the mountains, the broomship was low enough that they could see occasional animal trails crossing the melting snow drifts. Deep red crystals adorned rocky crags of dark stone, some jutting out like blades as long as their broomspan. Bonewise knew they had to be the famed blood-crystals, which had potent magical properties.

"There!" Shacklespurf exclaimed, pointing ahead. "Yond finger of rock looketh like what be drawn on the map."

The rock leaned westward from the peak, its eastward side encrusted with veins of blood-crystal. There was a nook in the mountain where the rock had apparently once been, before some tremendous force had pried it away.

"Think we can land in there?" Vilayne asked.

"Too risky," Bonewise answered. "Let's look for a more discreet landing site."

They came up the mountain from the backside and found a flat, wind-scoured shelf of rock to land on. The air was thin and cold, and drifts of white clouds brushed by, close enough to touch.

"Are you sure we can't just fly over there?" Fumble chattered, covering his ears and hairless head with a blanket.

"Tis nay far," Shacklespurf told him. "Breathe deep and pace thyself."

They hiked across the steep slope of crumbling stone; it took much longer than any of them would have liked, even though it had not seemed to be such a great distance from above. They climbed between a wide fissure in a cliff, feet scuffing against the bones of small creatures that had fallen into the crevice, discarded by birds of prey who roosted above in hidden alcoves. It was the dark of night, and Sueda struggled at the rear, being unused to traversing such terrain while unable to see the ground in front of her. She grit her teeth, suppressing whimpers of pain, for even though she had thickened the cloth wrapped around her feet, the layers offered scant protection against the sharp, bitingly cold rocks. She clamped her mouth, wishing she had stayed with the ship.

As they passed zigzagging veins of blood-crystal in the sundered stone, a faint light moved within the crystal as the bearers of the Source Stones drew near. They marveled at the light for a moment, but soon continued on. Sueda had an easier time of it, being able to see somewhat by the red glow emanating from them.

At last, they came upon the end of the narrow canyon, and the goblins huddled to peer out into a relatively flat area of packed stone. The moon had not yet risen above the bulk of the mountain. The darkness of the peak's shadow was diluted only by the light of stars between scattered swift-moving clouds that brushed the crystal crags.

The nook between the mountain and its dislodged slab was packed with rubble, mashed flat, presumably, by thunderous bird feet. A nest of woven tower-grass, grey with age, loomed in the center, as wide as the great gathering chamber of Kol'grathu. They could not see inside the nest from their vantage, but the exterior glinted in the starlight.

Ezme stepped out from the crevice, eyes fixated on the nest, but Vilayne grabbed her arm.

"What are you doing?!" Vilayne whispered.

"I'm going to look for chronic-stones, or whatever," Ezme whispered back.

"We should spread out," Trokar advocated quietly.

"No," Bonewise hissed, "we must stay hidden until we are sure there is no danger."

Fumble nodded. "Somebody should scout it out."

"Sneak around the nest, Ezme," Vilayne whispered to her, letting go of her friend's arm. "Check it out, then come back."

Ezme gave a nod, then walked carefully, rolling onto the balls of her feet with each step; the packed flakes of stone beneath her weight shifted slightly, crinkling. Several agonizing seconds later, she was next to the nest, pausing to listen. Only the icy breeze whispered against her numb ears.

She had made it a quarter-way around the nest when a cloud moved, and a beam of moonlight streamed down onto the nest over the lip of the mountain. Ezme could see that woven into it were innumerable treasures, like plunder from the belly of a great ship.

Tucked into the weft of the nest, next to Ezme, was a necklace of braided gold holding a web of jewels that would drape over the wearer's chest. Emeralds, rubies, and sapphires; it was the shiniest thing Ezme had ever seen.

Ezme hooked her claws under it and gently pulled. Half of it came free, but the rest of it was stuck, wrapped in the grass. She pulled harder and, rather suddenly, the necklace broke, a spray of gems clattering onto the stones around her feet.

Ezme froze, half of the broken necklace hanging in her hand.

A shadow fell over her as something big blocked the moonlight. She looked up, and a hawk-like, blue-feathered head with dark eyes gazed back at her, haloed by the moon as it closed in. She tucked the broken necklace back into the nest by feel, not daring to avert her eyes from the thunderbird.

Thief! the thunderbird shouted in Ezme's mind.

The others watched with terror from the shadow of the crevice, and Bonewise knew they could not survive a battle against such a powerful creature. The wisest thing to do would be to stay hidden, he thought, and he kept the others still with a gesture. Ezme was simply doomed.

The thunderbird came to rest, perching on the rim of the nest—a deft movement for such a massive body. Four whetted talons on each of its scaly feet gripped the woven tower-grass with the strength that could carry a whale. Its feathers shimmered with electricity, blending with the sheen of moonlight that danced across the interlaced filaments.

Ezme slowly reached for the zoharwood wand in her holster, the one The Wise Woman had given her.

That would be foolish.

"I'm sorry!" Ezme pleaded, and she raised her hands in a plaintive gesture.

Impudent goblin! I could vaporize you! The thunderbird opened its mouth a little, and snapping arcs of lightning fizzled between the razor-sharp edges of its black beak.

"I believe that! I didn't mean to steal from you . . . I didn't even know you were here!"

This nest is mine, whether I am here or not!

"Straight true! It's just . . . I was told there had not been any thunderstorms here for a long time, so—"

So you were unafraid to come here? Unafraid to take my treasures?

"I'm truly terrified! I'm really sorry! Your treasures are just so . . . so beautiful! It's the most amazing nest I've ever seen!"

Your envy does nothing to abate my anger!

"I never wanted to upset you! Please, can I just leave?"

You come to raid my nest, and you expect me to let you leave?

"I did not come to raid your nest, I actually came here looking for chronic-stones."

The thunderbird closed its mouth and tilted its head.

Bonewise could tell the thunderbird was speaking to Ezme somehow, but he could not hear it; he only heard Ezme's responses.

"Can we not help her?" Sueda whispered anxiously behind him.

It looked to Bonewise like Ezme had succeeded at confusing the thunderbird, at the very least, and a feeling in his gut told him that now was the time to act. He gestured for the others to stay, then walked out into the open, slingstaff clacking on the stones. The others listened, staying pressed to the walls.

The thunderbird did not turn its head from Ezme, but Bonewise was keenly aware that one of its eyes turned its attention on him.

"All-honored thunderbird of the tower-grass plains!" Bonewise bellowed. "Keeper of the Nargunul Mountains and Terror of the Sea! I am Bonewise of Kol'grathu, and we have come because the land is in great peril! I beseech you to strike down those who defile the land astride the great river!"

In an instant, the bird's head swiveled to him. *You dare to command my wrath?!* The wings of the thunderbird spread open, cascades of static crackling down its midnight-blue feathers.

"I *beg* you, my lady! Necromancers have brought a blight to the plains"—he gestured to the west—"and they are using the sacred tower-grass to make flying ships that they use to control more territory . . . such as *your* territory, mighty thunderbird."

I am well aware of what transpires in my realm! The thunderbird opened its mouth with a crackling of light. *The defilers have taken my egg!* Her eyes became wild, head craned back, and lightning struck her beak from a cloud above. The blood-crystals flashed red on the mountain and the thunderclap shook their bones.

"Then why do you not destroy them?!"

They will break my egg if I bring a storm! She folded her wings, one feather askew. *They promise to return it to me.*

"They cannot be trusted, my lady! They must be punished for exploiting you in this way!"

They will be. A predatory clarity came upon the thunderbird's eyes as it hunched. *As soon as my egg is returned, I shall destroy them all.*

"Permit us to help you! Together, we can reclaim your egg!"

No. If I move against them, they will crack it.

"They need not know that we have spoken to you, my lady."

The thunderbird's toes flexed on her nest, pausing to consider his words.

Bring me my egg.

Bonewise motioned Ezme to come toward him, and she ran. Together, they returned to the crevice, being watched the whole way. They hurried back through the fissure, then trudged to the Moonbeam in silence.

"So," Ezme said as she helped Bonewise onto the deck, "we go to the Moot now, right?"

"We have a bargain to uphold," Bonewise grumbled.

"You want to raid that cultist compound?!"

"We have little choice."

"Perhaps," Pepperbolt said, "if we go to the Moot, the new Big War-chief can command the other clans to help us root out these trespassers?"

"We don't need to root them out," Bonewise said, "we only need to un-steal an egg. The thunderbird will do the rest. If we hasten, we can get there before dawn."

"It's *your* call, Trokar," Pepperbolt reminded.

"We'll be in an' out of there before they know anything has happened," Trokar said cheerfully.

CHAPTER
TWENTY-ONE
THE RAID

Just before dawn, they set the Moonbeam down in the water upriver of the blighted land. The mist was thick in the air above, heavy with the blessing of Mawwu streaming from Sueda's lips. She swayed on the forecastle in a trance as the mist rolled up the empty banks of the river in the bluish pre-dawn light.

The goblins crept toward the encampment, following the mist, keeping ears primed to pick up any noise ahead. Pepperbolt was at the front, and he threw up his hand for all to stop when a tiny metallic tinkle caught his ear.

They all crouched down, and Pepperbolt rotated his ears, listening.

A story of his surroundings formed in his mind as more tinkles sounded, along with the clunk and thud of iron and bone. The stench of decay found his nostrils.

"You claim these witches have an army of the dead?" Pepperbolt whispered back to Trokar.

Trokar nodded and made a flapping gesture at his nose to indicate he smelled them too.

"I think they are wearing bells," Pepperbolt postulated.

"So if we attack them," Trokar thought out loud, "we alert the camp. Bonewise, what should we do?"

"We should make a wreath," Bonewise answered.

They hurried back to the river at Bonewise's behest and cut willow withes, weaving it into a circle big enough so that they could all stand inside. Bonewise incanted a charm of warding as it was created, then they carried it quickly back the way they'd come.

They slowed, shuffling along quietly when they picked up the smell of rot again. The willow wreath circled their formation, held at chest-level, with Bonewise in the center.

Bonewise thumbed his well-worn leather medicine pouch as they walked past the line of desiccated warriors that were draped with little bells. The bells swayed in the breeze, but the crinkled corpses stood still with listless resolve. He could feel their empty, dead eyes watching, but they did not stir; the blessing had worked, for even death magic must respect certain covenants.

There were no walls around the compound, and the goblins walked right up to the side of a large woven warehouse, the grass of its construction still green and connected to its roots. The buoyant arched reeds were reinforced with lateral willow withes, thatched on top with dry tower-grass. The fog was still thick, but the pink light of dawn was creeping up, and the goblin's collective anxiety was palpable.

Pepperbolt bent, putting his head near the ground to peer through the gaps of the fibrous shelter. He spotted large wooden troughs in the unlit interior, crates, and long racks of drying tower-grass.

"Clear," he whispered, unsheathing his knife, sharpened keen. He sawed at the grass wall until he could peel open a portion big enough for them to slip through.

Once inside, they slinked low along the troughs. The swollen wood reeked of chemicals, possibly what Gret had said they'd need to make them airworthy. They picked their way around crates to a corner behind a drying rack, where a clay-caked, willow-swaddled end wall met the arched living wall. They peeked through the gaps near the ground. Two pairs of boots stood on the other side.

"Milliwu nath morsun," a man's voice said. His tone was casual, as if remarking about the weather.

"Hoshoon tah nix loku," the man beside him said.

"Dunna-flugen hess marwick?"

"Sunna arimet alt *nixa,*" the other replied.

"Karkesh! Demorth lun adea munnpai azest elshak!"

The two men turned and clicked their boot heels together, answering, "Tova, desh Yavella!" They then marched toward a large circular canvas tent staked near a cluster of smaller tents, all dyed green and marked with numerical symbols. By the sound of their footfalls, the soil all about was battered to mud. All else was obscured by fog.

"Where is it?" Ezme whispered to no one in particular.

"It's there," Vilayne said quietly, pointing toward the circular tent.

"How do you know?" Pepperbolt whispered with clear skepticism.

"I just know."

"They just doubled the guard," Fumble commented as the two soldiers fell in beside another pair of guards posted by the tent's entrance. All of their uniforms consisted of banded armor and thick helmets with a T opening on the face of them for the eyes and mouth.

"They knoweth something is amiss," Shacklespurf mused.

"Or it is routine," Bonewise remarked.

"We don't have time to wonder," Trokar said. "We need a distraction."

"Is fire good?" Fumble asked with a waggle of his brow as he pulled out his crowbar.

Trokar grinned. "Fire is *very* good."

∼

A GROGGY SOLDIER with black hair finished his lukewarm, bitter drink from a small tin cup as he strode by one of the woven warehouses, his helmet jostling from a strap at his belt. He stopped when he heard creaking wood and squeaking nails from inside.

"Adiam?" the soldier queried, looking through the open entryway of clay-plastered wattle.

No one answered, and no one was supposed to be working with alchemical supplies until after morning drills. He tossed his cup to the ground and laid his hand on his sword hilt, stepping inside. Slowly, he walked around the stack of crates, then saw that the lid of one of them had been pried open. Clay jugs of alchemical oils sat in packing grass within the open crate, but several were missing.

Suddenly, a bottle tumbled across the room and smashed into the open crate. The soldier's shouts were drowned out by the explosion that engulfed him, and burning fumes leapt up into the thatch.

More shouts spread across the compound as soldiers were roused from their tents by the commotion. Men came running with buckets, spilling water to put out the fire. They organized themselves into a bucket brigade, passing water from a large barrel to the inferno, which lit the surrounding fog with an orange glow.

Trokar, Pepperbolt, Shacklespurf, Vilayne, Ezme, and

Bonewise ran through the fog, darting between rows of smaller tents until they approached the back of the big circular tent. Trokar sliced through the canvas with his sword, then pushed his way inside. A ginormous speckled blue egg rested upright in a little nest of woven towergrass. A well-dressed woman stepped into view from behind it, broom in hand. Her eyes widened at the sight of Trokar, and she reached to her belt, gripping a little rod of red crystal on a chain.

"*Shikkit!*" she recited, thrusting the jeweled tip of her broom at him, the crystal winking red.

Trokar's muscles clamped tight, and he could not move, his own strength working against him. He could not even draw a proper breath.

"*Goblin!*" the human shouted, but then a bone-tipped quarrel squelched through her skin, lodging in her neck. Shacklespurf pushed the rest of the way through the tear in the canvas and rushed the shocked human, driving her crossbow's bayonet through the woman's heart.

Two soldiers promptly arrived through the front of the tent as the woman fell to the ground, and Pepperbolt ran through the tear in the back, leaping into battle beside Shacklespurf; the men shouted, but there was shouting throughout the compound thanks to the fire.

Vilayne entered next and held the torn canvas open so Bonewise could fit through with his headdress.

"Trokar's stuck!" Vilayne informed him as the others flowed in behind. Bonewise laid his hand on Trokar's head and chanted an incantation, invoking the freedom of the Great River and its cleansing power.

Trokar sucked in a breath, relieved he could breathe again.

Ezme flicked her brass wand at one of the soldiers

embroiled in battle against Shacklespurf, striking him with bolts of energy. He fell, crashing against cubbies filled with scrolls. Pepperbolt got inside the second guard's reach and thrust the point of his sword deep under the man's armpit. The soldier collapsed with a gasp of pain, then went silent.

"Looks like the other two went to deal with the fire," Pepperbolt said with a peek out the front tent flap, using it to wipe the blood from his blade.

Another orange glow flared through the fog, illuminating the vague shape of a grounded broomship, one of its raised wings quickly catching fire. More shouts of alarm sounded, and the mood of the garrison shifted as they began to realize the fire was not an accident. Orders were barked, and they organized themselves to repel an attack.

"We have to move!" Pepperbolt urged.

Vilayne picked up the dead woman's broom and yanked the red crystal from her belt, breaking the little chain.

"This thing is a lot heavier than I thought it would be!" Ezme complained as she shoved against the egg, which was taller than her.

Trokar squatted at the bottom of the egg, hugging it. He lifted with all his might, but it didn't budge. It felt like at least five times his own weight. He clenched his buttocks and tried again, grunting through a strangled breath, and to his delight, the egg lifted from the nest.

On the other side of it, Vilayne concentrated on a spell of levitation. The Daystone glowed at her forehead, as did the red gem set in the top of the broom in her hand. She felt the weight of the egg like a ball of iron in her mind, but with the witch's broom, it was not beyond her limit. She directed the egg with a motion of the broom, and she brought it out the front of the tent. Trokar waddled underneath it, bracing it for support.

"It doesn't even feel heavy anymore!" Trokar exclaimed.

Vilayne kept silent, focusing on her spell. If she dropped it, at least Trokar would break its fall.

The others kept a circle around the egg as they rushed through the mud. The sun was rising, and the fog was lifting. More explosions sounded from somewhere in the compound. They had not made it far when they were sighted. The whole garrison had been roused, more than fifty men, by the sound of them, and twelve soldiers began running toward them, spears in hand.

Ezme drew her zoharwood wand from its holster, pointing it toward the onslaught of men.

Please, do something, Ezme thought. *Magic, work through me!* A rumbling came up from her gut, and a belch escaped unexpectedly from her mouth. At once, the earth rumbled and a hump of mud heaved up, barreling toward the charging men. They barely had time to react as a monster of mush buried them under a blanket of goop. The blob sprouted thick arms, swinging wildly and knocking down two others; the rest of the men stuck their spears into its amorphous, semi-fluid body to no avail.

"Thank you, magic!" Ezme said out loud.

"Go, go!" Shacklespurf exclaimed, shoving the stragglers of their group along.

They ran away from the compound, out onto open ground. The edge of the clearing was visible through what little fog remained, but there were also dozens of undead warriors shambling toward them from that direction, bells jingling.

"Fumble!" Bonewise called.

Fumble ran breathlessly from behind a burning warehouse, five soldiers pursuing him; the arrows in his quiver rattled back and forth.

"I'm all . . . out of . . . fire!" Fumble gasped. His throat burned from smoke and hard breathing. The humans were armed with short swords, and even with their armor, they were faster than Fumble, who slowed from utter exhaustion.

"Ancestors bones!" Pepperbolt cursed, pivoting toward Fumble.

"Fumble!" Trokar cried as he let go of the egg, not even noticing that it remained where it was, floating. He was already sprinting after Pepperbolt, drawing his sword. The men were almost upon Fumble, and Trokar could see that Pepperbolt would not reach him in time to stop the first blow.

Pepperbolt drew his knife with his free hand, flipping it in his grasp so he held the blade, then threw it. Fumble dove to the dirt as the knife twirled through the air, striking a soldier's hip and stopping his advance. Pepperbolt then closed the distance and rolled under a swinging blade meant for his head, cutting the soldier's ankle in the process. He came up behind him, deflected another cut with his sword as all but one of the soldiers closed in around him. The other continued to charge toward Fumble and Trokar.

Fumble scrambled on all fours in the slippery mud.

Trokar ran past him, clashing with the soldier who had been about to cut Fumble from behind. The fresh-faced man, big and well-armored elsewhere, was lacking a helmet, and looked almost as terrified as Trokar was. They maneuvered and swiped at each other, neither drawing blood.

"*Earless sprat-killers!*" Pepperbolt cursed, his gambeson taking many cuts, its colors there overtaken by the red of his blood.

In front of Trokar, a muddy tangerine-sized rock slammed into the soldier's unprotected face, and he toppled backwards. Bonewise crouched down to pick up another stone for his sling-staff, and Ezme fired slugs of energy from her brass wand to strike the injured man attacking Pepperbolt. A crossbow bolt streaked through air, embedding itself in the opening of the same man's helmet, downing him.

Shacklespurf cocked her crossbow, drawing the string back again.

Vilayne set the egg down and shot a concentrated beam of white light from the Daystone, burning the eyes of one of the soldiers who had turned to face Trokar. Trokar took advantage and knocked the man onto his back. The man stayed there, writhing in pain as he pushed his helmet off and clutched his eyes.

Pepperbolt deflected a thrusted sword, intercepting the other's strike with his free arm to grab the soldier above the wrist. At once, he pivoted around him, pulling the human off balance. Trokar moved in and, forgetting his revulsion of killing, thrust his sword under the man's helmet, delivering a fatal blow.

"*Kol'grathu!*" Pepperbolt shouted in battle lust as he pressed his attack against the one remaining soldier, and Trokar ran to flank him.

The man's fear was evident even through the bulk of his helmet, and he backed away, turning to retreat.

"Trokar!" Bonewise called. "The egg!"

Trokar swiveled to see the egg was floating and that his friends were moving away from him, Fumble now among them.

"Let's go!" Trokar called to Pepperbolt, but as he turned his head back to the grizzled warrior, a barrage of white-violet streaks slammed into Pepperbolt from three different wands, held by three witches on brooms.

Ten soldiers now approached as Pepperbolt fell to his knees, the morning sun glinting on the blood of his wounds before he slumped to the ground.

"*Pep!*" Trokar called, rushing to the goblin's side.

Another volley of magical projectiles was cast, and Trokar reflexively raised his hand to block them, for all the good it would do. Without meaning to, his thumb flicked the ring on his forefinger, the one he had taken from Audrel, and a glowing circle of runes appeared in the air like a shield. The flashes of energy that converged on him pinged and rippled off the disk of runes like drops of water.

He had been ignorant of the ring's power, and in his heart, he thanked the ancestors for his luck. Pepperbolt lay at his feet unmoving, his eyes open and unblinking. Keeping his sword handle hooked on his thumb, Trokar grabbed the collar of Pepperbolt's gambeson, dragging him across the ground. The muscles in Trokar's legs burned from exertion. *He's just unconscious*, Trokar thought desperately. *Bonewise will heal him.* He kept the magic shield raised, where it deflected more incoming bolts of energy.

The other goblins had stopped their retreat, blocked by the undead, and Bonewise began a chant to drive them away. Trokar looked back, finding the witches had stopped firing at him; they hovered above the soldiers on their brooms while the line of armored figures marched forward steadily, double-quick.

The thought occurred to Trokar that they could abandon the egg. They could push through and outrun the undead, lose them in the tower-grass. But no, he could not leave Pepperbolt. The ancestors would never forgive him. Perhaps they could surrender? But then the prospect of torture by necromancers crept into his thoughts, and suddenly, fighting the whole garrison seemed like a vastly better option.

"Bonewise!" Trokar called, on the verge of mad panic. But Bonewise was facing away from him, thumping his staff and chanting with unshakable focus. Vilayne was staring intensely at the egg. Shacklespurf shot a quarrel through the skull of a zombie—one down, twenty-something to go. Ezme was shaking her wand and arguing with Fumble, who had just dropped all of his arrows while trying to nock one.

A broomship flew near, headed straight for them.

I have failed them, Trokar thought in despair.

The broomship lowered down, turned, then thudded on the ground with a heavy *wump* that buried three undead warriors.

"Sueda!" Trokar cried. He could see her atop the aftcastle, holding the broomstick. The aft of the Moonbeam opened up as a ramp lowered where a rudder would have been on a seafaring ship. Gret was there, inside the modest cargo hold.

"Come!" Gret motioned, his little voice lost amidst the other sounds.

Vilayne levitated the egg up the ramp, and the others followed behind while Bonewise chanted at the undead who stamped their feet and wavered.

"We had a ramp this whole time?!" Ezme asked.

Trokar still had ground to cover, and Sueda popped open her bottle, spinning up a disk of wine just in time to absorb a volley of wand fire directed at her.

"Leaveth the fool!" Shacklespurf yelled at Trokar from the ramp.

Trokar refused. After all, he himself was a fool.

He prayed to his ten thousand squats with a guttural shout and stormed the ramp, dragging Pepperbolt roughly over the packed dirt. As soon as his feet hit the bottom of the ramp, Vilayne shrieked upwards for Sueda to *fly*.

The soldiers were running at them now, only a few strides away. The Moonbeam shuddered into motion, plowing the ground. It skipped a couple times, threatening to knock the goblins out the back, but they crouched and rode the bumps until they were airborne.

Gret struggled with the turning wheel that controlled the cargo ramp, flipping around with it each time he tried to give it a crank.

"Help!" Gret complained. Shacklespurf brushed him off and turned the wheel, raising the wall back into place with a thunk. The air stilled, and human shouts vanished.

"Get up there and help her!" Bonewise exclaimed to Ezme. She ran for the stairs, no argument.

"Someone want to tie this down?!" Vilayne asked gratingly, still staring intensely at the egg while trying to keep her balance on the tilting floor.

"Didst thou fix the rope thou chopped?" Shacklespurf asked bitingly as she began looking for it.

As Vilayne told her where to find it, Bonewise knelt beside Pepperbolt, where Trokar had been repeating his pleas for help and trying to put pressure on Pepperbolt's wounds, which were seeping much slower than they would have been had Pepperbolt's heart been beating.

Bonewise set his staff on the floor, put his hands on Pepperbolt's head and neck. He leaned down and put his ear over the slashed nose. Bonewise muttered something like a prayer under his breath, then looked up at Trokar.

"He's gone," Bonewise said to him, and stood up, leaving his sling-staff where it lay.

"I'm sorry," Trokar said to Pepperbolt's body, numbness seeping into his limbs.

"Rope!" Shacklespurf exclaimed, tossing the coil to Fumble, who succeeded only in catching it with his face.

"Trokar!" Bonewise said. "Help them tie it down!"

While the egg was secured in the hold, Ezme provided cover fire for Sueda, who was having difficulty keeping up her wine shield and steering the Moonbeam over the river at the same time.

The three witches pursued them on brooms in a triangle formation, right on their tail. The man in the middle of the formation fired at Ezme, who took cover behind the railing but still got a burn across her shoulder. The two women, both grey-haired, cast jets of fire from their wands and ignited both broomwings.

"We're on fire!" Ezme cried. She flung another bolt of energy from her brass wand, wounding the man in return, but Ezme had a splitting headache and her eyes stung. The magic she was dishing out was taking its toll.

Bonewise thumped up the stairs and ran to Sueda.

"I'll take it!" Bonewise said, and he grasped the broomstick below Sueda's hand. Sueda let go, and the ship dipped as Bonewise grappled with the running spirit of the Moonbeam. He let it dip down into the river, angling the ship's nose up a little to sweep the broomwings into the water, quenching the flames. The ship lurched as they dumped velocity, and Bonewise hoped the egg had been secured below.

Sueda centered one hand on her disk of spinning wine, and with her other made a lifting gesture. She called out Mawwu's name, and the wave made by their broomwings surged upwards, catching one of the women and knocking her into the river.

Bonewise skipped off the water, but couldn't turn in time to make a bend. The prow of the Moonbeam crashed through the willows and dove into the tower-grass. The reeds whined and whipped around the hull as Bonewise pulled up, but their scorched broomwings were heavy with water. Small birds scattered before them as he chanted through gritted teeth, managing to bring the ship up into the canopy.

"These earless corpse-lovers are persistent!" Ezme exclaimed as she pressed close to Sueda, favoring the winedisk as cover from incoming fire. She leaned out, daring to flick her wand. Nothing happened, but then, a moment later, the male witch was snatched out of the air by a giant mantis in the tower-grass. Ezme chose to believe it was not mere coincidence.

Vilayne hurried up onto the main deck just as the one remaining witch soared upward, well out of reach of any other ambush predators. The witch darted forward, coming up over the Moonbeam so her shadow fell upon it as the sun shone directly over her. Vilayne gazed sunward, letting the painful light drive her pupils to pinpricks.

She saw the magic coming as it was cast, a spell snare like the one she had heard the witch in the round tent seize Trokar with. Ezme, Sueda, and Bonewise were all held by the magic, and the Moonbeam sighed into the tower-grass. The buoyant blades dragged against them as they coasted, but Vilayne slipped through the net of the spell, gripped the chained red crystal she had taken, and echoed the same spell back at the witch overhead.

The witch was snared, and she tumbled from the sky, stiff as a board.

"Bonewise, breathe!" Vilayne bade him.

He grumbled, shaking off the spell of holding, and the Moonbeam began to rise again.

The wind whistled through the bones of his headdress as Bonewise skimmed the Moonbeam over the canopy, turning east. Waves of green undulated in their wake as they flew with haste. No one pursued them.

CHAPTER
TWENTY-TWO
REWARDS

Bonewise set the ship down on its landing legs, crunching the packed rubble beneath as the ramp was lowered. Vilayne guided the egg down the ramp of the Moonbeam in the light of the overcast afternoon sky, and the thunderbird watched vigilantly as the egg settled into her deep nest. Her eyes seemed to smile as she inspected the egg's strong, intact shell.

"My gratitude," the thunderbird spoke in their heads. She reached with her beak and plucked one of the smaller feathers from the top of her wing, extending it to Vilayne.

Vilayne fought the reflexive fear of being so close to the thunderbird's razor-sharp beak and mouth that could swallow her whole. She took the feather, as long as her own arm, an oscillating power embodied within it, crackling quietly through its filaments. Her hair lifted from static.

"Thank you," Vilayne squeaked out.

"You honor us with such a gift, my lady," Bonewise announced from the aftcastle. "We have but one favor to ask: We have need of the stones from your gizzard."

"Your kind are beyond my understanding. But if it means that much to you..."

The thunderbird made a deep sound in her throat. She repeated several times, electricity crackling up her breast feathers, then she dipped her head and opened her mouth. A pile of pearly lumps fell to the ground in a glob of translucent goo.

She straightened, rustled her feathers. *"Now, there is a matter to which I must attend. Do not be here when I return."*

With that, she leapt up from her nest and beat her wings. Gusts of wind buffeted them below, and a moment later, the thunderbird was a diminishing figure in the distance. The darkening cloud cover over the plains swirled, lit in flashes by lightning that traveled with the thunderbird. Then they could not see her anymore, but dozens of enormous, whipping lightning strikes converged on one particular spot on the horizon, and continued striking.

"Ancestor's bones," Trokar exclaimed in awe.

"We should leave," Bonewise stated.

"Ezme!" Fumble called in alarm, and they turned to see Ezme gathering up the emeralds, rubies, and sapphires that she had previously spilled.

"What?" Ezme asked innocently from her stooped posture.

Trokar and Shacklespurf ran over and grabbed her arms, shaking the jewels from her hands.

"Hey!" she squealed. "It's not like she's going to notice!"

"You just can't help yourself, can you?!" Trokar exclaimed. They pulled her to the ship as Fumble gathered the chronostones into a sack; he excitedly bottled some samples of the goo as well.

"THESE ARE *FRESH*!" Dreadfault stated in wonderment, feeling the film of slime still coating one of the chronostones. "How?"

"The thunderbird is still there," Vilayne answered. "We made a trade. It cost us the life of one of our crew."

Dreadfault looked up at her, ears drooped, then flicked his gaze across the others standing in his workshop.

"I'm sorry," he said, setting the stone back among the others on the desk. A moment of silence followed. The ancient goblin seemed to contemplate something, or perhaps he simply held the silence in respect for the dead.

"With your permission," Bonewise said at last, "we will make a cairn for him outside."

"Yes, yes of course. As for your reward . . ." He walked to a workbench, picking up a dark metal crossbow. "For you, soldier." He presented it to Shacklespurf. "Reliable, fast, and accurate. Pump-action lever allows for quick, automatic reload from a five-bolt, top-mounted clip. It's got a red dot laser sight, foregrip, and a detachable sling shoulder mount. I cast thirty carbon quarrels for it."

Shacklespurf let out a barely audible grunt, then took the weapon from him, tried the pump-action lever; the click resounded through the chamber.

"I shall taketh it as my due," Shacklespurf said coldly.

"You expressed interest in the portable hole?" Dreadfault asked the rest, directing their attention to the shimmering suspended circle nearby. "It's yours! You'll need this device to safely store and deploy it . . ." He picked up a metal ball that filled the palm of his hand, held it up to the circle and clicked a button. An aperture opened on the ball and the circle was sucked into it. He held the ball out to them.

Trokar stepped forward and took it. "Thank you, wise sage."

"Dreadfault," Fumble addressed, "I'm something of an alchemist, and I am curious about these chronostones. Is there anything I might be able to do with one of them with less sophisticated equipment?"

"An alchemist, eh? I don't know what tools you have, but without properly-attuned focusing crystals, a chronostone is useless. Well, except maybe as a time bomb."

"A time bomb?" Fumble's hairless brow lifted in interest. "Tell me more!"

"It would be a terrible waste of its potential! If it were broken, a chronostone will collapse into nothing, and a fraction of its power will fold local space back on itself, effectively reversing what you perceive to be 'time.'"

"How *much* time?"

"Well, this small one, for example . . ." Dreadfault took one of the smaller pearlescent lumps and wheeled aside a black chalkboard marked with incomprehensible diagrams. Behind was revealed a large, elaborate weighing scale. He placed the stone on the scale, squinted at several overlapping gauges.

"Looks like this one's density is equivalent to thirty trillion, nine hundred ninety-nine billion, nine hundred ninety-nine million, nine hundred and ninety seconds, give or take a few." He flipped the chalkboard, picked up a stick of chalk, and began scrawling dotted numeral loops. "If that crystalized time were to collapse, it would probably only translate one out of every ten trillion seconds of its full potency into the majorant curve for the finite-time convergent observer."

Dreadfault paused, cast a glance over to Fumble. Fumble's ears were flat, a look of bewilderment on his face.

"Uh . . ." Fumble said.

"Three seconds. It would reverse time by about three seconds."

"What about thunderbird gizzard goo?"

"Hmm? You have some? Let's have a look!"

As Dreadfault was preoccupied with Fumble, Vilayne went to the display case where the infinity die was imprisoned. She stared into its tiny, shifting facets.

Trokar stepped up beside her and peered through the glass.

"You want to ask him for this?" Trokar asked quietly.

"He won't give it to us," Vilayne answered.

"Seems a waste to let it sit behind glass forever."

Vilayne gave a shrug.

Trokar glanced over his shoulder, saw Dreadfault obsessing over something with Fumble, the others watching. He crouched down, felt around the pedestal.

"What are you doing?" Vilayne whispered, ears back when there was a click.

Trokar had found a hidden switch. He stood up, tilted the glass casing open, confident he'd disabled its trap or alarm. Without hesitation, he plucked the gem-like object from its prison, swiftly replacing it with a small chronostone he had pocketed.

"Are you *stealing*?" Vilayne asked.

"He's not using it, and he said we could have some of his inventions. If he even notices, he might think it turned back into a stone." He held out the infinity die to her.

Goblins do not steal from other goblins, Vilayne reminded herself. But the tessellating triangles of the gem danced with colors, reflecting feelings from her soul that tempted her with unending possibilities. She took it between her fingers. It was heavy for its size, like a lump of gold. She tucked it into a buttoned pocket inside her robe, hidden away.

Trokar gave her a wink.

THEY BURIED PEPPERBOLT, creating a cairn of dark stone in the clearing under the twilight sky. They sang the song of remembrance, which was always sung when laying a body to rest, welcoming the ancestors to be present and guide the spirit to the Shining Realm in the Heart of the World. Bonewise hoped Pepperbolt would find his way.

Bonewise had known Pepperbolt well for many years, when they had both been young. Pepperbolt had joined Bonewise and Thorn-Snub on a few hunting expeditions, and they had competed with one another over who was the better shot, Pepperbolt with his bow or Bonewise with his sling.

Pepperbolt had grieved when Creamfoot died. Bonewise did not know if they had been lovers, and it would have been rude to ask. Creamfoot's death changed them both, but Bonewise thought he had fared better against bitterness than Pepperbolt had done. Bonewise felt some guilt for having never reached out to Pepperbolt—so that they might have shared the burden and the gift of their grief.

Pepperbolt had transformed his pain into purpose, giving himself to the fight against the humans. He had been welcomed among the warriors for his zeal and meanness, and Bonewise had felt it was not his place to change Pepperbolt's path.

And now he was dead. He would be sung of as a hero back at the warren, Bonewise would see to that.

He noticed that Trokar was crying. Tears poured from his eyes while Fumble consoled him.

Pepperbolt had been hot-headed, obstinate, and as mean toward Trokar as any of Warface's hunters. And yet, Trokar felt compassion for him. Trokar had not blocked off his empathy like so many warriors.

And then Bonewise remembered that Trokar was not a warrior.

Bonewise considered this in the light that, in all probability, Trokar was about to be chosen as the leader of the warriors of every clan.

CHAPTER
TWENTY-THREE
THE MOOT

The meeting place for the Moot. It was a ruined silver tower atop a stoney ridge. The terrifying heights of the Nargunul peaks dominated the horizon to one side, with the rippling green sea of towergrass on the other. Its cylindrical, metallic surface was rusted powdery white—a soft, light metal no one could identify. The hanging outer wall that hugged the tower all the way up to its domed top was covered in flared alcoves that caught the wind and made it whistle and moan. It seemed that the outer wall once had rotated around the tower, but it had crumbled long ago and now rested slightly askew around the load-bearing inner wall.

Some said it was a temple to Utu, the Sky God, or some other god of the wind or heavens whose name was no longer remembered. Whatever it had once been, it had served goblin-kin as the secret location for the Moot since the first war-songs against the humans had been sung.

It stood in the western reaches of the Nargunul Mountains, a central location between the remaining goblin warrens, most of which were scattered across the western half of the vast continent. There had been many other warrens across Andril, but those in the east had fallen to the Faladian Republic, all except for the Pitshredder clan, who had to travel three times as far as any other warren to attend the Moot, either across the Naledzar Crags or through human-occupied territory.

The routes taken by each clan to the Moot were closely-guarded secrets, even from other goblins. The delegations from the clans always aimed to arrive many nights early, lest they miss the night of the election from delays and mishaps on the journey.

As they flew near, Vilayne could see the encampments of the various clans scattered around the tower, with a small fire lit in the plaza. The night of the full moon was upon them, after having spent the previous night flying and then the better part of the day recuperating at a creek on the edge of the mountains.

The ethereal creatures she glimpsed in the mountains were different than those she had seen elsewhere. There were shadow people—vague silhouettes, ranging from short to tall—standing amongst the rocks. Never moving, just there, always at a respectful distance. Until, that is, she and the others had bedded down to sleep.

The shadow people had sat on their chests, causing nightmares and difficulty breathing. She sent them away easily enough with light from the Daystone, but to rest herself, she had to place wards around the ship to keep them away. Despite her efforts, she had heard Trokar thrashing in his sleep in the cabin he shared with Fumble. At the end of the day, none of them had slept well.

As Bonewise made their approach, Trokar was as jittery as she had ever seen him, and he had obsessed over his appearance. Naturally, he wanted to make a grand impression, and at his word, Fumble conjured colorful sparks from the prow of the Moonbeam as they floated down.

Sueda was confined to below deck for the duration of the Moot, but she had offered no complaint. She said she would continue work on translating the many papers and scrolls in the captain's cabin, though she didn't have much hope for success, as she reported they seemed to be written not only in the northern human dialect, but in code. Fumble asked her to keep working on deciphering the labels on alchemical ingredients in the ship's small alchemy lab, as his method of poking and sniffing them proved to be not very accurate.

With luck, the Moot would reach a decision swiftly, and they could head back west without delay.

Dozens of warriors stood about the plaza, and more stirred from the encampments along the escarpments. They scurried and armed themselves as soon as they saw the flying ship, but then stood and gaped as goblin voices reached their ears.

Vilayne sang with the others: "The cliffs of Kol'grathu, thorny and cleat—fierce are the waters that beat at their feet!"

Bonewise set the Moonbeam down on the crumbling saddle of the ridge, the prow facing away from the tower. Shacklespurf lowered the cargo ramp, slowly, then Trokar walked down in full view of the encampments, followed by Bonewise and Vilayne side-by-side, with Fumble bringing up the rear. Ezme and Shacklespurf remained on board to "look tough," as Trokar had put it, to prevent any other goblins from snooping around. Ezme had complained about being made to miss the big meeting, but Bonewise reminded her that Sueda would not be safe unless the ship were well-guarded, and the young goblin's resistance crumbled.

They walked through the plaza, where distinct groups of goblins watched and muttered to each other. Trokar was the only one smiling.

"Pitshredders," Bonewise whispered to Vilayne, eyeing a large group of tall, muscular warriors covered in grey and brown furs, standing with long spears.

"Screamburners," Vilayne whispered back, looking the other way at a rusty-haired group wearing bandoliers of wax-sealed clay flasks.

"Dreadrot," Fumble added, looking at a group of warriors wearing lizard-scale armor, their hair gelled with dried blood.

At the end of the plaza, broken and tilted stairs went up to the tower entrance. A group of pale-powdered warriors stood at the base of them, and one of them stepped out to impede their path, a long-handled axe holstered at his shoulder.

"Hello!" Trokar said as amicably as he could. "Trokar," he thumbed at himself. "You must be Boneghost clan? I've heard a lot about you!"

"What . . ." the pale-powdered warrior asked gravely, "have you heard?"

"I . . . have . . . heard . . . that you ride wargs!"

"Yes. We *do*."

"But you did not ride them here?" Trokar asked, his ears turning and hearing no wargs.

"They are hunting," the warrior snarled pointedly. "They will return with some of the meat."

"Nifty! Well, the moon is rising, so we better get up to the Moot!" He moved to step around the warrior.

"Who *are* you?" the warrior demanded, stepping in front of Trokar again. "How is it that a ship can fly?"

"It's magic!" Fumble called from behind Vilayne and Bonewise.

"We are the delegation from Kol'grathu!" Trokar said grandly, calling the warrior's eyes back to him.

"Kol'grathu, huh? I did not see any of you here three years ago, or three years before that! Where is Warface?"

"Warface is dead!" Trokar declared. "I am the new war-chief, and this is my war-council." He gestured behind him. "We have a right to attend the Moot, now step aside!"

Trokar walked around the warrior, who made no further attempt to stop him. The others followed, and they entered the tower through its modest round entryway, the rusted metal door laying on the rocks outside.

A steel stairway spiraled up the inside of the inner wall, into shadow. The only source of light streamed in through the doorway at the bottom, so Vilayne asked the Daystone to shine a little, illuminating the space. The walls were covered in goblin graffiti close to the ground and around the stairs. The stairs themselves were rusted, but they looked sturdy enough. There was also a massive steel rod that disappeared into the floor at the bottom and went all the way up into the darkness at the top, partially screened by enormous braided coils of green-rusted copper. All of the copper had been sheared off from the floor to about a quarter-way up, and broken, rotted remains of wooden scaffolding lay in heaps around the dusty floor.

Vilayne held her broom ready, just in case the stairs decided to collapse that night. She had spent her idle hours while on watch trying to connect with its magic; she had even managed to float, but balancing on top of it was more difficult than she had imagined. It tended to flip her underneath, so she learned to manage her posture. She then figured out that she did not need to *ride* the broom, but rather transfer its levitation magic into herself, which was aided by her contact with it.

The stairs held firm with only a few metallic groans, accompanied by the constant moan of the wind flowing around the tower and whistling against the oddly flared surface of the outer wall. After a long climb, at last, they reached the chamber at the top. The windowless space there was lit by a jagged beam of moonlight that slanted in through a break in the ceiling. A rust-bearded rod of steel, less in girth than the one in the stairwell, had broken free of its gear casing and hung at an angle from a hole in the ceiling, likely a hole it had created. Clay oil lanterns the Screamburners made burned around the perimeter of the room, illuminating giant vertical gears that ringed the chamber along a track, and one fallen gear resting on its side served as a table. There were various leather maps placed upon it, as well as five small objects.

Around the table stood five silent goblins who watched them approach. One at the far end smoked a pipe, the moonlight bouncing off the curl of bluish smoke that drifted up above.

Following the wisps up, Vilayne spotted a pair of feline eyes shone silver in the girders of the ceiling. She could make out its hulking outline as that of a tiger-bat, the most feared flying predator of the Hucancha Jungle.

Five quilted banners hung from the wall, showing the emblems of the various attending clans, bordered with pictographs of their histories.

"Aw crap," Trokar whispered to Bonewise, "I left our banner at home."

"Who are you?" a green-speckled goblin woman asked, her black hair tied back in a plume of red feathers.

"I am Bonewise of Kol'grathu," Bonewise said quickly, cutting off Trokar, "apprentice to The Wise Woman of our clan. Warface was killed in Shal'draaken. This is our new war-chief, Trokar." He gestured to Trokar, who stepped forward and nodded in greeting.

Trokar's smile was stricken with the sudden nervousness of meeting the long-rumored war leaders of other goblin warrens. The first thing that came to his mind about the goblin standing before him was that she was the most muscular woman he had ever seen.

"I am Dart-Tooth," the woman said, "of the Spiderclaw clan. We had just begun our deliberations."

"Well-met, Dart-Tooth!" Trokar greeted with a forced smile. "I—" He then remembered that he had already been introduced, ". . . am curious to see what offerings you all have brought!"

"I was just explaining my clan's contribution. Come, this is Kol'grathu's place, here." She gestured to a vacant spot, between two teeth of the giant gear.

As Trokar stepped into the nook, a profound unease settled upon him. Warface had stood there in Moots past—the goblin he had murdered to seize political power. Their most ancient laws allowed it, but it was not ever what he wanted to be. He felt disgusting for wanting to believe that Warface had deserved his fate. All the years of judgment, of belittling and ridicule, circled beneath the surface of his mind, bringing with it the echoing tides of rage.

You are no warrior, the memory spoke to him. *Fraud. Pretender.*

The other war leaders were sizing Trokar up. He saw in their faces the same disapproving look he knew well from

Warface . . . *and Bonewise*, Trokar thought. He stopped his ears from falling, and, desperate for a distraction from his inner thoughts, forced his attention onto Dart-Tooth, then he noticed the golden sling on the table in front of her.

"As I was saying," Dart-Tooth said, "this is the Golden Sling of Boulders, taken from dangerous and haunted ruins near the human colony of Bayminster. Our spell-singers banished its ghosts and unraveled its secrets. Do not let its small size deceive you, for it is a powerful weapon."

She picked up the sling, which seemed to be spun from fine threads of gold, embroidered with dwarvish runes. She held up a small pebble for all to see, then placed it in the sling. She stepped back from the table and with one mighty swing, she released the stone. It sailed across the room, growing in size as it went, then crashed into one of the large vertical gears on the opposite side of the room. The thick steel gonged, then the stone clattered loudly to the floor, roughly the size of a goblin head.

"They get bigger the farther they travel," Dart-Tooth said with a sharp smile. "Better than Screamburner artillery."

A tall fur-clad goblin across the table guffawed, and a portly goblin with mismatched eyes scowled at him, then gave the same expression to Dart-Tooth.

"I have led many successful raids of the logging camps around Bayminster," Dart-Tooth said, "halted their expansion. My hunters are the best trackers—"

"In the jungle . . ." the portly goblin grumbled.

"With our poisons," Dart-Tooth continued, shooting the portly one a glare, "my warriors can kill with a single arrow—a single prick from a dart! My tiger-bat can fly me silently over any battlefield, and with *this* sling, I can rain death upon our enemies! This I promise."

Finally, after a deliberate pause, she nodded curtly to the goblin on her left, the portly one with one eye bigger than the other, and different colors—yellow and blue. He straightened his posture and composed his expression, picking up the object in front of him. It was a small weathered wooden bird with a golden bill.

"I am Boomeye," he said for the newcomer's benefit, looking at Trokar, "of the Screamburner clan." He looked around the table and lifted up the carved bird; it resembled a toy more than anything. "This is a magic *boat*, taken from the arcanist's tower at Bastow." He tapped the golden bill three times, then tossed it up over the table. It shuddered and creaked, growing to the size of a two-oared rowboat as it came down on the gear with a crash. It rocked a little but shuddered to a stop. A cavity folded open on top, completing its boat-like transformation.

"What is it?" the tall goblin on his left asked with a quizzical scrunch of his nose.

"It's a *duck*," Boomeye replied, then he heaved himself up onto the table and tapped the duck-boat's golden bill three times again. It shuddered once more and shrank back to its original form, which Boomeye scooped up into his hand. He straightened and looked around the table imperiously from his newfound height. "I've been leading raids since most of you were sprats! Every one of my warriors counts for a *hundred* with our firepower! I know where and when to strike, so that even a whole *den* of *wizards* cannot withstand us."

He lowered himself back down to his spot and gave a decisive nod to the tall goblin next to him.

"I am Tombtongue," the tall, muscular goblin said, shooting a glare toward Trokar, "of the Pitshredder tribe." He picked up a long woodworker's saw. "I *destroyed* an entire dwarven caravan, overran their magic metal wagons, and cut their beards from their arrogant heads! I took this tool as a prize, the power of which I will now show you." He turned and clicked his tongue twice, whereupon two of his warriors emerged from behind him, from a vertical gear that bore the Pitshredder banner. They carried a section of tree trunk. They placed it on the table so that one end stuck out, then withdrew to lurk in the shadows once more.

Tombtongue braced one hand against the log and sawed off a section of it with three solid strokes, an action which should have taken dozens of such motions, even with his strength. He laid the saw back on the table, gestured his warriors forth again, and they removed the log.

"I have decimated entire towns in the east, where the humans are strong. We have defended our warren against countless incursions by their *earless* armies, stopped them *dead* with our trenches. We are the most numerous of the clans, and the strongest! It is *my* warriors that do the dying in the summer raids when it is not Pitshredders who lead! Trust in me, and I will crush the humans so decisively they will be desperate to march against our trenches again."

He nodded to the goblin on his left, distinguished lines of age marking their white-powdered face. They puffed their fractured smoking pipe of carved bone.

"War-chief Blackpipe," the pale goblin said in northern goblin dialect, shaking the golden rings on their ear with a twitch. "Boneghost clan." They lifted an elegant sword, one hand under the flat of the blade, tilting it so the mirror-like blade reflected the moonlight. "The famous sword of the Silverwood Ranger."

Eyebrows went up around the table, and Vilayne noted

the shift of the mood, the surprise that shook each of their auras.

"Who's that?" Fumble asked Bonewise in a whisper.

"Someone famous," Bonewise replied evenly, not wanting to encourage a conversation that would disrupt the meeting. He had heard of the ranger, a long-lived elven huntress who was a notorious goblin slayer.

Vilayne could see the magic auras of each of the objects presented, but the silvery radiance of the mirror-like sword was keenly bright, rivaled only by the golden glow of the sling. She also noticed Trokar's aura was pulsing with red and purple irregularly, colors she had learned to associate with anger and disgust, and it troubled her.

"This sword was taken as a prize from the former hunting lodge of the menace herself," Blackpipe said.

"Former?" the petite goblin to their left asked.

"Burned the lodge to the ground."

"Is she dead?" Boomeye asked.

A moment of hesitation from Blackpipe.

"She escaped, though not *unscathed*. We outsmarted her and all her hunters, nonetheless. Place leadership in me, and we shall see many such victories."

They bobbed their pipe at the petite goblin to their left, who was on Trokar's right, and Trokar's anxiety began to grow as his turn fast approached.

"Wotakx," the petite goblin introduced himself with a glance to Trokar, "of the Dreadrot clan. I offer the Moot this magical Ring of Climbing, taken from the sacking of Neray Castle. My infiltrators took both the outer and inner gates without raising any alarm . . ."

As Wotakx regaled the story of his successful raid, Vilayne watched Trokar's aura wobble and bloom with more red and purple. There was no reason for him to feel anger and disgust, she thought. Then she saw it; an aura hovering behind where Trokar stood.

Wasting no time, she stepped into the shadow of one of the giant gears, drew a circle in the dust with her finger, then added the pictographs for "spirit" and "binding."

Touching the red crystal hanging from the little chain at her belt, she whispered: "Vengeful soul, I bind you from your evil goal. I bid you speak to me, so must it be!" she repeated it once, then twice.

The spirit rushed at her through the giant gear, hovering an arm's length away, caught in the magic circle.

"You dare to command me?!" Warface growled in Vilayne's imagination, but it was not herself who was imagining it.

"An honorable ancestor does not sabotage the living!" she whispered.

"He will bring our clan to ruin!"

"We are already in ruin! Every clan is! We have just begun to reclaim the power of our ancestors, and yet you would cling to your anger and your pride? This is our chance to change things. If you are not going to help, then leave us."

He hovered there, festering in a red bile of rage.

"Leave us!" She swiped her finger through the pictograph depicting a spirit.

He disintegrated into a cloud of static-charged dust.

"Give Dreadrot your vote," Wotakx concluded at the table, "and every stronghold we attack will fall as easily." He gave Trokar a nod.

Trokar stood there in the sudden vacuum of his own mind. The self-deprecating thoughts had ceased, but a crippling fear of failure lingered. A dramatic pause stretched, but if it went on much longer, he would bungle his first impression.

Bonewise saw Trokar's hesitation and muttered a prayer: "Benevolent spirits, guardians of Fate's doors, grant him courage, now and more, grant him bravery, may it stay, for him to follow his path, to have his say."

Trokar straightened, glancing around the table; he decided to tell the truth.

"I am Trokar of Kol'grathu," he said. "I am one of the strongest goblins of our clan, but that does not make me a warrior. I have killed in battle, but that does not make me a warrior either. I have even been trained how to fight by a warrior . . . but being able to fight does not make me worthy to lead you."

"What makes me worthy . . ." he continued, "is that I know how to beat the humans. And when I don't, I have friends who advise me when I'm wrong." He gestured behind him to Bonewise, Vilayne, and Fumble.

"And when I say 'beat the humans,' I don't just mean harassing their borders or taking some of their stuff . . . I mean bring down their fat empire from the inside out. Strike at the very heart of their power!"

The other war chieftains were listening intently, and Tombtongue was outright grinning.

"This is grandstanding," Boomeye grumped. "How do we know this upstart can make good on this ambition? What gift does Kol'grathu offer to this Moot? I see nothing here!"

"Ah," Trokar said with a smile, holding up a finger, "our gift is too big to fit in this room! If you look outside, we will show it to you. Is there a window up here, or balcony, or something?"

"Yes," Dart-tooth answered. "There is a way to the top

—this way." She led them to another stairway that went up to a hatch in the ceiling.

"This better not be a metaphor . . ." Boomeye muttered as he followed along.

"Vilayne?" Trokar called. "Will you bring it up, please?"

Vilayne mounted her broom and hoped her magic would not fail her. If it did, it was a long way to the ground. After two skips, she was airborne, keeping her center of gravity low against the top of the reed-binding, with the handle angled upwards. She floated up through the gaping hole in the ceiling, eliciting stares of disbelief. Her heart lurched when she saw the tiger-bat wiggle its rear in its instinct to pounce at her, but then she was past it, and it simply watched her soar up into the night sky, eyes big as saucers.

She directed her focus down toward the Moonbeam, and the broom darted that direction. She had never actually *flown* on the broom before, and she held on for dear life. In seconds, she was over the deck where Ezme and Shacklespurf stood watch, and she strangled her momentum, landing on the aftcastle.

"All good?" Ezme asked.

"All good," Vilayne answered with a huff of relief. "Just like we planned."

She kept hold of her broom in one hand, taking hold of the Moonbeam's broomstick in the other. Vilayne chanted to shift her connection, and Ezme joined in support. The ship lifted up, and Vilayne signaled Shacklespurf to lower the wings.

Trokar and the other chieftains emerged on the tilted top of the broken tower, steadying themselves against gusts of wind.

"I give you the Moonbeam," Trokar announced over the wind, "the flying ship of Kol'grathu!"

Vilayne spiraled the ship up around the tower, then soared above it, tilting so she could keep eyes on it. The magic of the ship was perilously strained, both from the burnt tips of the wings and from the elevation. She felt her knees buckling so she tilted the prow down and let the ship glide toward the plains, dropping halfway to the ground before turning around and lining up for an approach back to their landing site.

Trokar could not contain his grin as the chieftains breathed various curses at the sight.

"We boarded it during a mighty battle," Trokar regaled loudly, "dispatched the humans, then flew over the battlefield and rained fire down on armies of zombies!"

Eyebrows arched high at that.

"That's right!" Trokar continued. "We raided the forces of the Witch Queen! With this ship, we can cross the continent and the seas—strike anywhere! We will be unstoppable!"

The wind chilled him, and without further preamble, he climbed back over the broken metal and through the open hatch, down into the meeting room.

Except for the shuffle of feet and the moan of the wind, the room was quiet as the leaders assembled once more around the gear. Tombtongue clicked again, and his two warriors brought stacks of planks, which were passed out 'round the table, one plank per leader. The numeral glyphs for one through eight were already marked on the left side of the planks from top to bottom.

"The presentations are complete," Boomeye said, breaking the silence. "Let the ranked vote be done."

Trokar waited and watched the others begin. They

unsheathed their knives and began scratching clan sigils into the wood. Trokar deduced that his first choice was to be placed next to the number one, his second choice next to the number two, and so forth.

There were only six clans present, but there were nine goblin clans in the known world. With eight ranking choices marked on the plank, Trokar guessed that it was not allowed for a clan to vote for themselves. He did not want to seem a fool by asking. Could they vote for clans that were not in attendance, he wondered? That didn't seem likely. He decided to vote for Spiderclaw as his first choice, for no other reason than its leader was the most attractive of the lot. He scrawled the Screamburner emblem next, because its war leader was the most senior; Pitshredder next, then Boneghost, then Dreadrot. He left the last two numbers vacant. While some of the others were still scratching their votes, Trokar spent the extra time to embellish his renditions of their emblems.

When next he looked up, all the others were watching him, waiting for him to finish. He smiled and set his plank down.

Boomeye facilitated the counting of the votes, done in plain sight of the others. He scratched tallies onto a separate plank. None got more than half the votes in the first count, so Dreadrot, having the least, was eliminated from the runoff.

Bonewise thought that seemed appropriate, for he thought the Ring of Climbing was the least impressive of the relics, even though it allowed Wotakx to climb up the walls like a spider. Still, he wondered at the politics beneath the surface. Fumble beside him was doing a remarkable job refraining from commentary as he sipped from a flask.

Spiderclaw, Pitshredder, and Boneghost clans all ranked

Kol'grathu as their second choice. With more than half of the vote, Kol'grathu was the undisputed winner, without need for further rounds.

"It has been decided," Boomeye announced. "Trokar of Kol'grathu shall be Big War-chief for the summer."

Relief swept over Trokar, Bonewise, and Fumble. It was done.

There were resigned sighs around the table, a couple breathy curses, but no one challenged the vote. Dart-Tooth turned to Trokar and held out the golden sling.

"May Spiderclaw's contribution . . ." she said diplomatically, "serve you well on the war path, Trokar."

Trokar took the sling with a nod and a gracious smile. One by one, all the leaders came around and presented their relics to him with similar words, until they were all arrayed on the gear's surface before him.

"I am honored to be chosen to lead you all against our ancient enemy," Trokar said, his ears high.

"What is your war plan?" Tombtongue asked.

"Here's what we will do"—he placed his hands on the gear and leaned forward, remembering what he and the others had discussed over supper with Sueda the day before—"all of you will conduct raids in your own territories during the first moon of summer. Nothing out of the ordinary. This will lead the humans to believe this year will be like any other. During the second moon, we will move through the hills around the mountains, toward the headwaters of the big river that flows to the south sea." He looked at one of the maps spread out on the table.

"Spiderclaw, Screamburner, and Boneghost clans will take the pass between the Nargunul Mountains and Naledzar Crags. Dreadrot, that's your territory. You said the human castle there was sacked?"

Wotakx gave him a nod of affirmation.

Trokar decided to improvise with the original plan. "How long ago?"

"Two years."

"Link up with those who come through the pass and attack it again. Take it. Use its food stores for the journey along the river, then hide in the forest. Let the humans think you've taken the spoils back to your strongholds. In the east, Pitshredder clan will use their numbers to attack multiple targets, keep them guessing so they won't concentrate their armies."

He paused, looking at another map.

"Any word from the other clans?"

"Thunderbite, Bloodpeak, and Ironskull clans are no-shows," Dart-Tooth answered. "No word."

"Let's hope they will do some raiding on their own and add to the confusion. During the third moon, we will converge our forces around the human capital and strike before they have time to marshal their armies. The goal is not to take the city, but to capture the leaders of their government. Once we have them, their resistance will fold!"

"What about their ships?" Blackpipe asked. "Perhaps they will evacuate their leaders by sea?"

"Or reinforce the garrison from their coastal fortresses?" Dart-Tooth added.

"Ah, but we have a ship, too! We can strike from above, sink their ships with boulders, perhaps?" He chanced a wink at Dart-Tooth.

She gave him the slightest smirk in response.

"This plan is nutty as a binkle-fruit cake," Blackpipe said, blowing smoke.

"I think it could work," Dart-Tooth said.

"And if the rest of us get boxed in," Tombtongue said, "your *pet* can fly you to safety, along with his flying ship, while me and *my* warriors throw ourselves on human spears!"

"The humans will have no reason to expect an attack against the center of their power," Boomeye said. "But their walls are high."

"Trokar!" Fumble called from the sidelines. Trokar turned his head. "Maybe you should tell them how we can make a hole in their defenses!"

"Ah!" Trokar exclaimed with a smile. "Kol'grathu's leading alchemist is right to remind me." He pulled the portable hole carrier out of a pouch at his belt, stepped back from the table and unleashed the shimmering circle onto the metal floor. He drew his sword and then casually dropped it through. It fell, landing with a clatter distantly below at ground level. He retrieved the hole with the press of a button, then replaced his erstwhile sword with the famous silver blade.

"Handy for getting in and out of government buildings." He winked at Wotakx.

Wotakx grinned, perhaps even salivated a bit.

"Well," Blackpipe said, letting out another puff of smoke, "perhaps we can pull this off, after all."

"Where will *you* be during the moons leading up to this grand assault?" Tombtongue asked Trokar.

"I will travel the skies, coordinate our forces, seek out the human's other enemies and invite them to join our attack."

"*What* other enemies?"

"The . . . Uh . . ." He could not dare to mention working with the human rebels.

"Ogres!" Fumble called.

"Yes! The ogres! They *hate* humans!"

"Ha!" Boomeye barked. "They are as likely to eat you as talk to you!"

"We shall see about that! Rest assured, I shall be working to bolster our forces. Perhaps I can persuade the Thunderbite clan to join us. In any case, three moons from tonight, we shall launch our big attack and overthrow the human empire!"

"If this plan doesn't work," Tombtongue said, "I'll have your ears." It was a serious threat.

"I'll cut them off with my own blade if you're not satisfied!"

"I'll hold you to that, W*ar-chief*." Tombtongue gave a bitter smile.

THE MOONBEAM FLEW west over the tower-grass canopy, carried by the wind. Behind them, the first light of dawn peeked over the mountains, brushing the night away with golden fingers. It was Vilayne's turn at the ship's broomstick, but Bonewise stood close by. Everyone was above deck, including Sueda, who was glad to breathe the fresh air after so many tense hours confined below. Vilayne noticed Shacklespurf gazing southward over the railing.

"Bonewise," Vilayne asked. "Do you remember how to find that glade, above Zalenthas?"

"I could find the way from the ground," he grumbled, "between there and home. Not from here."

"We promised Shacklespurf we would take her there," Trokar said, overhearing. "Sueda, how did you find it?"

"I have a map of where we thought it might be," Sueda

answered. "But in truth, we found it by luck. We came up the coast from the south."

"If we fly around enough clearings, I'm sure we'll find it," Trokar said cheerfully.

"Take nay such trouble," Shacklespurf spoke up. "If thou canst find some other to guard this flying tinder-box, I wouldst like to see thy warren, mayhap eat some real food. I grow weary of salted fish. The dead of Zalenthas canst wait a few more days."

"I would love to show you Kol'grathu!" Trokar beamed.

"It's probably pretty rustic by your standards," Fumble said, "but the bug-butt bread is top-notch!"

"Trokar," Sueda began, "after we take Shacklespurf to Zalenthas, I must meet with Jalimac, my superior in the rebellion. He will be eager to meet all of you, I'm sure."

"Where is he?" Trokar asked.

"The rebellion is based in the mountains north of the Mirror-sand Desert. He is likely to be there."

"Then that is where we shall go! If he is as open-minded as you, Sueda, then I'm sure we will work together famously!"

"'Open-minded' is not the word I would use to define Jalimac, but he is . . . *dedicated* to the cause."

"How dedicated?" Ezme asked. "How will he feel about an army of goblins attacking the human capital?"

"I think he will see it as an opportunity to take the Republic by surprise. But please, do not punish the ordinary people of the city! They are also victims of slavery and oppression. We must get the senate to surrender to the rebellion, with minimal loss of life."

"Don't worry, Sueda," Trokar said, "we will figure something out!"

As the others talked, Vilayne gazed at the collage of

their auras, patched with joyful greens, golden anxieties, and blue hues of grief. Wind snakes danced around them.

She remembered The Wise Woman's prophecy, that a warrior would bring disaster, or that the warrior would fall victim to it. It was not clear. Perhaps the time of that prophecy had already been concluded when they retrieved the Geostone, or perhaps it had been fulfilled when Pepperbolt was killed.

Warface had warned that Trokar would bring ruin to their clan, and spirits often knew things about the future. Then again, the former war-chief had been blinded by his anger, and even in death, he could not be trusted. She had a feeling he would continue to haunt them.

Vilayne resolved to ask The Wise Woman the first possible chance she had when they got back home.

For the moment, she was content to let the westerly wind carry them to the limestone cliffs of Shipwreck Bay.

. . . TO BE CONTINUED . . .

ACKNOWLEDGMENTS

Many thanks to my friends Frances Yackley, Jordan Mackay, Shawnna Young, Kevin "Tank" Rex, Theresa "Gopher" Swanson, Donna "Salty" Wyrik, Susan Schramfield, and many others who took part in the crafting of this story. Their playful, creative minds gave the characters a dynamic life of their own.

Thanks to my parents, Linda and Greg, who initiated me into the world of tabletop RPGs.

And thanks to Kindra Tia for illustrating a beautiful front and back cover!

ABOUT THE AUTHOR

Azul Gregorson is an emerging author of dystopian science fiction and fantasy novels. This is Azul's second book, the first being Foregone Future.

He currently serves as the environmental coordinator on the board of directors for Havenroot, a campground near Veneta, Oregon. He lives on his family farm nearby and when he is not growing food or writing stories he spends much of his time doing ecological restoration work.

Between the time humans came to the world,
and the time of reckoning beneath the red sun, there was an Age undreamed of.
The Great Civilizations of myth and legend have risen and fallen.
Deep caverns, vast and mysterious, permeate the world, and seas of dry silt flow across
great swaths of the windswept lands. Nature reclaims once great cities, and powerful
bloodcrystals dominate the deep beneath the continent of Andril, piercing the stone like a
long-neglected briar-patch of ancient gods.

And unto this...Goblin Quest!

Seen as little more than monsters by "civilized" folk, a vicious cycle of war dominates
goblin history. Few know that goblin-kind once maintained a thriving civilization, led by
the mythical Goblin King. After a civil war that ended with the Goblin King's banishment,
goblin-kind embraced the ways of their ancestors, living for art, music, and simple
pleasures, until their lands were taken from them. But a time of change has come, a time
of destiny, and a few unlikely heroes from the cliff caves of Kol'Grathu will undertake a
quest to reclaim the power once wielded by the Goblin King in ancient times, to disabuse
their people from those who see them as their lessers. Guided by dreams, instinct, and
cunning, a fellowship takes form as Vilayne, Trokar, Fumble, Ezme, and Bonewise set
out to uncover ancient secrets, and join forces with a courageous human priestess. The
balance of power is about to be upset. Very upset.

Made in the USA
Coppell, TX
10 February 2026